MW00612815

The Highlander's Stolen Heart

by

Donna Fletcher

This is a work of fiction. Names, characters, places, and incidents are either the product of the author's imagination or are used fictitiously, and any resemblance to actual persons, living or dead, business establishments, events or locales is entirely coincidental.

The Highlander's Stolen Heart
All rights reserved.
Copyright June 2014 by Donna Fletcher

Cover art
Kim Killion Group

Visit Donna's Web site
http://www.donnafletcher.com
https://www.facebook.com/donna.fletcher.author

Table of Contents

Chapter One

The Highlands, 1432 AD

"How can you wed when your heart is not in it?"

Heather shrugged. "It is the way of things, Patience. Father is not well enough to lead the Clan Macinnes and with no sons, and I being the eldest daughter, it is my duty. And need I remind you that you did not have to accompany me on this journey to meet my intended," —Heather smiled— "though I am most grateful you did."

"And leave this lot," —Patience nodded at the warriors who rode in single formation ahead of them— "to look after you and Emma? Absolutely not. Where is Emma anyway?" Patience rose up on her mare to glance around.

"Right here," Emma said from behind her sisters.

"You were not there a moment ago," Patience turned her head and scolded. "What did I tell you about remaining close?"

"An unfamiliar plant caught my eye and I had to take a look," Emma explained.

"You could have been snatched up and abducted in seconds by a band of rebels. There has been much mischief afoot in these parts lately, and there is no telling what lurks in the surrounding forest. Do not wander off again."

"Patience is right," Heather agreed. "There has been talk of rebels pilfering the area."

Emma drew her mare up alongside Heather. "I heard it was mercenaries out to claim land promised to them." She lowered her voice. "They say the Dark Dragon has returned to claim his due."

"Hush up," Patience warned. "No one speaks that vile name. Besides, I have heard tell that King James has paid him well for his services and sent him on his way."

"More likely that the Dragon provided much needed funding to King James and took his own leave home," Emma said, "and home I heard was the Highlands."

"Enough," Heather scolded with a shiver. "Let us not speak about such evil. It is a joyous time. In a few short hours, I will meet my intended, Rogan of the Clan MacClennan and in a month's time I shall wed." She forced a smile. "Then in no time at all father will find you both suitable husbands and we will all be happily wed."

Patience snickered. "I will wed who and when I want, and he will not be giving me orders."

"I think we should stop for a rest soon," Emma said. "I will go and alert the warriors."

"How foolish my remark," Heather said after Emma rode ahead.

"You are not the only fool. I should not have boasted about choosing my own mate." Patience stared after her sister. "I worry so about Emma. She buries herself in the running of father's land with no thought of a man."

"Can you blame her? Father has tried several times with little success to arrange a marriage for her. Too plain of features and too smart of wit, that is what father has been told time and time again."

"I do not understand it." Patience shook her head. "My features are fair enough that men find me appealing. Your features are so stunning that father has to beat the men away with a stick, but Emma?" Patience shook her head again. "Her features are so plain that no man glances her way or they make snide remarks."

"Not in your presence," Heather said.

"Anyone who does will suffer for it, though it is Emma who has suffered the most. I wish she had not heard father tell you that when he had approached Angus, laird of the Clan MacClennan about an arranged marriage between Rogan and Emma that Angus laughed at him. The old warrior insisted that it be you his son Rogan wed or no one. And to hear tell, the son was adamant about the choice himself."

"And since our lands border, it was an arrangement father could not refuse," Heather finished. "I cannot believe Angus had the gall to request that Emma accompany me so that she could advise him on how to enhance his land's production."

"That is the only reason anyone is interested in Emma. She is brilliant in producing abundant crops, preserving food, multiplying stock, and keeping illness from claiming many, not to mention her studies with the various foliage and trees. Have you seen how she painstakingly continues to record everything in that monk's parchment book?" Patience sighed. "Her name should be Patience, not mine."

"Remember how often Mother had reminded you that she named you such because she instinctively knew patience was something you needed to learn."

Patience smiled. "I am trying." Her smile faded. "I wish there was something we could do to help Emma."

"We do help her," Heather said. "We are always there for her and we always will be."

"It is not enough. You cannot tell me that she never thinks about falling in love and having children. She may speak mostly about her interests, but you cannot tell me that the thought of being kissed, held, and made loved to, has never entered her head."

"I think the incident with Daniel, the miller's son, turned her against ever trusting another lad."

"And Daniel got what he deserved from me—two black eyes and a split lip."

"You cannot fight her battles all her life," Heather warned.

"I can and I will."

"Mother should have named you Obstinate."

"And she should have named you Sweet," Patience said wrinkling her nose. "What should she have named Emma?"

"Lonely," Heather said sadly.

~~~

Emma rode in the front near the lead warrior James. He would talk with her on occasion, though his focus remained mostly on his surroundings. Older than the other warriors with a paunch to his stomach and graying hair, he nonetheless was a fierce fighter and one of her father's most trusted warriors and also his closest friend. He also was a bit of a champion to her, since he would admonish any of his warriors if they cast a disparaging remark about her.

She had thought she had convinced herself that it did not matter that she was plain and that no man found her appealing. She had her interests and that was enough. But when Heather had mentioned that they would all be married one day, it was as if someone had reminded her of what she would never have.

The only way she thought she would ever wed was if her father offered a hefty dowry, but that had failed to prove true. He had offered to make Rogan laird of the Macinnes clan if he would wed her and he had refused the generous offer.

It pleased her that she had had enough intelligence when she was young to have realized that marriage would never be in her future. It was the reason she had turned her attention to exploring various areas of interest and had become proficient in most. She kept herself busy with studies, research, and documenting all she had learned and continued to learn. She had a good life and a loving family.
~~~

Her father was a wonderful Da and she didn't know what she would do without her sisters. She loved them dearly. They had helped raise her after their mum had died seven and ten years ago when Emma was barely two years. Actually, it had been Heather, three years older than Emma, who had taken their mother's place. And she did not want to think of life without either one of them.

She was happy. She did not need a man, but then no man ever glanced her way. They were too busy staring wide-eyed and slack-jawed at Heather. Her sister was a beauty, a few inches over five feet, a perfectly curved body, long wavy blond hair, blue eyes and a face that stole a man's breath. While Patience could not compete with Heather's gorgeous features, she at least was attractive. A few inches taller than Heather, she had a body defined by her love of strenuous activities, tree climbing being a favorite of hers, and long black hair that she forever drew back with a leather strip. She had lovely green eyes that would brighten when she cried, which she rarely did. It was usually other people she made cry.

Whereas she... she sighed inwardly. Emma did not know how to define herself. Plain features, brown hair, though on occasion some blond streaks shined through, and the shortest of the sisters at about four inches over five feet. She gave another inward sigh at the thought of her body. Even though Heather had tried to convince her many times that she had a lovely body, she wore loose tunics to hide her shapelessness. Her gracious words were always lost on Emma, for she did not believe her sister.

Enough, she silently scolded herself. Her life was full and she was happy. At least, she would be once she was home again. She had no desire to meet Rogan of the Clan MacClennan. She did not believe that it was only the laird who had refused the proposal for his son to wed her as her father had told her. She was certain that Rogan himself had voiced his opinion on the matter and had gotten his way. He would marry the beautiful Macinnes sister, not the plain one.

Emma almost refused to accompany Heather on this journey, knowing what she would face upon arrival at the MacClennan keep. People would stare and whisper hurtful remarks, thinking she could not hear them, but she would hear them. Unfortunately, refusal was not an option for her. Her father had beamed with pride that the stubborn Angus had requested her help.

Her father was the only man who had ever told her that she was pretty. And he had promised her that he would find her a handsome husband who would treat her good. She did not have the heart to tell him that it was a dream that would never come true.

Her father had been more devastated than she had been when Angus had turned down his offer for her and Rogan to unite along with making him laird of the Macinnes clan. Her father had been willing to give up all he owned to see her wed to a handsome and good man.

She recalled seeing Rogan on the few occasions that he and his father would visit with her father.

She had not paid him much heed nor had he acknowledged her. She had not seen him in years, though he had been a handsome one when he was young. She could only imagine what fine features he must possess now. Patience had teased Heather unmercifully when the arrangements had been made. She had gone on about what beautiful children the two would have, and she was right. They would make beautiful children.

"There is a spot ahead where we can stop," James said, catching her attention, "but not for long. We are not far from MacClennan land and I wish to reach the keep before nightfall."

"As you say," Emma said pleased. She would take the brief time and opportunity to forage in the forest and see what it had to offer. It was early spring, planting time weeks away but the forest did produce early seedlings, and she hoped to gather a few interesting ones.

A small clearing could be seen after the bend in the road and most likely that was where James intended to stop. She grew eager to reach it, eager to dismount, and beyond eager to explore.

She urged her mare forward, hoping to get there and be off foraging before Patience had the chance to object, and no doubt James would agree. With a smile on her face and no longer caring about her arrival at the MacClennan clan, Emma pressed forward.

The attack came so fast that Macinnes warriors barely had time to react. Men dropped down from trees, rushed out of the forest, and sprung from behind bushes. Emma quickly pulled a dirk from her boot and turned her horse in an attempt to reach her sisters.

Not one of the attackers tried to stop her and as she maneuvered her way through the melee she realized why. While the warriors were kept occupied fighting off the surprise attack, Patience was bravely fighting off three men who were trying to get to Heather.

It struck Emma then, the men had come for her sister, but why?

Emma did not wait. She hurried her mare, giving anyone in her path a hefty kick. No one was going to take her sister if she could help it. She reached Heather's side as a man reached out to grab her. Emma swung her dirk at his arm, splitting it open and with a forceful kick sent him tumbling to the ground.

Emma and Patience fought wildly, trying to keep the men from capturing their sister. And it appeared as if they were winning. Several of their attackers scurried back into the woods, presumably to lick their wounds, but not so. As the wounded foe disappeared into the dense forest, a deluge of men emerged from it, swords drawn.

In seconds, they were surrounded. The Macinnes warriors fought tirelessly, but to no avail. Heather was scooped off her horse and carted away while Emma and Patience fought to get to her.

Once the forest swallowed Heather and her abductor, the other men swiftly followed and in minutes all was quiet around them... all except Patience.

"Get on your horses now, we are going after her," Patience shouted and turned furious eyes on James. "Do not attempt to fight me on this. The men who are able go with me or I go alone. Leave a man to watch over the injured and you go and alert father to what has happened and return with Macinnes warriors."

"I will send a man, but I stay here," James protested.

"You will do as I say," Patience snapped. "You ride faster than the others and you know the best warriors to return with, so do as I say. We waste enough time arguing."

James reluctantly agreed and began gathering available warriors.

Patience turned to Emma. "You take the wounded to the MacClennan keep and tell Rogan what happened. Make certain he gathers his men and returns here to follow my trail. You know how to track. I taught you when you were young."

Emma nodded.

Patience reached out to Emma and they locked hands. "I will not return until I rescue Heather."

"And I will not rest until the three of us are united again."

They hugged and Patience whispered something to Emma before she stepped away, mounted her horse, and rode off into the woods, leading the warriors.

James had men gathered in no time and with a word of warning to Emma to stay with the wounded while Dunnan went to get help from the

MacClennans, he took off.

This was one time men wanted Emma—when they were injured. The wounded warriors knew that her healing knowledge could save them. So, they reached out to her. It did not take her long to assess the injuries and determine that all, save for Dunnan, would prohibit travel. That was until she noticed how Dunnan held his arm close to his side and winced now and again as he prepared to leave.

She hurried over to him. "You have been wounded." She did not wait for him to reply, she grabbed his arm.

He let out a holler. "It is nothing."

"Sit," she ordered, pointing to a stump.

"Time is wasting. I need to be on my way."

"Not until I see to your wound," she said and stepped between him and his horse.

Dunnan mumbled, but sat.

One look told her what she feared. "The wound is too serious for you to travel."

"Wrap it, I will be fine."

"No, you will bleed to death before you reach MacClennan land."

"Nonsense."

She jostled his arm. He let out a yell, blood running down it, and paled considerably.

"I will tend it and you will use it as little as possible so that it will heal properly."

"Who will go and fetch the MacClennans?"

"I will," she said as if it was a command. She would have no choice. There was no one else fit to go. She would have to go alone.

Dunnan protested her decision the whole time

she tended his wound, insisting her father, and most of all Patience, would have all their hides if they allowed her to continue on unaided. The other warriors agreed, saying they would not let her go.

"I waste precious time standing here arguing with all of you," she said hands on hips, facing them. "I have already wasted time caring for your wounds. I will go on alone and return with help, and I will hear no more about it. You will obey me on this."

Not another objection was made. Dunnan, who knew the land well, explained the trail to her and told her not to rear off it.

"The woods are thick in these parts and you will be lost for sure," he warned.

She paid heed to his words, but did not let him frighten her. She often searched the woods on her own and always managed to find her way home thanks to Patience. She had taught her how to mark a trail and it had helped her on many an occasion.

With one last check on the wounded, she mounted her horse and was on her way. She kept a good pace and kept her focus on her task. She would not fail Heather or Patience. She would bring help and find them both.

A roll of thunder had her casting a glance to the graying sky. "Please, please don't let it rain," she whispered. The rain would wash away any tracks and make following Patience that much more difficult.

She rode hard, praying as she went. The rain started a short time later. It was not long before it was pouring buckets and not long before she was soaked through, her wool cloak doing little to keep her dry. She kept going, wiping the rain from her eyes and holding back her tears.

The MacClennan village came into view over a small rise. She halted her mare to have a look. Cottages comprised most of the outer bailey, while the inner bailey held the stables and storehouses and beyond that lay the large stone keep. A high stonewall encircled them all. She hurried the horse along, entering through two tall, thick wooden doors that stood open with not a guard in sight. Once in the village, she headed for the keep. No one was about, though when she reached the steps a young lad suddenly appeared.

"You be a Macinnes," he asked.

"I am," Emma said.

"I am to tend the horses."

He looked around, expecting others to be with her, but he would not ask. It was not his place to question. She handed her mare's reins over to him and hurried up the few steps to the keep.

She paid no heed to her appearance, though knew she had to look a sight, soaked through as she was and her hair dripping wet. She rushed into the Great Hall, not as many warriors or villagers there as she had expected, but her greeting was exactly what she had expected.

"The plain one leads the way," Angus MacClennan shouted from the dais with a raise of his tankard in welcome. "We were worried the storm would delay your arrival, though it appears it got you good. You look like a drowned cat."

She ignored Angus's thoughtless remark, seeing that he was far into his cups and would be of no use to her and demanded, "Where is Rogan?"

"It is not your place to be asking about him, lassie, he belongs to your sister," Angus said, standing, though swaying. "I made that clear to your da."

Emma noticed that though Angus had pure white hair that lay to his shoulders and some wrinkles around the eyes, he had fine features and his body was well-honed for a man of his years. She recalled his wife had been a beauty and a kind woman and from what her father had told her about him, Angus still grieved her loss these past three years now.

That did not, however, give him cause to be rude. She would not be put off by this man. Her sister's life was at stake. "I would speak to you, but you are too far into your cups to be of help. I will speak to your son *now*."

The wooden floor began to tremble and Emma turned to see a small group of warriors march into the room. Their leader wore a dark brown cloak, the hood pulled down over his head concealing his face.

"Rogan, Emma Macinnes demands to see you," Angus shouted.

The cloaked warrior threw his hood back and stopped right in front of Emma. "Where is my intended?"

Emma never had her legs turn weak at the sight of a man, but this man caused her legs to tremble until she thought she would collapse. He towered over her and muscles ran thick and hard beneath his shirt and across his chest. His shirtsleeves were rolled up to his elbows and black leather arm cuffs covered the remainder of his arm to his wrist. His dark brown hair fell away from his face to an inch or two passed his shoulders. However, it was his face that made her breath catch. Never had she seen a man with such stunning features. Even the scowl he wore could not diminish his exceptional good looks. The young handsome lad she had once seen had grown into an even more handsome man.

"Answer me, lass."

He did not shout like his father had, but there was a command to his tone that she imagined all obeyed without questions... as did she.

"Heather was taken by a band of rebels."

His hand shot out and grabbed her arm so tight that it squeezed the rain water from her sleeve. "Where? When?"

"About four hours ago we were about to stop at a small clearing along the road when we were attacked. My sister Patience went after her with those of our warriors who were able. Those who suffered injuries wait for my return. You must get your warriors together and go with me now."

His dark eyes remained fixed on her, and she could see that he was giving thought to her words. Her heartbeat quickened, upset that she had gotten no immediate reaction from him. When he did speak, she grew angry.

"You will tell me everything about the attack while you dry by the fire and eat. Night falls within the hour and the rain already hampers our vision.

My warriors and I will leave at first light."

Emma tried to free her arm, but she could not budge it. His grip was much too strong. "That is too late. We must leave now."

He released her arm, though remained beside her. "That would be foolish for us to do. You will do as I say and stay here while I go and go and bring your sister home."

She was more shocked than angry that he was not running from the keep ready to rescue Heather. She could not hold her tongue. "Since you are a *coward,* I will go find my sister myself."

Gasps echoed throughout the hall, but Emma ignored them and turned to leave. Before she could take one step, a strong arm locked around her waist and she was swung around and slammed against Rogan's steel-hard chest.

"No one accuses me of being a coward and lives," Rogan said his nose pressed against hers.

Fear rushed through her, turning her stomach and shivering her flesh, but she refused to pay heed to it. It did not matter that this powerful warrior threatened her. It only mattered that her sister was rescued and returned home. "Then kill me and be done with it or let me go so that I can do what you will not."

He let out a roar that Emma swore shook the rafters, then he grabbed her, tossed her over his shoulder, and headed out of the room.

Chapter Two

Rogan dropped Emma to her feet once in a small bedchamber and slammed the door, then turned on her. "You will watch your foolish tongue or suffer for it the next time. I understand you are upset and that you have ridden hard to get here and get help for your sister, but you are here and you now have the help you need. There is no more you can do. I will see to this from here on."

"No!" Emma shouted, stepping away from him, the width and breadth of him much too intimidating. "Heather is my sister, and I will not abandon her. I go with you or I go on my own."

"It is good I chose Heather over you for a wife, for you are a willful lass."

Emma's chin shot up defiantly, though his thoughtless remark stabbed at her heart. It was one thing to assume that a man did not want her, but another thing to hear it from him. "I do not care what you think of me, and I am blessed that you will not be my husband. And since you will not be my husband, you have no say over me. I will not let you stop me from seeing my sister safe."

"You think I cannot stop you?" he asked incredulously.

"I am not blind," she said, recalling the ease in which he had hefted her over his shoulder and the strength of his muscled arms that had held her firm. "You are a mighty warrior, but I am a determined sister. I will not be left behind."

Rogan itched to reach out and grab her and—throttle her. He did not need her interfering, getting in his way, being more of a hindrance than help. Rogan caught the shiver that ran through her and silently swore. Dampness was probably seeping into her bones from her wet garments.

"Get out of those wet clothes," he ordered.

Her eyes popped wide. He could not expect her to strip naked in front of him. Could he? "Or what?" she dared him. Two long strides had him leaning over her and planting his face so close to hers that she could see that his dark eyes were dotted with specks of gold.

"Or I will strip you myself. Not that I will take any pleasure in it. You are soaked and need to get dry."

Another thoughtless remark that tore at her, not that she would want him to touch her, but of course he had to let her know that stripping her would be a chore.

"I have no other garments," she snapped, feeling pity for Heather that she should be stuck with this rude man—if they could find her. The thought of possibly never seeing her sister again caused her legs to go so weak that she had to grab the back of the wood chair, she stood beside, for support.

He saw that exhaustion and worry were taking their toll on her. She needed to get dry and rest. And if he was lucky, she would sleep through his departure. Then there would be nothing she could do but remain here while he saw to rescuing her sister.

"Sit," he snapped frustrated with her foolishness.

"No!" she retaliated sharply. "I will have your word that you will take me with you or I leave now and see to finding my sister myself."

His hand snapped out and grabbed her wrist, yanking her from behind the chair and slamming her against his solid chest once again. His dark eyes blazed with fury, and she feared she had gone too far.

"Listen well, Emma, for my warning is not to be taken lightly. I rule here and I will not be disobeyed. You will do as I say or I will see you locked away in the tower until I return with your sister."

His threat sent a chill to settle deep in her bones, but courage did not fail her. "You may rule here, but you do not rule over me."

"Do not test me, for you will surely lose." He released her, shoving her away from him.

Though she wanted to unleash her tongue on him, she wisely held it. Arguing with him was pointless. He would do as he wished no matter her protests, though one thing was certain—she would not be left behind.

"Finally, some sense settles over you and your tongue stills."

Emma had to clamp her lips tightly shut to keep from spitting out her anger at the frustrating warrior. Poor Heather, her lot would be heavy with Rogan as her husband, and Emma felt a twinge of guilt for being grateful that he had refused to wed her.

"I will have food and dry garments brought to you. While I go find your sister and make the culprit pay for abducting her, you will look over my land and see what can be done to improve it."

Emma stared at him stunned. He truly believed that she would concentrate on his land while her sister was in danger?

"Warm yourself," he said with a nod toward the hearth. "Someone will be here soon to see to your needs." With that he left the room, shutting the door behind him.

Emma stared at the closed door, feeling as if she had been dismissed without an ounce of regard to her concerns. Rogan obviously was accustomed to being obeyed, especially by women. His handsome features and fine body probably had all women easily obeying his every command and seeing to his every whim. She, however, was not most women. Being plain in feature and mostly disregarded by men had made Emma view men differently than other women. No man had ever impressed her in speech or actions. They blustered and demanded and were never nearly as important as they thought they were.

She had paid mind to none. Even her father had had a difficult time with her. He could never understand her interest in things that most women cared little about. In a way, she had realized that she had been lucky to be born plain, for she had not wasted her time on a man, but had pursued her interests. She knew more about the workings of the land and animals than most men, and learned knowledge had greatly benefitted her clan.

A shiver ran through Emma and she quickly stepped in front of the hearth to try and warm herself, though it would do little good. She was well aware that she needed to rid herself of her wet garments if she hoped to chase the chill. But this would do until dry garments arrived.

A plan was already forming in her head. She would need to make certain that she shed her wet garments, ate, and got some rest before taking her leave. She had no intentions of being left behind no matter what Rogan had said. She intended to accompany him in his search to find Heather, and Patience as well, though she hoped that Patience had already found Heather. She was certainly a persistent and skilled enough warrior to do so. But if not, Emma was confident that Rogan would find her sister, and she would be there when he did.

Emma jumped, startled by the door flying open, and a short, stout woman with a generous smile hurried in. It was easy to see from the numerous wrinkles around her mouth that she smiled often and her soft green eyes greeted as generously as her wide smile.

"Good lord, you will catch your death in those wet garments," the woman said, shaking her head and hurrying over to Emma. "Now you just let Bertha tend you and all will be well."

Before Emma knew what was happening, Bertha had her out of her soaked garments and a blanket wrapped around her and seated before the hearth.

"We will get you all warmed up, food in your belly, and then you will sleep."

The woman was as authoritative as Rogan, though in a more pleasant and caring manner and Emma could not help but like her.

Servants arrived with blankets and trays of deliciously scented food that had Emma realizing that she was hungrier than she have thought. And her limbs were beginning to complain from the hard ride in the rain. She needed to rest, but not too long. She had to leave before Rogan or she had no doubt he would do as he had warned and lock her in the tower.

"Here is a nice warm nightdress for you," Bertha said, handing her a soft wool garment. She then gathered up Emma's wet garments and boots. "I will see that these are dried and ready for you tomorrow, after you are well rested."

"They can dry by the fire," Emma said.

"Nonsense, they will dry faster by the larger fireplace," Bertha said. "Now you get straight into bed and sleep and leave the task of finding your sister to Rogan. He will not fail to bring her home."

Emma realized then that Rogan had ordered her garments taken from her, leaving her no recourse but to remain at the keep. What pained her heart even more was that she was losing her sister to this beast of a man. This would be Heather's home soon and Emma would miss her greatly. But first Heather needed to be found, and Emma intended to be there when she was.

If Rogan thought that by taking her garments he would stop her, he was wrong. She would travel in her nightdress only, if she must.

Emma dared not chance lying on the bed, for she would surely drop into a much needed, and much too deep, slumber. She remained in the chair by the fire after slipping on the nightdress. She would doze until she felt the time was right to take her leave. She had eaten well, which would help to give her strength and with rest she would be fit to take to the road again.

The warmth of the fire lulled her to sleep, though she woke on and off in the hours that followed. It was well into the night when Emma decided it was time. She worried that Rogan may have posted a guard outside her door, but when she eased it open, no one was there. She supposed depriving her of all but a nightdress made him think he had solved the problem.

She kept her steps cautious and was relieved when she found the Great Hall empty, though she crept silently through the large room in case someone lingered nearby. She was thrilled to find a hooded, fur-lined cloak lying on one of the table benches. She hurriedly swiped it up and draped it over her shoulders to protect her from the chill of an early spring night. She was, however, disappointed not to find any boots. So, she left the keep with her feet bare.

The rain continued to fall, though not as hard as before. It took her a bit of time to locate her mare and ready her to ride. She searched the stable for boots, but found none. Like it or not, she would go barefoot. But it was little to suffer when she thought of what Heather might be going through. As she rode away from the keep and across MacClennan land, she prayed that her sister was safe and that they would find her before any harm could befall her and that Rogan MacClennan would not be too angry when he found her gone.

Chapter Three

"What do you mean she is gone?" Rogan roared.

"She is nowhere to be found and her horse is gone," Bertha said.

"I ordered you to take her garments from her," Rogan snapped as he looked around for his cloak, having recalled leaving it on one of the benches last night.

"I did take her garments and her boots as well."

Rogan's eyes narrowed and he shook his head. "Do you mean to say that she has gone off in only a nightdress?"

"The cloak you look for is missing, so she does have that, though she is most assuredly barefoot," Bertha said with a firm nod. "She certainly is a determined lass."

"She is going to be a sorry lass when I lay my hands on her."

"Emma is not your wife," Bertha reminded.

"Thank God for that."

"Perhaps," Bertha said with a shrug, "though it takes a strong woman to flee nearly naked in the rain to go after someone she obviously loves very much."

"It is well known how close the three Macinnes sisters are and Donald Macinnes confirmed it himself, but Heather is to be my wife and I will come before her sisters. Emma will learn that fast enough."

Bertha grinned. "Will she now?"

Rogan rolled his eyes. "I need none of your age-old wisdom right now."

"Later then," Bertha said, her grin firm, "for you will surely need it."

Rogan ignored her and shouted to a passing servant to fetch a cloak from his bedchamber. He looked back at Bertha. "You will watch over Da for me."

"As I always do, though if he does not stop drowning his sorrows in drink he will soon join his beloved Anna, which is what I believe he wants more than anything."

"It was bad enough losing Mum. I don't want to lose Da as well, but I am helpless of what to do for him."

Bertha shook her head. "There is nothing you can do. Your Da will do as he will just as you do, a trait common to the MacClennan men."

"Are you telling me that I am stubborn?" Rogan asked his brow narrowing, though a slight smile touched his lips.

"You are," Bertha said her smile spreading, "but you may have met your match in Emma." She snatched a wrapped bundle off the bench and held it out to Rogan. "Clothes for Emma."

A heavy frown gripped Rogan, and he snatched the bundle out of Bertha's hands and stormed out of the keep, a servant hurrying after him with his cloak in her hands.

~~~

Emma reached the injured Macinnes warriors by daylight, though gray skies greeted the morn. Thankfully, the rain had stopped halfway through her ride, leaving her wet but not soaked. She did not care for the scene she came upon. The injured warriors had not fared well through the rain-soaked night. They needed shelter, warmth, and food, and she knew where she would get it for them.

Dunnan appeared the heartiest, his wound minor and his stamina strong. His hands went to help her off the horse, but she shook her head and slid off with ease.

"You will be using that injured arm enough when it becomes necessary. You do not need to waste it on me when I can fare for myself."

Dunnan's eyes turned wide as he looked her over.

Emma realized how she must look, her hair hanging in wet strands, her bare feet caked with mud and wearing only a wet nightdress and cloak.

She shrugged. "I had to leave in a hurry."

Dunnan scowled. "Did someone try to harm you?"

"No, but someone would not let me join in the search for my sister."

Dunnan smiled. "He will be here soon?"

"He will," she said with a nod, "and he will insist that I return to his home with the injured, and that I will not do."
~~~

"Then you best be on your way. I will get the men ready to leave."

"No message from Patience?" Emma asked, though knew it would have been the first thing Dunnan had spoken of, if there had been one.

Dunnan shook his head. "Nothing."

"You will have shelter, care, and food soon enough. Stay with the MacClennan clan until you hear from a Macinnes. I want to have a quick look at the injured before I leave and let them know they will be safe and tended to soon."

Dunnan joined her as she took time with each warrior, assuring them they would do well and seeing to changing a bandage or two before she was finished.

Dunnan walked her to her horse, though she would not let him help her mount. "You be careful, lassie, and remember the things I taught you about the land. She will keep you safer than people will."

Emma nodded and, though fear gripped her stomach, she gave Dunnan a nod and took off to search for any signs Patience had left for her, knowing that it would not be long before Rogan caught up with her.

~~~

"She has what?" Rogan asked, shaking his head at the large warrior, not believing what he had just told him.

"Emma has gone to find her sister," Dunnan repeated.
~~~

"You let her go off on her own?" Rogan continued shaking his head. He had never met such a willful woman in his life. No wonder her father had such trouble finding her a husband. Not only was she plain of features, but she was too damn obstinate for any man to want.

"Emma is," —Dunnan paused and chewed at his lower lip for a moment— "an independent lassie."

Rogan laughed, though it held a bitter tone and had his warriors and the Macinnes warriors turning their heads to stare at him.

"Mule-headed is more like it," Rogan said, though giving it thought he realized that Emma was also shrewd. She had known that he would have sent her along with her warriors to his home, so she made certain that the option had been taken from him. But now he had two women to find, three if he counted Patience, though what he knew of her, she was an accomplished warrior in her own right.

"Emma is a good woman and does well by her clan," Dunnan said loudly.

Macinnes warriors began getting to their feet and the ones who could not were helped by others to stand. While none were in any shape to fight, they all made the effort of showing that they would defend her name and honor regardless of their weakened conditions.

Rogan was impressed. Emma was obviously well thought of by her clan, but then her unique knowledge of the land and animals had greatly benefitted her clan. So, they would be likely to hold her in high regard.

"It would take the devil himself to stop her from

searching for her sister," Dunnan added and the other warriors agreed with nods and shouts.

It was clear that the Macinnes warriors were letting him know that they would not take kindly to him preventing Emma from joining in the search for her sister, but then Rogan did not take well to threats.

"If Emma can best the devil, then she has the right to search for her sister," he said loud enough for all to hear and the MacClennan warriors smiled.

Dunnan did not take well to his remark and turned to walk away.

"I am not finished," Rogan said, stopping him.

Dunnan turned back around reluctantly.

"Carts have been brought to carry your wounded back to my home where you all will be cared for until you are well enough to return home."

"I was told to wait there until I hear from a Macinnes."

"Then wait you shall," Rogan said and took a step closer to the man, "though make no mistake, my word is law there and if I say otherwise you will obey."

Dunnan nodded, not fool enough to argue with the chieftain. He had heard stories about Rogan MacClennan and what a fierce and fearless warrior he was. And from the look and demeanor of the mighty warrior they appeared to be true.

A tall, slender warrior, with long brown hair and fine features approached Rogan.

"Did you find her tracks, Liam?" Rogan asked.

The warrior nodded. "It is an easy enough trail

to follow."

"Not good," Rogan said, "if we can follow her trail so easily than others can as well."

"There were no signs of anyone following her," Liam confirmed.

Concern for Emma had Dunnan speaking up. "There had been no signs that we were being followed before the attack. They came out of nowhere, some dropping from trees, others appearing as if they materialized out of thin air, they were upon us so fast. And once they had Heather, they all vanished, even the injured ones."

"Are you saying that the attack was for the sole purpose of abducting Heather?" Rogan asked the suggestion difficult to believe.

"What other reason could there be? They took nothing, only Heather, and if they were after women, why not take Patience and Emma as well?" Dunnan argued.

Rogan did not like what he heard. If that was so, then this was no random abduction. It had been planned. But why only take Heather? For now, he could only ponder the disturbing questions, time being of the essence in his search for Heather. The more time he wasted, the more difficult it would be to find her. He needed to locate her trail and track down the culprit who had had the audacity to capture his intended and make him pay and bring Heather home safely.

"Liam, set us on the right trail," Rogan ordered, and then turned to shout. "We leave now."

He and his warriors mounted their horses in minutes, and after orders to his warriors to head directly home and stop for nothing, he and his troop took off.

~~~

Emma had come across a babbling stream, the tracks she had been following having taken her off a well-worn path. While her horse drank, she discarded her cloak and knelt beside the water and got a distorted glimpse of her reflection, which made her look even worse than she already did. Dried mud spotted her face here and there and her hair hung in strings over her shoulders. Her hands were a mixture of dried mud and scratches, and she wished she had remembered to use the salve in her satchel before leaving the stable. The mixture was her own concoction she had scented with lavender and it kept her hands in fine shape, not to mention soft and smelling nice. But she had forgotten about it and now she had no time to care for her hands, or for that matter herself. She looked affright, and she doubted that even a brief washing would change that.

She went to dip her hands in the water when she caught another reflection shimmering just behind hers. It towered over her and the breadth of it made it seem like it was about to devour her.

"You deserve a good dunking in there for disobeying me."

She released the breath that had caught in her throat, realizing it was Rogan, though there was a threat to his words and for a moment she wondered
~~~

if he would actually carry through on it. She quickly got to her feet and turned to face him.

Why was it that he seemed larger than last time she saw him? His shoulders appeared broader, his chest thicker and of course muscles rippled everywhere over him. She had to admit that she had not seen many warriors built as powerfully as him. Many were thick and solid, but Rogan was more defined, almost as if he had been sculpted by a skilled craftsman.

She shook her head, chasing away the observation since it seemed to cause a strange stirring in her and focused on what was more important. "Then you would do me a favor, for I require a good washing."

It took a moment for Rogan to comprehend her response. He was much too engaged in the way her wet nightdress clung to her curvaceous body. Her loose garments had hidden well the treasure beneath. Her plentiful breasts would spill over in his large hands, and such a narrow waist tempted to be stroked. Then there was her full hips and rounded backside that had his hands aching to take hold and squeeze. But the place his eyes lingered the most was the triangle of dark hair between her slim, hard legs, the passageway to pleasure that turned him hard.

With an angry growl, he dismissed his foolish thoughts, and said, "I have garments and boots for you. Clean yourself up, dress, and then we talk."

"If you have more of the same to say, then do not waste your breath."

Rogan clenched his hands at his sides. "If you

were my woman, I would—"

"But I am not your woman and glad of it I am. I would not want a husband who thought me so dimwitted that he felt the need to dictate to me all the time. My husband will be my partner or I will not wed."

"Then that will be your lot in life, for there is not a man alive who would wed a harridan like you."

Emma recoiled, once again feeling as if he had struck her. He not only thought her bad-tempered, but old-looking as well. Did she truly appear aged and unappealing when he looked upon her? She had been called many things through the years that hurt more than if she had been hit with a stone. This was one of them.

Rogan bit at his tongue for his heartless remark. Emma might not share the beauty that her sisters possess, but she certainly was not unattractive. And old she was not, her fine body attesting to that. He was not used to being defied and Emma certainly had a penchant for defying authority.

Emma tossed her chin up and glared at him. "Then I am lucky, for I will be free to live my life as I choose, instead of being saddled with a husband who has not half the intelligence that I do." She pointed a finger at him. "Now go so I may wash and dress."

She actually thought herself more intelligent than a man and she was dismissing him like a common servant. Never before this day had he wanted to throttle a woman as badly as he did

Emma. Not that he would. After all, she was a mere woman and a powerful man did not raise his hand against the weak. But then Emma had proved herself anything but weak.

Rogan crossed his arms over his chest. "I will turn around, but I will not leave you to your own devises, since I cannot trust you to take off again on your own."

"I am where I need to be —"

"With me," Rogan finished, "and you will not go off on your own again or I will bind you and see you sent home on the back of your horse. And do not bother to ask if it is a threat or a promise, for it is both, and you will do well to remember it." After tossing the small sack of clothes to her, he turned his back, signaling that the discussion was over.

She did not waste her breath arguing with him. He was much too pig-headed to see reason. She got busy washing up as best she could and getting dressed, though she found the garments a bit big and the boots as well. She supposed her clothes had not dried in time and she had been sent another's to wear. She wished she had taken the time to retrieve some of her own garments before leaving the injured men. But after having checked on the wounded, she could not have spared another moment or she would have risked being caught and sent home. And that had been something she had made sure had not happened, nor would it. Her sisters were counting on her, and she would not let them down.

When she finished, she ran her fingers through her hair, working through the stubborn knots with several grimaces before she was done. Then she twisted her long hair and secured it in a tight knot at the nape of her neck as Heather had taught her to do.

She rolled up the wet and muddy nightdress she had used to dry herself, intending to wash it first chance she got. With no garments to spare, it could become useful along the way.

Emma did not bother to glance over herself one last time. She looked as she did and there was no changing that. Besides, how she looked did not matter in the least.

She called out, "I am finished and ready to ride."

Rogan turned around ready to lay down the law—his law—to her since he had no choice but to take her along, but he was struck silent when he laid eyes upon her. Her hair was drawn back tightly away from her face and her cheeks were spotted red from the fresh scrubbing. Her eyes seemed a bit larger. Or was it that their lovely green color that reminded him of meadows and hills on a fine spring day made them more appealing? Were her lips a bit plumper than he had first noticed? He grunted beneath his breath annoyed that she had caught his eye in a manner he had not expected. He also grew more annoyed that he could not get the image of her enticing body in the wet nightdress out of his mind. He would be wise to remember her quick tongue and willful ways and that her sister Heather was his intended. Still, he could not ignore that the sight of her had aroused him twice in a very short time. If he had not lain with a woman recently, he would have blamed it on too much time between a good and satisfying poke. But it had been only a day that he had shared a lively and gratifying evening with a lassie that had been more than willing.

So why the bloody hell had this woman, plain in features and defiant tongue, aroused him?

He grunted low again and advanced on her with a quick step. Her eyes narrowed, her chin went up, and she held her ground, which surprised him since more often than not such a sudden move intimidated a person, but obviously not Emma.

"Since I have no choice but to take you along, listen well to what I say. You will obey my every word, for I have no time to deal with your foolish antics that serve no purpose but to delay my search for my intended."

"Delay your search?" she repeated incredulously. "You did a fine job of that yourself. And my foolish antics found the trail of those who took my sister, so I warn you, I will let nothing get in the way of finding my sister—not even you."

Chapter Four

Rogan was the last to mount his horse and with the furious look on his face, his warriors wisely gave him a wide berth. He guided his stallion next to Emma's mare and in an even, though threatening tone said, "Issue me such a warning again and I will see you bound and draped over your horse and sent home to your father."

Emma smiled pleasantly. "You would have to catch me first." With that, she rode off in an easy trot, her head turning from side to side, studying the muddied path as she went.

Rogan glared after her. Her wit and tongue were much too quick. There would come a time that he would call her to task for it and see her disciplined for such improper behavior, but now was not that time. He had Heather to think about. Sweet. Beautiful Heather. Wagging tongues spoke of her kindness and her generosity and how not a harsh word ever passed her lips. Heather would prove a good wife and their marriage beneficial to his clan.

His musings were interrupted by his tracker Liam as he rode up alongside him. They had been friends from when they could first walk and that friendship had grown stronger through the years. Liam was one person he knew without a doubt that he could trust. Though his wife Ina was another good friend, two years younger than Liam, she had forever dogged their steps. Mostly though, it had been Liam she had followed around. It was as if she had claimed him for herself on first sight and refused to let go. Liam had never seemed to mind and no one had been surprised when they wed five years ago. They had yet to welcome a child, though it had not been for lack of trying, as Liam had confided, but at least they had each other. They had always had each other. They were meant to be, and they did make a fine pair. Liam tall and slender and Ina petite and pretty and with a head of flaming red hair that curled every which way. They got to wed for love. Something Rogan would never be able to do. His father had once encouraged him to find a woman to love as he and Rogan's mother had. But time passed and with no prospects of love on the horizon and Rogan having recently turned twenty and five years, it was time for him to wed. It had been his choice to seek a bride, to see his duty done and his father had not argued.

Liam nodded toward Emma. "She is skillful at reading the land. Those tracks were not easy to find after the rain."

"It is a shame that she does not do as well with holding her tongue."

"Can you blame her, Rogan? If Ina had a sister she would not let me rest until she was found. And I would be wise to do as she asked or suffer for it."

"Still, Ina knows when to hold her tongue."

Liam laughed. "When did Ina ever hold her tongue?"

A smile tickled the corners of Rogan's mouth. "I remember when she was but six years and claimed that she loved you and that you would one day be her husband, then continued to remind you of it through the years."

Liam nodded, his smile growing wider. "And reminded me of it yet again just before we took our vows, though I think it was more of an I-told-you-so."

"You are a lucky man to have a woman who loves you that much."

"That I am, and grateful for her every day."

Both men watched as Emma turned her horse and rode toward them.

"You are the tracker?" Emma asked, fairly sure he was since she had seen him earlier studying the ground.

"I am," Liam said proud of his skill.

"Then what are you doing here prattling on like a gossiping woman when tracks need to be watched?" She did not give either man a chance to respond. "Come with me, I want to show you something." Again she gave them no chance to respond. She rode off, expecting to be followed.

"One day..." Rogan said through gritted teeth.

"I was waiting for her to discover the problem," Liam said.

"What problem?"

"There are two sets of tracks. They divide where Emma had stopped. The question is who do the two tracks belong to and why would the two diverge?"

Rogan followed Liam to see for himself.

Emma slid off her mare and studied the tracks. If one did not have a good eye for tracking, the fact that one set of tracks converged with the other would not be noticed. She followed along the one trail a few feet, and then turned and followed the other one.

Liam dismounted and did the same.

Rogan remained on his horse watching the pair, though his eyes mostly followed Emma. It did not surprise him that her extensive knowledge included tracking. It was widely known that her unique skills had greatly benefitted the Macinnes clan. Their harvests were more than bountiful and their livestock well-bred. Winters saw no shortage of food for the large clan and, due to Emma's expanding knowledge of plants, illnesses were not as rampant as in other clans. It was the reason his father had requested that she accompany Heather. He wanted her to show him what needed to be done so that the MacClennan clan could flourish like the Macinnes clan.

Liam turned to Emma. "It would appear that the group that captured Heather divided, leaving your sister Patience to make a choice as to which trail to follow."

"So it would appear," Emma agreed, "though knowing Patience she would have sent a warrior or two along the other path so as not to choose the wrong one and waste time following a worthless trail."

"That would mean that since no reverse tracks are here that she had chosen the correct path to follow," Liam said with a satisfied nod and looked to Rogan and pointed. “We go that way.”

Rogan and Liam were both surprised when Emma mounted her mare on her own. With her own strength, she pulled herself up and onto the horse and without a glance to either man, she followed the trail her sister Patience had taken.

Once on his horse, Liam turned to Rogan. “I will scout ahead.”

“Keep an extra eye out,” Rogan warned. “Emma had said that no one had been spotted before the attack. Her injured warriors had also commented on how their attackers appeared out of nowhere like ghosts.”

Liam stared at him for a moment, as if fearful of speaking what he thought.

“I know what you are thinking, for I have thought the same myself. It sounds like the work of the Dark Dragon. His warriors appear out of nowhere and vanish to God knows where.”

“No one has ever tracked him or at least lived to tell about it,” Liam said. “But what would he want with Heather?”

“My thought exactly. And though many reasons have run through my mind, none make any sense, except one.”

Liam felt his gut tighten, for he was sure he had reached the same conclusion as Rogan.

“The Dark Dragon wants Heather for himself,” Rogan said, fighting to keep his anger at bay.

“No!” Emma said empathically.

Both men turned, seeing that she was only a few feet from them.

"Do not say such a thing. A vile creature such as he could not have Heather." Emma fought back tears at such a horrible possibility. She turned pleading eyes on Rogan. "Please, we must find her."

"We will," Rogan assured her, his gut wrenching at the pain he saw in her eyes, and he turned to Liam. "Follow the trail ahead and alert us to any changes. Keep a fast pace, for we shall as well."

Rogan did as he said. They traveled at a sharp pace, not deviating from the trail Patience had taken. Emma was sure that her sister had kept a fierce pace, not wanting to take a chance that Heather would be lost to them. And she felt the same. She hoped, though more prayed, they would come upon her sisters safe and waiting from them to come to their aid, but as the day wore on her hope faded.

It was just before nightfall that Rogan ordered his troop to stop, and though Emma wanted to protest, she knew it would be a foolish thing to do. They had ridden long and hard and needed the rest so that tomorrow they could begin anew. Patience had always warned her that strength needed to be maintained if one was to succeed in her endeavor. Whether hungry or not, one was to eat and whether tired or not, one was to sleep. Otherwise a battle, a mission, a task would fail.

Emma ate heartily when presented with food that night, her sister's words ringing in her ears, reminding what she must do, though her stomach had no use for sustenance. Sleep was harder for her to achieve, and she found herself staring at the flames until, unable to deal with her worrying thoughts, she sat up.

She walked soundlessly around the camp, listening to the warriors snoring and wishing she and her sisters were home and that this was nothing more than a nightmare.

"Sleep eludes you?"

Emma startled, though gave no shout of alarm, another thing Patience had taught her. A sharp cry could alert the enemy to your whereabouts, and Patience had put her through grueling tests until Emma no longer yelped in unexpected fright.

"More like worry keeps sleep at bay," Emma said as she approached Rogan's shadow on the outskirts of the camp. "You stand guard?"

"I do not ask of my men what I would not ask of myself."

"My father felt the same until his illness intruded."

"Your father is a good man and a wise leader. I was sorry to hear that he had taken ill."

"He has improved, though has not returned to his full vigor—in time—I hope." Emma was glad for the dark, for she did not want this mighty warrior to see the tears that stung her eyes. She worried endlessly about her da. He was, as Rogan said, a good man, but more than that he was a wonderful father. She could not bear the thought of losing him, which was why she worked so hard in treating his many maladies.

"I am sure he will do well, especially with a

daughter such as yourself to help him. I am pleased he has agreed for you to remain with my clan for as long as necessary to show me what must be done to make the MacClennan clan thrive like the Macinnes clan."

Emma found herself speechless, though only for a few moments. "My father made no mention of such an arrangement to me. I was to show you what I could while my sister visited with you, and then I was to return home with her."

"He probably forgot," Rogan said, thinking nothing of it.

It was possible, Emma thought. Her father had seemed a bit forgetful of late, but to agree before discussing it with her was not like her da. And though she and her sisters had not agreed with all his decisions regarding them, his word was always final, and they respected and obeyed it—with a little of their own meddling of course.

"I suppose," Emma said, "but until I hear it from him, I will not be extending my stay at your home."

Rogan stepped further out of the shadows and closer to Emma. That he was an impressive size did not fail to catch her breath. And the faint light from the sliver of the moon fell across his face and made her breath catch twice and her stomach clench. Never had she seen such a handsome man. Heather and he would make a perfect pair, one more beautiful than the other.

Rogan placed his face an inch from hers and his words suddenly caught in his throat. Shadows wrapped around her like a protective cloak except for her face. And he could not help but see how flawless and smooth her skin was, not pale like many women, but more creamy as if it begged to be touched and kissed.

He realized at that moment he was growing aroused and he grew annoyed, and his tone grew brusque. "You will be staying with me as long as I want you—and need you."

His words gripped at her heart, though she was well aware that he did not mean it as her heart had taken it. And why had he paused, brief as it was, to add *and need you*? And why did her body feel as if it had suddenly come alive? It was as if her skin was more sensitive and she could feel the heat that drifted off his body tickle her flesh and send gooseflesh running over every inch of her.

She fought against the pervading sensation, though she would have much rather surrendered to it. The sinful thought had her coming to her senses and she gave her chin a toss. "You are not my father or my husband, therefore, I do not take orders from you. I will do as I please.'

Why the bloody hell was her defiance spiking his arousal? More annoyed than ever, he said, "You will do as I say."

"Not likely."

He gripped both her arms and her bright green eyes challenged defiantly.

Kiss her.

The thought was like a punch to his mid-section. Whatever the hell was he thinking? He did not want to kiss her. Then why had he grown so aroused?

She was a bold, mule-headed woman who needed to be—*kissed.*

Rogan let go of her and stepped away. He had no right thinking such thoughts. She was the sister of his intended.

"Go and sleep," he ordered, wanting her away from him since his hands itched to reach out and take hold of her once again and give her a good solid kiss. God help him, but he ached to kiss her senseless. Never had he felt such a strong desire to kiss a woman as he did right now. "Go," he ordered again."

Emma turned and hurried off, her stomach fluttering as madly as her heart. She stretched out on her blanket and shut her eyes tightly. Whatever was the matter with her? For a moment, a sheer moment, she thought Rogan was about to kiss her. And worse, she wanted him to.

This was utter madness. He was Heather's intended and even if he was not, he was a mighty warrior who dictated far too much to her liking. She had to keep her distance from him. She had to, or chance doing something she would regret.

Chapter Five

Morning had dawned cloudy and Emma prayed that it would not rain. Tracks would be that much harder or impossible to follow since the previous rainstorm had already done a fine job of making tracking difficult. Add to that possibility, her sleepless night and troubling thoughts and the day was proving more than challenging, and it was only mid-morning.

Emma had done her best to avoid Rogan, spending more time with Liam. He was an exceptional tracker and Patience would have been impressed by his knowledge and want to learn more from him. But they had to find her first and find Heather. Emma would not return without her sisters. She would search no matter how long it took, though she prayed endlessly that they would come upon them soon and all would be well.

The attack came without warning. Warriors rushed from the woods and dropped out of trees so fast that Rogan's men barely had time to react, leaving quite a few injured before swords were drawn.

Emma watched the melee in stunned silence. Not once did an attacking warrior approach her. It was almost as if she was invisible or she was ignored on purpose. Rogan and his men fought valiantly and impressively, yet the attacking warriors outfought them at every turn. It was as if they could not be touched, as if the warriors were ghosts.

The attack ended almost as quickly as it had begun, the enemy warriors disappearing as fast as they had appeared. Several of Rogan's men lay wounded on the ground, though none had lost their lives. And not a single one of the foe lay dead or wounded badly enough to have been left behind.

Rogan was the first to move, his men looking around as if in shock, as if not comprehending what had just happened. Emma followed his lead, dismounting and hurrying to tend the wounded.

"You know what to do," Rogan shouted and his men startled and hurried to obey.

Warriors formed a circle around the area, swords in hand, in case the ghost warriors returned. Others warriors went to help the injured, though when they realized that Emma knew much more than they did, they followed her command.

Rogan went to Liam. "You saw no signs of this?" He did not accuse. He was more shocked, Liam never having failed to alert him to anyone in the area when they traveled.

"Not a single sign," Liam said upset. He shook his head and ran his fingers through his hair. "I cannot believe I missed this."

"What you and I cannot believe—do not want to believe—is that we were attacked by ghost warriors, which means that the Dark Dragon is involved in this."

"They barely left a footprint," Liam said, as if not believing his own words. "They struck with such precision, and then vanished. Look around. They have wounded half of our men."

Rogan did not have to look. "I have already realized that. They weakened my troop." He knew what that meant and he knew what would be his wisest move.

Liam voiced Rogan's thoughts. "They will attack again and keep attacking until you have no warriors left and have no choice but to retreat. You need to return home and gather a larger contingency of men."

"I do that and I take a greater risk of not finding Heather."

"They will not stop. This is only the beginning of their assaults. And since we cannot see them, we will not know when they will strike again, leaving us vulnerable." Liam voiced what Rogan already knew, but then they thought much alike.

Emma approached the two men. "Injures are either leg or arm wounds, leaving them unable to fight. It would be best to send them home, since I do not have everything I need here to tend them, and they will require rest to heal."

"Then you will go with them," Rogan said, seeing a problem that had plagued him since last night, now solved.

"I will not," Emma said most empathically.

"You will," Rogan ordered just as strongly.

"Have you learned nothing?" Emma said her finger rushing forward to jab him in the chest.

Rogan's hand grabbed her wrist just before her finger could hit him, his large hand circling her delicate bones with ease. One good squeeze would see it crushed, so he was careful as to how hard he gripped her. "I have no time for your nonsense. You will do as I say and that is final." He let go of her wrist with a toss and turned and walked away.

"The best way to help your sister is to do what Rogan says," Liam advised.

"You have eyes for tracks, yet you see nothing else?"

Liam scrunched his brow. "What do you mean?"

"Did you not see that I was completely ignored during battle? It was as if they could not see me or purposely avoided me. For some reason they have kept their distance from me, which means I am safer than anyone else here. I do not care if I am the last one left, I will continue to search for my sister or perhaps they will take pity on me and bring me to her. But either way, I will not be leaving."

Liam watched her turn and walk away, going once again to tend the wounded. He turned and hurried to Rogan and related what Emma had said.

"I saw that myself when I made ready to go and protect her. She was removed from the battle, not a single warrior charging her. I thought it odd, though I had no time to reflect on it. Now, however, it seems so very strange."

"This whole abduction is strange," Liam said. "You should return home and—"

"I cannot. I must continue my search for Heather."

Liam gave a nod toward Emma. "She will not be left behind."

"She has no choice."

"If you force her to go, she will leave the troop and follow us or, Lord forbid, go on her own."

Rogan shook his head. He had foolishly thought his problem had been solved. The idea that she would try searching for her sister on her own angered him and made his stomach clench, as if a hand had gripped it and twisted tight.

"As Emma said, she is in less danger than any of us," Liam said.

"But for how long? How long before her persistence grows unwelcome? Then what?" Another twist to his gut had him spewing several oaths.

"She twists you in knots," Liam said with a grin. "I have never known a woman who could do that to you."

"Mind your mouth that it speaks such foolishness."

"Too bad you are already spoken for," Liam said, his grin growing. "Emma might just be the one who could challenge and win against a pig-headed bastard like you."

"You are lucky that I call you friend."

"And you are lucky I call you friend, since there is no one else who would speak so truthfully to you," Liam said, "which is why I say turn around now and go home."

"You know I cannot do that."

"Duty," Liam said sadly. "It forever haunts you

and you are forever beholden to it."

~~~

When Emma finished seeing to the injured men, she approached Rogan. She was not sure what she would say. She only knew that she could not be sent home, especially his home. She had to keep on her sister's trail. She had to find her before it was too late.

"You cannot send me away," she blurted out when she was but a few steps away from him.

He saw the desperation in her eyes, the rise of her chest as her breathing labored and how her hands trembled even though they were locked together. She had been unsure about approaching him and yet she had done so anyway. She had not let her fear stop her and for that he admired her.

He could try and send her away, but knew it would be a worthless attempt. She would find her way back again and possibly create more turmoil than already existed. He would, however, not let her know that.

"I know not how to make you understand why I must remain with you."

"I am listening," he offered, his arms crossed over his broad chest and his expression stern.

"Truly?" she asked with a shake of her head.

"You question my word?" he asked surprised by her audacity, even though her hands still quivered.

"How can I not when you stand there, sounding as if you could care less with what I have to say?" She shocked herself and him when she stepped
~~~

forward and placed her hand on his crossed arms. "I need you."

Damn if his loins did not harden in an instant, and it was not only her gentle touch, but her innocent words that ignited his lust. The question was why did this wide-eyed, plain-featured woman affect him so?

"I am not foolish enough to believe I can find my sister on my own and even if I could, what then? Patience speeds ahead of us and is expecting me to bring more warriors. Heather knows we will not rest until we find her. I must be there for them both—they are expecting me."

He could make this easy on himself and send her home with his men. It would be the sensible thing to do. And even though her impassioned words were spoken from the heart, he knew it took the wisdom of a seasoned warrior to make difficult decisions, but nonetheless necessary ones.

So why then did he say, "Obey me and you may come with me." He did not have time to ponder the notion since he saw how she bit at her lower lip, no doubt trying to keep a sharp retort from spewing out. Her bold tongue would condemn her and send her home.

"As you say," she said with a slow bob of her head, so that he could not see the fury in her blazing green eyes. She answered to no man, since no man wanted her, and she wanted no man. She reminded herself that this was for the good of her sister. Besides, their time together would be limited, which was for the best after what she had experienced last night when she had briefly spoken with him.

Rogan did not, for once, believe that she acquiesced so easily. “You tell me you will obey, give me no trouble, follow my dictate. I have your word on this?”

She raised her head, looked him straight in the eyes and spoke the only way she could—with honesty. “No, I cannot give you my word.”

Her green eyes glowed with an angry passion and he was suddenly struck with an image of her naked beneath him, her green eyes glowing with heated lust as he plunged into her repeatedly. The image dissipated, but not so the arousal that had grown along with it.

There it was again that look in his eyes and this time her body flushed with heat and once again her skin felt as if it came alive. She fought the urge to move her hand off his arm, to slip it beneath his chest and feel, oh God, how she wanted to press her hand against his naked chest and feel him, truly feel him.

Wisely, she stepped away from him, turning for a moment to catch the breath that had lodged in her throat before turning back to face him with as much control as she could muster. “I cannot lie to you. With my sister in such dire straits, I can give you no such promise, for my tongue will surely be more bold than usual.”

Damn, now he wondered exactly how bold her tongue could be. He shook away his unseemly thoughts, though they refused to entirely leave him, clinging to the nether regions of his mind, not to mention his groin.

It took him a moment to gather coherent thought and when he did, he tilted his head and narrowed his eyes as if just realizing something, and said, "Your tongue is bold and—honest."

"Sometimes my honesty is worse than my boldness," she said with a faint smile.

"Then give me your word that you will be honest with me in all things, and you can continue on the search for your sister," he said.

"That I have no problem doing. You have my word that I will be honest with you in all things." A shiver ran through her and she was struck with the sudden thought that she had just sealed her fate.

Chapter Six

Rogan sat his stallion, his eyes alert and his thoughts concerned. It had been three days since they had been attacked and while they continued to follow the trail, he had begun to believe they were deliberately being led off course. When Liam rode up alongside him, Rogan voiced his thoughts.

Liam nodded. "I recently thought the same myself. We are being led instead of following a trail, but where to—on a wild goose chase or into a trap?"

"Do you have any idea where we went wrong?"

"That is the problem. The tracks have not changed. We follow Patience's troop."

"Then she was led falsely as well," Rogan said.

"I do not believe that," Emma said, coming up from behind them on her mare to keep pace alongside Rogan. "Patience cannot be easily fooled. She trusts nothing and questions everything."

"So you believe we are on the right trail?" Liam asked.

"I cannot say it is the right trail, but it is the trail Patience chose to follow, and I trust her decision."

"Then we remain on the trail and see where it takes us," Rogan said.

Liam gave a nod and rode off to see what more the tracks could tell him.

Emma turned to Rogan. "You believe differently, yet you follow my word?"

"You spoke honestly as you promised you would and you know your sister, I do not. Therefore it was not a difficult decision to make."

"But this trail concerns you."

"Not a question, more perception?" Rogan asked.

"Your eyes betray your thoughts."

"How so?" he asked concerned that she would be able to see that she spiked his passion far too often.

"You scrunch them when concerned, which you must do frequently since the lines between your eyes are deep."

"And what else do my eyes tell you?"

"That while you dictate, you also care. You are not heartless as I first thought," she said, as her green eyes brightened and a faint smile emerged.

How could a plain-featured woman appear beautiful? He had no answer and yet there was a beauty to her face that could not be denied. He addressed her response with a smile. "You will keep my secret then?" Her soft laughter rippled over him, turning his groin hard, and he silently cursed his reaction.

"I am glad to know you have a caring soul, for you will make a fine husband for my sister."

He did not need to be reminded of that at the moment, not when he found himself growing aroused for the wrong sister. "Tell me of Heather." Hearing her fine qualities would surely help divert his inappropriate thoughts away from Emma.

"Many speak of her beauty, but her beauty comes from her generous and loving heart. She forever has a good word or warm welcome for all those she speaks to and meets. And she has this way about her that makes all who meet her feel loved and cherished. My father calls her his angel and some believe she is one. While she is my sister, she is also like a mother to me, though there is only four years between us. She looked after me and Patience, after our mother died, as only a mother could. She was always there, drying our tears, mending our scrapes, listening to our complaints, and she took over the running of the keep for Da when she was barely eight years."

"Heather appears a kind and dependable woman."

"She is that and much more."

"And she has never loved a man?" Rogan asked curious.

Emma's eyes darkened. "You would have to ask Heather about that."

"I am asking you," Rogan said all the more curious that she had avoided answering.

"Rogan!"

At the shout of his name, he turned to Liam and saw that he was waving him over.

Rogan had not finished with Emma. He wanted an answer from her concerning Heather, and he would eventually get it.

He rode over to Liam. "Something wrong?"

"I cannot be sure, perhaps it is simply instinct, but I do not think we are alone."

Rogan did not hesitate. He shouted to his men and they hurried to dismount, but too late. Warriors began dropping from trees and some looked as if they stepped out of the base of the trees. The brief warning, at least, gave Rogan's men time to react, though the troop suffered injures almost immediately. This time, however, the attacking warriors descended on Emma, to her surprise.

Rogan cut his way through the melee, striking at anyone who got in his way. He reached Emma in no time, battling those around her. He swung his sword with such potent force that the muscles in his arms strained against his shirt to the point she thought the linen would tear apart. A feral snarl rumbled from his chest and tore loose in a savage roar that had his foe stumbling and dispersing swiftly. His stallion pawed the ground and snorted at being kept with a firm hand so that he would not give chase. The two mighty males stood guard in front of her, daring anyone to cross paths with them.

Once again, the attacking warriors vanished as fast as they had appeared, leaving many of Rogan's warriors injured, though not a one of their own. Once again Emma went to see to the wounded, but this time Rogan stopped her.

"Stay where you are," he ordered as she went to direct her horse around him.

His abrupt edict had her halting quickly.

"Until I can ascertain that you are safe, you stay where you are—behind me."

Emma thought to protest, but when Rogan turned his head and looked at her, the forceful glow in his dark eyes that had the tiny golden specks burning bright had her holding her tongue.

After several minutes, though it seemed like hours to Emma, he allowed her to go tend the wounded. He followed along after her, but she knew it was to see for himself the damage done. And it was substantial. More men than before had suffered wounds that left them unable to fight. An arm sliced enough so that the warrior would not be able to use it for weeks, a cut to the hand that would not allow a sword to be drawn, a leg that left a limp until it could heal, or a broken limb. It was almost as if every wound had been inflicted on purpose rather than randomly. But how could that be possible?

"I will say it again, though I doubt you will heed my advice," Liam said when he and Rogan walked off where they could not be heard. "You should return home and regroup. You need more men and you need more knowledge about the Dark Dragon if you hope to defeat him."

"And if it was not for Heather, I would. But the longer I delay, the more I risk not finding her, and the more her fate is sealed," Rogan argued. "I am her intended. It is my duty to rescue her."

"And what of Emma? It seems that our foe have changed their minds and have now targeted her, but to what end? Do they wish to kill her or take her captive? And look how little men you have left."

"Which makes your task even harder, for you will leave with the injured, though set your own fast pace, and return home to gather a large contingency of warriors. Macinnes warriors must have shown up by now and are either on the trail or at the keep. Do not let them ride alone. Make certain our men and theirs ride together. The larger the troop, the safer you all are. Return as fast as you can."

"And you?"

"I continue on."

"Emma?"

"If they plan on abducting her then she is safer with me than anyplace else."

"I will help gather the injured and get them on the road, then I will set my own pace for home." Liam placed a firm hand on Rogan's shoulder. "I will return with haste."

It took time to get the injured settled. Walking sticks had to be made for a few, a carrier, to be hauled behind a horse, needed to be assembled for another, before all was settled and the group took their leave.

"I expected you to turn around and return home," Emma said, standing beside him and watching the men disappear down the road. "I am relieved that you continue to search for my sister."

"Heather is my intended. I will not desert her."

"I am most grateful you are such an honorable man."

He almost laughed. *Honorable*. Not with the impure thoughts that plagued him every time he looked at Emma—his future sister-in-law—not his intended. And how many times must he remind himself of that? And need he remind himself that their lives were presently in danger and distraction could be costly for all concerned?

"Why did you not send me home?"

He kept his eyes on the road as he said, "You are safer with me."

Remembering how fiercely he fought to protect her, she definitely agreed. She was safer with him. She posed a question that had been troubling her. "Why did the ghost warriors come after me now and not before? It is as if someone issues orders, and then changes his mind."

"Or it is someone who knows exactly what he is doing?"

Emma shivered. "I have only heard tales of the Dark Dragon, but they were enough to frighten me senseless."

"Most tales have a basis in fact, so while some may be nothing more than fables, others hold a ring of truth to them."

"It is said that he has never been defeated, that his enemies never see him or his men coming until it is too late. And that has proven true. It would be unlikely for us to defeat him in battle. So what then do we do?"

"Find his weak spot," Rogan said. "Everyone has one."

Emma had to ask, "And yours is?"

You. Damn. What the bloody hell was he thinking? He wasn't. His groin was thinking for him. He had to stop this ridiculous nonsense. Emma was not the type of woman he wanted and that was the end of it.

"Family," he answered, "I would do anything for family."

"A weak spot we share."

"Damn it," Rogan said, a fierce scowl spreading

across his face.

"What's wrong?" she asked anxiously.

"He knew I would go to protect you—future family—leaving my men more vulnerable. He planned it. He showed no interest in you, leading me to believe that you were safe from him, so that I would not assign warriors to protect you. Then when he struck next, he had his warriors go after you, knowing I would not hesitate to protect you, thus giving him a better chance to dispose of more of my men."

"But to what end and why do it in increments? Why this cat and mouse game? Why not simply attack once and be done with it? And what of his plans for Heather? Why in heavens name did the Dark Dragon abduct her?" she asked frustrated for herself and fearful for her sister.

"His cat and mouse game is obvious. He weakens my troop with each attack, and he delays my chance of finding Heather, though his reason for taking her escapes me. The answer, however, could prove beneficial to our search."

Emma shivered again. "I know what you imply. The reason he abducted her could determine where he has taken her. If he plans to sell her for a good profit, then we must go where such transactions take place. If it is money he demands from my family, then he will hide her somewhere until he receives it, and if," —she did not want to think it let alone voice it— "he took her for himself, then we will never find her, for no one knows where the Dark Dragon resides." She turned her head away, fearful that she could not stop the tears that threatened to fall. She was frightened, so very frightened that she would never see Heather again.

Her head whipped around when she felt him grip her shoulder. She looked down at his hand resting there, felt its warmth spread through her and wished, oh how she wished, she could rest her cheek upon it.

His hand had moved instinctively, offering her comfort, though he would have much preferred to reach across and yank her off her horse onto his. Then he could wrap her in his arms, press her to his chest, wipe away the tears that were about to spill, and kiss those plump lips that forever begged to be kissed.

"If I must go to the Dark Dragon's lair to rescue Heather I will," he said with a reassuring squeeze to her shoulder before dropping his hand away.

She missed his touch already. She had never known a man's comforting touch and, therefore, had not known how good it would feel. There was strength to it and it was so different from her sister's comforting touch or her father's, when he would attempt to hug away her tears. It lingered with her, almost as if he had left an imprint of himself on her, and she did not want it to ever go away.

"We will find Patience as well."

"Patience," Emma said on a long sigh. "I think more of Heather than Patience when she could be captured by now herself." She almost laughed at the thought.

"Your eyes worry, yet you grin."

"If by chance Patience has been taken, they will

return her fast enough."

Rogan grinned along with her. "She does not epitomize her namesake?"

She laughed lightly. "Heather and I agree that Mum must have instinctively given her that name, aware that it was a trait she would be in dire need of learning."

"And she has not been successful thus far?"

Emma laughed again. "Not even close. Father swears there is not a man alive strong enough or foolish enough to wed her. And any man that has shown interest usually loses it as soon as she begins to best him in almost everything."

"It sounds as though there is no need to worry about her," he said, hoping to quell her fears about one sister at least.

"That is true. She is probably more concerned as to how I am faring than her own fate."

"Patience must have had confidence in you since she sent you off on your own to get me."

Emma scrunched her brow. "Patience did not quite send me."

"What does that mean? She either did or did not. Was someone else supposed to come for me? Bloody hell, did you usurp your sister's orders?"

"I had no choice and since I was the only one left with authority, I did what needed to be done."

"Make a foolish decision," he argued.

She jabbed, in the air, at him. "Foolish or not. It was mine and mine alone to make. It got us what we needed—help."

"It could have cost you your life."

"But it didn't."

"You will listen and follow my orders or else," he snapped.

"Or else what?" she challenged with a smile rather than anger.

He had not expected a smile, a teasingly challenging one at that. And he bloody well had not expected his body to react to it. It was like a punch in the gut, stealing his breath, robbing him of words and of all things, arousing him. Then suddenly, without thought, words shot from his mouth like an arrow from a bow, and once released could not be drawn back. "I will show you just how dishonorable I can be."

Chapter Seven

Emma stared at Rogan's back as he left her side to ride ahead and join the warrior who had replaced Liam as their tracker. What exactly had he meant that he would show her how dishonorable he could be? And why did his threat feel as if it lit a spark inside her?

You want him to touch you.

She cringed at the sinful thought. He was Heather's intended. She had no right to think such fanciful thoughts or have improper feelings. He spoke of punishment and she foolishly took it as passion.

Heather. She had to concentrate on Heather. They would find her, and she and Rogan would wed and have beautiful babies and a happy life together. While she, Emma, would live her life out with her father, seeing to the land and the livestock and tending the ill. It was her lot and she had to accept it.

Emma raised her glance to the heavens while stifling a sigh and realized that the sky was gray, though no heavy clouds lingered. It would be an overcast day with a slight chill to it. A few weeks into spring and the weather had proven unpredictable, warm one day, chilly the next and a few nights of shivering cold. She was glad winter had left them, though she had been more pleased that she had paid close attention to the signs as to how the approaching winter would be. With heavy fog in August, the pine cones growing larger than usual, the animals' coats thickening early and the bees gathering heavily in the trees having warned of a cold winter, she had made sure the clan had been prepared.

She had ordered the last of the crops to be harvested early and was glad of it when a few nights later it had turned bitter cold. They would have lost a good portion of their winter food if she had not been attentive. More hunting had been done and more meat preserved. Her clan had done well this past winter and before leaving, she had reminded them that the ground needed preparing for planting. She had also instructed Maura, the woman who shared the duty of caring for her father with her, in how to prepare the potion she gave him in case he should require more while she was gone.

His illness had seemed to come on so suddenly and he had grown weaker before her and her sisters' eyes. His illness had been a deciding factor in his decision to see, at least, one of his daughters wed. This way if anything should happen to him, there would be a strong warrior to become laird of the Macinnes clan.

Patience had hoped that their father would have seen how valuable a laird she would make, but their da had had other ideas. If only the three of them had been left to decide their own futures, they would, at this moment, be home safe.

It was an hour, perhaps more, when the small troop of men was suddenly brought to a halt. Emma tried peering past the broad-shouldered warriors that sat attentive to their surroundings, but could see nothing. She did not hesitate. She wound her way around the warriors. None stopped her. None paid her heed, but then it was not uncommon for men to ignore her.

"What is it?" she asked anxiously as she approached Rogan.

He turned to her and his stomach clenched at the worry in her eyes, but he did not hold the truth from her. "The tracks divide again, but which way your sister travels is not clear."

Emma felt as if someone gripped her heart and squeezed tight, and she shut her eyes against the pain. She could not lose both her sisters. She could not. When she opened her eyes, she was stunned to see that her hand was firmly gripping Rogan's forearm and while it was not proper for her to touch him with such familiarity, it mattered not to her. Holding onto him, feeling the strength of his taut muscles gave her some sense of hope, so she refused to let go.

His hand hurried to cover hers, giving it a reassuring squeeze. A strange sensation rippled through her, a shiver yet not a shiver, for she felt no chill. Whatever it was made her feel cared for and protected, as if she was loved.

The strange reaction to his touch had her gripping his arm more tightly, as if she never wanted to let go of him.

Patience's voice suddenly echoed in her head. *Keep your wits about you or all will be lost.*

A reprimand and a lesson all in one, and it almost brought a smile to Emma's face. She focused her thoughts on Patience. She was skilled in so many areas. What would she have done?

It came to her in an instant. "Patience divided her men so that whoever followed had to divide their men as well."

Rogan nodded as he spoke. "It would weaken both forces."

"It would also enable her to search a wider area."

"Then it matters not which trail we follow since no doubt your sister gave orders for her men to eventually meet in one place."

Relief flooded her and she eased her hand off him, though she thought she felt reluctance on his part to let her go. Again, a fanciful thought she had no right thinking.

The skies grew heavy with storm clouds as they continued traveling and thunder rolled in the distance. Emma could not help but think that the heavens warned them of proceeding any further. Or were dark forces threatening their journey?

"What troubles you?"

Emma turned to Rogan, riding beside her on his horse. "I cannot decide if the heavens warn or dark forces threaten."

It was strange how often her concerns mirrored his own, though he dared not tell her that. Or was it that he did not want to admit that they often thought more alike than not?

"Ominous weather brings gloom along with it," he said.

"I suppose, though being attacked by warriors that materialize and vanish like ghosts does not help."

"They are not ghosts. They are well-trained warriors who can suffer a blow from a sword just like any warrior," he insisted. "I am sure the Dark Dragon is pleased with the mythical tales told about him. It makes people fear him more when in all actuality he is nothing more than a man like myself."

"A potent warrior who wields a sword with confidence and not an ounce of fear," Emma said. "Yes, why should anyone fear such mighty warriors?"

He was more than confident when it came to wielding his sword, at least that's what the willing lassie he had tumbled last had told him. And he had no doubt he would have Emma feeling the same. *Hell and damnation*. Exactly what he would suffer if he did not stop thinking about Emma this way. How many times did he have to remind himself that she was not his intended? He had no right having such carnal thoughts about her. And where had this attraction come from and why was it growing ever stronger?

"Something concerns you?" Emma said.

Rogan shook his head to clear it and when he turned to her, he saw that her hand rested on his shoulder. Her concerned touch shot heat straight to his groin, hardening him in an instant. His nostrils flared, his lips tightened, and his eyes narrowed in anger at his uncontrollable response to her touch.

Emma quickly withdrew her hand when she saw how annoyed he had gotten at where her hand rested. Whatever was the matter with her, touching him as if she had the right to? She had never laid a hand on a man with such familiarity. She had never felt at ease to do so, not after the one and only time she had done it. The consequences that had followed had hurt and taught her never to do it again. And she had not. But now... now she laid her hand on Rogan without thought or consequences and that was not good. Especially since every time she did, her body sparked to life. It was as if something long dormant was awakened, and she so badly wanted to shake it fully awake.

"Everything concerns me," Rogan finally answered, especially his damn hard arousal that had him shifting uncomfortable on his horse. "Though at the moment, I would say those dark clouds in the distance take priority."

Emma glanced and shook her head when she saw the clouds that seemed to grow darker and larger before her eyes. "A storm."

"And a good one at that."

"A heavy rain will wash away what few tracks are left from the last rain," Emma said, feeling a sense of defeat settle over her. *Your wits, Emma, your wits.* Her sister's scolding voice in her head had her asking, "Are there some crofts in the area? Perhaps someone has seen something that may help us."

"There are some, but not on the path we travel."

Rogan's brow knitted. "Perhaps we travel the wrong path."

Emma thought to follow him as he rode off without a word to her, but then thought better of it. She had wondered herself if perhaps they had missed something along the way. The one thing that bothered her was that they had not met up with any injured Macinnes warriors. How had Patience's troop avoided being attacked? She did not want to think of a more logical answer. That Patience and her troop had been captured. Patience was too skilled to allow that to happen.

Please, Lord, let it be so. Let both my sisters be safe.

As soon as she saw that they were changing course, she realized what Rogan was doing. He was taking them to where there was not just endless woods or barren land, but to crofts where people may have seen something. She prayed his decision was right.

It was a couple of hours later when the sky looked about to dump a torrent of rain upon them that they crested a small hill and spotted a farm, smoke billowing from the chimney. There was a cottage and two outbuildings and empty lean-tos that could shelter the horses.

Welcomed or not, Emma did not think they would be turned away. The occupants would most likely be too fearful of being inhospitable to a small troop of warriors and bid them welcome whether they wanted to or not.

An old man with long white hair and beard and

lean frame stepped out of the cottage as they approached and called out, "You best hurry and secure those horses out of the rain that's about to descend on us in buckets." He gave a nod to Rogan. "Your men can make use of the outbuildings, while you and your lady are welcome to share my cottage."

The old man had assumed that Emma was Rogan's lady, and Rogan had not corrected him, but then there was no time for that since the sky burst open, releasing the rain.

Rogan was off his horse in an instant and his hands went around Emma's waist just as fast, yanking her off the horse. He rushed her to the door, shoving her in as the old man quickly stepped aside.

"Stay put," he ordered and turned to take care of the horses and see to his men.

"I take it that you are not an obedient wife, since he warns you to stay put," the old man said with a chuckle.

"I am not his wife," Emma said, going to the hearth to dry what little of her garments that had got wet. If Rogan had not reacted so quickly and pulled her off her horse, she would have gotten soaked. His first thought had been about her, not anyone else, and while she should not waste her time thinking more of his gallant gesture, she could not help but do so.

"Not wed yet," the old man said with a wink, "but at least you know how he will treat you once you are, and you cannot miss the love in his eyes for you."

Emma's mouth dropped open as she turned to

stare at the old man. Was he joking or simply daft?

"I have only a broth of pot herbs to offer. You and your intended are welcome to join me, but his men will have to see to providing their own sustenance."

Emma was about to thank him and finally make it clear that she was Rogan's future sister-in-law, not his future wife, when the door opened and Rogan entered. He threw his hood back off his head, and she was reminded of the first time she had laid eyes on him at his keep. Even now it was still difficult to believe a man could be so handsome that one look could turn a woman senseless and how often had his fine features stolen a woman's heart?

"Your hospitality is much appreciated, sir," Rogan said with a nod before he walked over to the hearth and draped his cloak over a chair that he drew close to the fire's flames.

"Samuel," the old man said, "the name is Samuel."

"Thank you again, Samuel," Rogan said. "I am Rogan and I hope we will not be too much of a burden on you."

Samuel dismissed his concern with a wave of his hand. "Nonsense. It is you who do me a favor. I am alone, and it will be most pleasant to share a meal and conversation for a change. Rest while I see to the meal."

"Please allow me to help," Emma offered, though she did not wait for him to answer. She pitched right in to help.

Soon the three of them were seated at the table

enjoying, surprisingly, the tasty broth made of nothing more than pot herbs and also bread hot off the stone.

"So we are your first visitors in some time?" Rogan asked.

"First to stay," Samuel said, dunking his bread in the broth. "A couple of warriors wounded, not badly, in a fight were here for a few hours. They rested and I fed them, then they were gone. Heard them say they needed to catch up with the others."

"Did they happen to say what clan they were with?" Emma asked.

"No," he shook his head, "though I thought it odd when I heard one say Patience will wound us worse if we do not hurry and bring her the information."

Emma almost gasped, but held her tongue. Macinnes warriors had been here and they must have found out information about Heather. Hope filled her heart and she turned to Rogan, her hand going out to grasp his arm. Too late, she realized her gesture was, once again, far too familiar, and she saw Samuel smile and nod, as if confirming what he had first thought—they were to wed.

Not wanting to snatch her hand away and appear guilty, she eased it off Rogan's arm. As she did, she noticed that his lips were set tight, and she thought she saw him give a slight shake of his head. It dawned on her then that he was warning her to hold her tongue.

Trust no one. Another reminder from her sister, and she took heed.

Samuel did not seem to notice their brief

exchange. He kept right on eating and talking. "I tell you, it is those ghost warriors. They have invaded the area and no one is safe."

Emma and Rogan exchanged looks, and Rogan was about to comment when the old man went right on talking.

"They drop from the sky, step out of trees, rise out of the ground, and then they vanish as mysteriously as they appeared. But what do you expect when they belong to the Dark Dragon." Samuel shook his head and lowered his voice. "He has got dark powers he does. He rules the dead and raises them when he needs them, then sends them back to hell to wait until he calls upon them again."

Emma shivered, knowing the old fool talked nonsense and yet his words still frightened.

She jumped when she felt Rogan's hand on her arm. He gave it a reassuring squeeze, then he slowly ran his hand down until it lay on top of her hand. Then, as if it was common place for him to do so, he pressed his fingers intimately between hers, gripping her hand from atop. Emma stared at their attached hands. What was he doing? His actions clearly showed his claim on her, but why? He had no such claim.

"The Dark Dragon is a man and no more. He does not command the dead, though he is a shrewd leader of man," Rogan said.

Samuel shook his head slowly. "He is more than shrewd, his men more than common warriors. He conquers all in his path and once captured, there is no escaping him. You are his forever."

Tears stung Emma's eyes. She did not want to think of her sister being in the clutches of one so evil or that there was no possibility of rescue. She would not rest until Heather was freed or she was a prisoner along with her sister.

"The most powerful weapon the Dark Dragon possesses is fear," Rogan said. "And he uses it wisely. He fosters myths and lets them grow, giving him more and more power. I do not fear myths, and I do not fear him."

"Then you are a fool," Samuel said sadly, "for myths hold a kernel of truth."

"And the kernel grows, but not the truth," Rogan said, "which leaves the Dark Dragon nothing more than an exceptionally skilled warrior."

"I hope you never have to face him, my son, to prove your theory," Samuel said and sipped at his broth.

Emma admired Rogan's courageous and persistent nature. It meant that he would not give up on finding Heather, and she was ever grateful for that. And she truly did not mind at all that he still kept his hand firmly locked with hers. It gave her hope and made her feel so pleasantly strange.

"Please, you and your intended take my bed. I will make use of the floor."

"Nonsense," Rogan said. "I will not see you put from your bed."

"I keep a pallet for those cold nights when it is wiser to sleep close to the hearth, so I do nothing that I have not done before. Besides, the lady will be warmer with you wrapped around her than only the thin blanket I can supply."

"Then I thank you for your generous hospitality."

Emma continued to wonder as she got into bed how it was that Rogan and she would be sleeping together tonight. Why had Rogan not corrected Samuel's assumption? Why did he let the old man go on believing that she was his intended?

Once in bed, she realized it was narrower than she had thought. How they would fit, she did not know. She found out soon enough when Rogan finally joined her.

"On your side," he ordered, "it is the only way we will fit."

She turned and he slipped in, resting against her, his hand draped over her waist.

"The least strangers know the better, since we do not know who to trust," he whispered near her ear.

Patience would certainly approve of his prudence, though Emma did not know if she would approve of her sleeping with Heather's intended. But then she and Patience would do whatever needed to be done to find Heather. And she could not say it was a chore lying next to Rogan in bed. She had wondered what it would be like to share her bed with a man. Now feeling the warmth and strength of his body against hers, she had to admit that it was much nicer than she had imagined. But then she felt safe and comfortable with Rogan and that probably made a difference.

Emma tried to ignore the little sparks nipping at her flesh, but how could she when several sparks hit her nipples, turning them hard. Then there were the sparks that tickled and dampened between her legs. If he could evoke such a response from lying harmlessly against her, what would happen if he touched her in such intimate places?

The thought rushed a heavy blush to her cheeks and she was glad he could not see her embarrassment. She shifted her body, hoping to ease away from him a bit.

"Uncomfortable?" he asked once again, settling close against her.

"Restless, is all," she whispered quickly, not wanting him to know how he stirred her.

He pressed his face near her ear, and whispered, "We will find Heather, I promise."

And she will be all yours, Emma thought and for once in her life she was jealous of her sister. Tears quickly rushed to her eyes and she let them fall quietly, not wanting him to know she was crying. Not wanting him to know how ashamed she was of her thoughts. She soon fell asleep with wet tears staining her cheeks.

Rogan gently wiped her tears away as soon as he felt her body go limp with sleep. He was startled by how attuned he was to her body. It was as if her senses were magnified and he could feel each and every one of them as clearly as his own. He had felt her quiet intake of breath and felt her body grow taut when her tears started to fall. Her sorrow had stung him as strongly as if it had been his own.

But what startled him the most was when with one shift of her body, she had become aroused by their closeness, and he had had to fight his own quick mounting arousal. It was not the time for him to be growing hard when lying so close against her. If he was more truthful with himself, he would admit that his decision to sleep with her had not been purely due to trust as he had claimed. He had wanted to join her in bed to prove to himself that his stirrings for her had been nothing more than harmless lustful wanderings.

But now lying here in bed with her, his thoughts, body, feelings so attuned to hers, made him wonder over this plain woman asleep in his arms. What was it about her that set his heart to beating more strongly whenever he laid eyes on her, set his glance always in search of her when she was not near, set his manhood constantly stirring for her?

Move away from her. Keep your distance, his thoughts warned.

His body responded, tucking her closer against him and tightening his arm around her.

Chapter Eight

Emma did not want to open her eyes and fully wake. She was much too comfortable and content where she was to allow anything to disturb her. The chores could wait a while, and she was not yet hungry for the morning faire. So, she much preferred to linger in the pleasant warmth and comfort of her bed. She wrapped her arms tighter around the solid yet comfortable form and cuddled closer, tightening her leg around it. She nestled her face against the linen, inhaling a rich, robust scent that stung her nostrils most pleasantly.

She could not recall the scent, but surely it was one of her flower and herbal blends that she had the servants use when scrubbing the bed linens. She sighed and soaked in the favorable scent as she buried her nose in it.

Hard so hard, she thought.

Her eyes shot open and she bolted up in bed, the realization of where she was finally dawning on her. She looked down at Rogan and thought she saw lust, hot and heavy, stirring in his eyes. Had he gone that long without a decent poke that lust had gripped his loins for her? Or was she simply imagining that he could actually lust after her?

The latter seemed more likely and left her feeling lonelier than ever. Men might lust after her as a last resort, but no man would willingly lust after her or love her. The sad thought left an ache in the pit of her stomach, and she made a quick move to climb over and away from him.

When she felt his stiff manhood brush against her, she froze. Then she realized it was Rogan's strong grip on her arms that kept her from moving.

He stared at her, his rock-hard arousal jabbing at the point between her legs. Her body suddenly fired to life, stinging her with such potency that her only thought was to slip down on him and take him inside her.

"Those wicked thoughts will get us both in trouble," he warned in a curt whisper.

Good God, was her passion that transparent? Heat rushed to stain her cheeks as she ordered sharply, "Let me go."

He released her after he swung her off him and the bed, landing her on her feet. She hurried away from him and over to the fireplace, glad Samuel was not about.

Rogan bolted out of bed, grabbed his cloak from the peg, and without a word to Emma walked out of the cottage. He stood stock-still outside the door a moment in an attempt to regain his sanity. He had woken aroused and for a good reason. Emma had been wrapped around him, her leg over his, her face rubbing against his chest, and he had had all he could do not to touch her. She had been warm, soft, and persistent in her need to get closer to him. He had seen in her eyes how very much she had wanted him. For a moment, a brief moment, he had thought she would mount him and, God help him, he had wanted her to.

This was not good, this strong desire he had for her. It was so much stronger than the lust he felt for the occasional willing woman he would enjoy. It was more a hunger that needed to be fed, and damn if he wasn't salivating for a taste.

"Good you are awake," Samuel said with a smile as he approached Rogan. "I did not want to disturb you two. You both looked so content wrapped around each other. You are lucky to have found such a strong love. But the morning is running on and you will need to eat before you take your leave, which I assume you want to do posthaste since the rain has stopped, though the gray skies remain."

Found love.

More duty than love was what had Rogan wedding a woman he did not know. He barely gave thought to love. He had no time or want for it. Duty was something he knew and understood. Love was... something he never thought he would experience.

With a shake of his head, Rogan turned his attention to the weather. His mind had been much too occupied with Emma. Casting a glance around, he saw that the land had received a good soaking, which meant mud had swallowed the tracks. Now what did they follow?

"Let me provide you with a good meal before you take your leave," Samuel said and eased past Rogan to open the door and enter the cottage.

"First, I will see to my men," Rogan said and

walked off, needing time away from Emma to collect his thoughts and ease his arousal.

Samuel watched the mighty warrior strode off and smiled, then turned and entered the cottage.

Emma turned with a jerk as the door opened. She was not ready to face Rogan, was not ready to admit to her own body's traitorous reaction to him. So, she was relieved to see it was Samuel who entered.

"Gray skies, but no rain," he announced and immediately got busy preparing food.

Emma offered to help, but Samuel insisted he needed none and ushered her to a chair at the table as he continued to work.

"Do not worry so," Samuel said. "You will find your sisters soon."

"I do not know what I would do without them," Emma said with a tearful sigh.

"And you will not have to," Samuel insisted. "You will find your way to one another and all will be well."

For some reason his words reassured her and a distinct calm settled over her that she had not felt since she had been with her sisters.

"Tell me about Patience and Heather," Samuel cajoled.

Emma smiled and was soon spilling stories of her sisters, laughing as she did.

~~~

Rogan never joined Emma for the morning
~~~

meal. Samuel packed a sack of food for them and after giving her a loving hug, wished her well and told her that Rogan and her love would see them through the most difficult of times.

Emma thanked him for his generosity, though wondered over his words. The old man's eyes had to be failing him if he thought he saw any love between Rogan and her. Ignoring his foolish remark, she mounted her horse.

Rogan was already astride his horse and she had no doubt that he had purposely stayed away from her and was continuing to do so. With him keeping his distance, old hurtful memories stirred in her. It was what many a young lad had done to her, claiming her too frightful to look at and to be around.

Heather had always been there to comfort and reassure her and that reminder had her missing and worrying about her sister even more.

The small troop's movement shook Emma from her musings and she quickly followed, hoping the day might find them successful, at least in some small way. The day wore on with nothing to show for it. If anything, the heavy rain had left it more difficult to locate any tracks and Emma wondered if they were going in circles.

At least, the gray skies brought no rain, though by the time they camped for the night there was a sharp chill in the air. Rogan continued to avoid her and that was fine with her. However, when it came time to bed for the night, she was missing the warmth and comfort of his solid body.

She shivered most of the evening, the ground as

chilled as the air, and did not fall asleep until well into the night. When she woke, she found a blanket had been added to her own and wondered who had been so thoughtful. When no one stepped forth to claim it, she rolled it up and packed it away with her own, grateful to have it.

Gloomy gray skies greeted them again the next day and a grumpy mood spread amongst the few warriors. It was growing ever more obvious that the men thought it a hopeless and dangerous venture and mumblings about returning home were growing louder.

When they stopped for a brief rest and the few warriors huddled with Rogan, Emma feared what they were discussing. The logic of their concerns was not lost on her. With few men left, no tracks visible, and danger lurking at every turn, the wise decision would be to return home. But that would mean a delay in finding Heather or could possibly prevent Heather from ever being found. The realization that her sister might never be found suddenly hit her like an arrow to the heart, and she turned away as tears rushed to fill her eyes.

Rogan's tremendous roar ripped through the air and had her swerving around to see warriors rushing out of the woods—too many warriors. They would never be able to defeat them.

Fight, she heard Patience yell in her head and Emma did not hesitate. She grabbed a sword from the sheath of a warrior's nearby horse and joined the melee.

Rogan's warriors fought bravely, though

outnumbered, and Emma did as her sister had taught her. She continuously swung her sword so none could get near her. But none of the ghost warriors actually seemed interested in her. They concentrated on the few warriors, especially Rogan. He was outnumbered.

Emma quickly made her way to him, ducking, darting, and maneuvering as best she could around the warring warriors. But just before she could reach Rogan, one of the three men he was fighting struck him on the head with the hilt of a sword. As soon as she was close enough, she lashed out at his attacker as he delivered another blow to Rogan's head that sent him collapsing to his knees.

The ghost warrior turned on her, striking her. The blow to her shoulder sent her stumbling backward and before she slumped to the ground, she watched as a final blow was delivered to Rogan. His face hit the ground as all went black around her.

Chapter Nine

Rogan stumbled to his feet, ready to fight, though pain radiated in his head. He looked around, rubbing at his bleary eyes, not believing what he saw... or what he did not see. Not a ghost warrior remained and not one of his warriors was in sight. The only person besides him was Emma. She lay on the ground, blood seeping out beneath her and pooling in the muddy grooves around her. With clarity, he recalled how she came rushing at his attacker, sword swinging, and just as clearly he recalled how the warrior had thrust his sword back without looking and speared her shoulder.

He rushed to her side, his head continuing to pound, though not as badly as his heart on seeing Emma lying there so lifeless. He sunk to his knees beside her. The blood was coming from a wound to her shoulder. She was pale and did not respond to his touch. He needed to see to her wound, needed to get her to safety. He wondered where his warriors were, but had no time to dwell on them. He had to stop a few times, growing too dizzy to move as he gathered their two horses, the only ones there. His warriors had not only disappeared, so had their horses.

With no time to give the matter serious thought

and his head hurting too much to linger on any heavy musings, he returned to Emma. He examined the wound as best he could and saw that the blade had pierced her shoulder, though had not gone clear through. He took his dagger and cut a strip of cloth from a blanket and wrapped the wound with it as best he could. It would have to do until he could get her someplace safe, if there was anyplace safe left to them, and sear it closed.

He draped her over her horse until he mounted his own, then he reached out and moved her over to his horse and tucked her in the crook of his arm so she could rest against his chest. The closest place he knew where he could get help was Samuel's cottage, and he intended to ride straight through until he reached it.

She began to stir after they were traveling for about an hour. When she attempted to stretch her way out of Rogan's embrace, she let out a howl and slunk back in his arms. Her eyes fluttered open, tears ready to fall.

"You have suffered a wound to your shoulder. You must stay as still as you can to keep the blood from flowing."

She scrunched her face against the pain that shot like hot coals through her shoulder. "And you? How have you faired?"

She worried about him when she had suffered far worse than he had? That she cared should not surprise him. He had seen the way she had treated Macinnes warriors, as if each and every one was important to her. She had a generous heart. And that he had failed to protect her, failed to find her sisters, failed to keep his men safe... stirred deep anger in him.

"A blow to the head," he informed her.

"More than one," she said, as if just remembering and winced at the pain that seemed to be growing worse with each pounding of the horses' hooves.

Rogan muttered several oaths, though offered no apology for the rough ride. It was necessary. He could do nothing about it. The day wore on, tiring them both and shortly after night fell, Emma begged him to stop.

"Please—the pain—I need to rest," she pleaded. "And drink, I am so thirsty."

Rogan did as she asked, not that he wanted to, but he realized that she needed rest as did he. He found a cropping of rocks and set up camp behind them. She drank and ate from what Samuel had generously given them.

When she finished and looked ready to sleep, her eyes heavy with fatigue, Rogan said. "I need to look at your wound."

He carefully removed the strip of blanket he had used to wrap it and saw that while the bleeding appeared to have stopped, the blood around it was still wet. It had yet to cake, and he worried that the rough ride kept the wound bleeding. It needed to be seared closed or she would continue to bleed. There was also fever to worry about, not to mention the possibility of the wound turning putrid.

"The wound needs to be seared so the bleeding stops," Rogan said.

"Then do it and be done," she said. "Tomorrow as we ride, I will instruct you on how to use the herbs in my pouch that will help keep fever at bay and how to prepare a poultice that hopefully will keep the seared wound from turning putrid."

He spoke his thoughts aloud. "You possess much knowledge."

"I enjoy the pursuit of knowledge. It fills my days. Now please listen carefully, you will need to cut away the cloth around the wound. But first you must take some of Samuel's brew and use it to clean away the blood before searing the wound. Use my dagger to cut away the cloth while your knife heats in the fire, for if the blade is not stinging hot, it will not close the wound sufficiently."

Rogan could not help but marvel over how calmly Emma gave him instructions. She was in pain. He saw it in her eyes and the scrunch of her brow, yet she did not groan or cry out. He wondered if she would be so brave when he laid the hot blade to her flesh. The thought that he would cause her such pain turned his stomach, but it had to be done or she could possibly die.

He retrieved a rolled blanket from the back of her horse and with a gentle lift of her head placed it beneath it. "So you have a better view when I tend the wound and can tell me if I do anything wrong."

Rogan placed his knife in the flames, then took her dagger and carefully cut away the bloody cloth around the wound.

"Take the sleeve if you must and whatever else is a bloody mess. Leaving it will do me more harm than good," she encouraged.

By the time he was done, her sleeve was discarded and her one breast lay exposed down to the nipple that had puckered at the night chill or had it been his touch? Not something he should be thinking of at the moment, but her breast was quite plump, far more than a handful, though blood covered most of it. His brow knitted, thinking of the blood she had lost, and he quickly got busy cleaning off the blood with the brew so he could close the wound.

Emma wondered why his brow knitted so deeply when she saw that his eyes focused on her breast. Did he find her lacking? She shut her eyes against the ridiculous thought. Whatever was she thinking? She had been injured and he was tending her. It was nothing more than that.

Rogan concentrated on his task at hand. He refused to let himself linger over how lovely her breast was or how rosy her puckered nipple was after he finished cleaning it. This was neither the time nor place to think such things, and she certainly was not the woman he should be lusting after. He reminded himself over and over that it was her sister who was to be his wife as he continued cleaning away the blood.

When it was finally done, Rogan wrapped a cloth around the knife's hilt and pulled the hot blade out of the fire and looked at her. "This is going to hurt like hell."

"A cloth," she said and when Rogan handed her a piece of the torn blanket, she stuffed it in her mouth and nodded.

He hated what he was about to do, but he was quick about it. He was surprised when she did not faint from the pain, though it would be better if she had. Her eyes turned wide, she clamped down hard on the cloth, and her whole body stiffened against the excoriating pain that would linger after it was done.

He pulled the cloth from her mouth when he finished. "Are you all right?"

Her eyes drifted closed and she nodded. "Do not wrap it yet. Place a cloth over it until morning."

He did as she told him, then said, "Rest, we leave at first light."

She nodded, her eyes closing and was asleep before Rogan laid his blanket on the ground on the opposite side of the campfire. His head still hurt, though was no longer pounding. He found he had no urge to sleep just yet. He kept an eye on Emma while his mind began to stir with the events of the attack. He was concerned for his missing men. What had happened to them? They were loyal warriors and would not run off and leave him to fight alone. That meant they had been taken by the ghost warriors, but why had he and Emma been left? And why had they both been left alive or had they thought them both dead?

Rogan sat staring into the darkness that surrounded them. Were they alone now or were they being watched? Never had he come up against warriors that were not seen until it was too late. While he was a skilled warrior, he was one man with an injured woman to protect. He needed to get Emma to safety and let her heal, and then he needed to return home and devise a plan to find Heather.

Morning dawned with the sun fighting back a few clouds. With the day looking promising, Rogan felt renewed, though he had gotten little sleep. He hated waking Emma, knowing rest was what would serve her best right now, but he had no choice.

Her movements were slow as she instructed him on how to bandage the wound. She winced in silence as she settled in his arms once mounted on his horse and fell asleep shortly thereafter. She woke a short time later, though it was more like she roused herself from sleep.

"A fever is setting in... I can feel it. I need you to listen and do what I tell you," she said and grimaced, at the hot pain that struck her.

"I am listening and will follow your instructions," he assured her.

She detailed how to prepare the herbs in her pouch and how and when to use them. Once she finished, she laid her hand on his arm.

Her hand was limp and much too warm, and Rogan's concern grew.

"If my skin grows hot you will need to keep me cool. Do not ply my body with blankets. Strip me down to my shift," —she hesitated— "strip me bare if you must, but keep me cool until my fever breaks."

"As you say," he said and her eyes drifted closed once again. Her strength continued to amaze him. And that she should tell him to strip her bare of her garments if necessary meant one thing—she trusted him.

~~~

Rogan was relieved to see the cottage, but as he drew closer he grew concerned. There was no smoke from the chimney. The few farm animals Samuel had were nowhere to be seen. The place looked as if it had been deserted.

He approached more cautiously, wondering if the ghost warriors had attacked and taken the animals. Could they have taken Samuel too? But why? They would have no need of an old man or food, since it was said the Dark Dragon provided well for his warriors.

Rogan felt much too vulnerable with Emma in his arms. If attacked now, he could not defend them. He eased off his horse, holding Emma firm, and pushed the front door open with his shoulder. He entered cautiously. The place was empty, the hearth cold and cleaned of all ashes as if it had not been used in some time.

He placed Emma on the bed and pressed his hand to her brow. She was much too hot. He did not know what had happened here that the place should seem deserted, but he had no time to give it thought. He had to see to Emma and to securing their safety.

With quick steps, he returned to the horses and secured them in the lean-to, supplying them with food from the trough and water from the rain barrel. He then gathered their bedrolls and weapons and hurried back to the cottage.

He made sure the door was firmly latched against unwanted intruders, then he laid the items he carried aside, rid himself of his cloak, and went
~~~

to Emma. She looked so pale, and when he reached out and pressed his hand to her brow, his breath caught.

She was as hot as Hades.

Rogan did not waste a minute. He began to undress her. There would be no saving her shift. It was beyond repair. And with her fever raging, he would have no choice but to strip her bare. He was careful as he maneuvered her in his arms, trying not to cause her any pain. The squint of her brow and the small intake of breath let him know that as hard as he tried, his good intentions still caused her to suffer. And the thought ate at his gut.

Finally, she lay completely naked and he would have pulled the soft wool blanket he had placed at the end of the bed over her, if he did not recall her words. *Strip me bare if you must, but keep me cool until my fever breaks.*

She was burning. He needed to leave her as she was—naked.

He could not help but admire her gorgeous body. She might be plain to look upon, but her body was perfection. Plump breasts, narrow waist, flat stomach, rounded hips, firm thighs, all perfectly proportioned, as if sculpted by a skilled artist.

He shook his head. *She is not yours. You have no right to touch her.*

She groaned and moved uncomfortably in the bed.

His hand went instinctively to her head and with a tender caress, he said, "Rest, Emma, I will take care of you. You have nothing to fear."

She quieted, and he was reluctant to leave her to see to the brew, but it had to be done. She had to be healed. It was bad enough that he had failed to find her sister. He would not lose Emma to death.

After he started a fire in the fireplace and set water to heat, he returned to Emma to check her wound. He slipped his arm beneath her back and lifted her gently to place a rolled blanket beneath her head. Her head lolled against his chest, her heat searing him. He shifted his one hand to the back of her head while he slipped his other hand around her waist to ease her as gently as he could back down on the bed.

Her hand suddenly latched onto his arm and though her eyes remained closed she said, "It is all a lie. You lied to me. You never meant what you said."

It took Rogan a moment to realize that she was not truly speaking to him. At first he thought she was accusing him of not keeping his word about finding her sister. But it was obvious that her fever had taken her to another time and place when next she spoke.

"I am not ugly." A tear slipped from her eye. "Heather! Heather, where are you? Daniel lied to me. Please, Heather, I need you."

Her anguish gripped at his stomach. Had Emma once been in love? Had the man wronged her? His anger grew at the thought, far more than he would have expected.

It pleased him to know that Heather had consoled Emma in her time of need and no doubt protected her as well, especially with Emma being the youngest of the three sisters. His da had warned him that the Macinnes sisters were close and that it might cause a problem for him. But seeing Emma so determined to find her sister, no matter the cost to herself, made him realize how strongly she loved. His mum and da had loved that strongly, which was why his da was having such a difficult time since her death.

"Heather," Emma cried, another tear spilling from the corner of her eye.

Rogan caressed her brow again, wishing he could rid her of her pain. He hoped she could hear his words and that they helped ease her suffering. "We will find Heather. I promise, Emma, I promise."

Whether it was his words that calmed her or that her dream had dissipated, he did not know, but he was relieved to see she had quieted.

He reluctantly left her side to prepare the brew as she had instructed, his thoughts weighing heavily on him as he did.

Duty. It was something that had been drilled into him from a young age. He had an obligation to his clan since he was not only the lone son, but also the only child. His clan's survival weighed heavily on his shoulders. So duty took precedence over all else—especially love.

He did not search for Heather out of love as Emma did, but strictly out of duty. He felt nothing for Heather. How could he when did not know her? He had recalled seeing her when he had visited the Macinnes clan a few times, but that had been some time ago. He had looked forward to getting to know her. With so many people having spoken so highly of her, he had felt fortunate that his da had secured such a fine woman to be his wife.

Though now, having met and spent time with Emma, he found himself attracted to her never-wavering courage, her persistence in searching for her sister who she loved dearly, and for her exceptionally vast knowledge. There was also her luscious body.

Rogan refused to turn and glance at her stretched out naked on the bed. She was racked with fever and he had no right admiring her body. But damn if it was not a sight he would never forget. The image was forever embedded in his mind and he feared he would never rid himself of it. And worse, he did not want to. And worse yet... the urge to make love to her was growing ever stronger.

He shook his head, though it was not that easy to chase away nagging images. What was it about this plain woman that had him having such salacious thoughts about her? He gave his head another shake and forced himself to focus on the task at hand. Besides, he had to pay attention and get the mixture right or it would not help Emma.

It proved easier to prepare the brew than to get her to take it. He finally got a few mouthfuls of it into her. Afterwards, she seemed to settle into a comfortable sleep, and he took the time to take stock of the cottage, particularly to see if there was any food available to them.

Shortly after nightfall was when Emma grew restless and her fever spiked. He did everything

Emma had instructed him to do to bring down the fever, but he feared the fever worsened rather than improved.

She was so restless that he worried that she would somehow cause the wound more damage, so he made a decision. He decided it was best to join her and keep her still in his arms. The one problem was that he feared his garments might worsen her fever.

He could think of only one solution. He stripped naked and got in bed with her, taking her in his arms. She nestled contentedly against him, as if she had been waiting all along for him. And not only did she drift comfortably off to sleep... but so did he.

Chapter Ten

Rogan woke before Emma the next morning and was relieved to find she was no longer hot, though she was warm. Her fever still lingered, though gratefully not as bad as yesterday. It was easy to ascertain that her fever did better, since her naked body was sprawled across his. Her breasts were pressed against his chest and her leg hugged his so hard that he could feel the soft snatch of hair between her legs nestled against his thigh. Her arm lay draped across his middle, as if laying claim to him, which all had served to turn him hard instantly. She had not stirred a slow arousal in him... no, she had turned him rock-hard in mere seconds. Something he had never experienced before.

He had to get out of bed and away from her and get his engorged lust under control. He began to ease himself away, a task more difficult than he would have thought since Emma clung greedily to him as he tried to slip out of her grasp.

He soothed her with reassuring words and the worry that knitted her brow and scrunched her eyes eased. His own brow creased when he realized how pretty she was in sleep. All her features softened and he noticed that she had the most beautiful skin. It was flawless, not a scar or blemish stained it. Beauty was there, if one only bothered to look.

His gentle words relaxed her hold on him enough for him to finally ease out of her relentless embrace. It was with great reluctance that he finally left her in bed alone.

Sometime during the night he must have pulled a blanket over them, and he used it now to partially cover her. She was not completely free of fever and he didn't want to make it worse by warming her up even more with blankets. But for his own sanity and to get his arousal to fade, he needed to at least cover her partially.

He quickly donned his garments and stepped outside, sword in hand in case he needed it.

A gray sky and chilly day were the only things to greet him. He checked on the horses and looked around. The place appeared deserted. He could not understand how that could be when only a couple of days ago it had been occupied by an old man who had looked as if he had resided on the small croft for years.

He saw to his needs, then he further explored the woods behind the cottage. There did not seem to be signs of anyone, but that meant nothing as he had learned over the last couple of weeks. He could only hope that the ghost warriors had gotten what they wanted and were finished with him and Emma. He would let them think that they had won, but the battle was far from over.

More warriors would be needed in his search for Heather and with the combined efforts of the Macinnes and MacClennan clans that should be no problem. He was confident that they would be able to find Heather and bring her home. What was presenting a bigger problem to him was his attraction to Emma. It was growing stronger by the day. What troubled him the most was that it was not merely a physical attraction, he also enjoyed her company. Conversations with her were not only interesting, but stimulating, something he had never found with any woman. But then Emma was not any woman, at least not to him.

He shook away the troubling thoughts and headed back to the cottage. Emma was still asleep when he entered, and he set another brew to simmer so it would be ready when she woke. He ate more of the food Samuel had given them and realized that it would last only today. He would have to hunt tomorrow.

Rogan glanced over at Emma and wondered how long it would be before she could travel. He wanted her home, at his keep, where she would be safe. Until he could get her there, he worried for her safety. One minute the ghost warriors seemed ready to snatch her and the next they ignored her.

Her eyes fluttered and she stirred, and Rogan went over to her. He rested his hand to her brow and though it was not hot, warmth still lingered there.

Her eyes drifted open and before drifting closed again, she whispered, "You do care." And with a weak smile, she returned to her fevered slumber.

Rogan's brow wrinkled in thought. For some reason he did not think she was talking about him. And from her previous feverish mumblings, he believed it had to do with a man who had once hurt her heart. The thought that some man had been cruel to her fired his anger, though he recalled his da telling him that no man had ever paid interest in the plain Macinnes sister. He wondered if it could have been a secret liaison that she had had and only confided in her sister Heather. He grew all the more curious to find out.

~~~

Emma felt uncomfortably warm and shoved the suffocating blanket off her, desperate to rid herself of the heat. It would be a hot day. She would need to see that the crops did not go dry and if some were in need of harvest. But at the moment, she did not feel like moving. It felt like all strength had been drained from her body, leaving her exhausted.

She allowed herself to drift off, then after a moment, admonished herself for being terribly lazy. There was work to be done and she needed to get herself out of bed. She fought to get herself moving, but the more she did, the more difficult it seemed. It felt as if something was holding her there, refusing to let her get up, and suddenly frightened by the thought, her eyes sprang open.

"Easy, I am here with you and you are fine. It is the fever you battle."

Emma glared at Rogan. It took her a moment to realize that she was not home and to recall where she actually was and why. The fright drained from her body as soon as she did, though some apprehension remained when she realized that she lay completely naked in front of Rogan.
~~~

He realized her worry, and said, "You instructed me to keep you cool, naked if necessary to accomplish that."

She was about to thank him, and then thought better of it. It did not seem proper to thank a man for stripping her naked. But then it was not proper that he see her naked at all.

"The brew?" she asked.

"I have more ready."

He left her side and for a moment panic gripped her. She suddenly felt vulnerable and alone and she feared she would submit to tears. Her worries eased as soon as he returned.

He slipped his hand beneath her head and gently lifted it as he brought the goblet to her mouth. "Slow and easy," he advised as the liquid touched her parched lips.

Once she finished taking several sips, she asked, "How long have I slept?"

"Through the day, night fell hours ago."

"I have no strength," she said frightened that she lay so helpless.

"The fever drains you, but your strength will return. Until then, I will be your strength. You have nothing to fear."

Emma could not stop a tear from falling from the corner of her eye. Never had she thought she would hear a man say that, least of all from the man promised to her sister.

Rogan was quick to wipe it away. "You are safe with me."

She gave him a weak smile. Yes, she was safe with him. She was safe with all men, since none found her appealing. Another tear slipped down her cheek as her eyes closed, and she once again returned to her feverish slumber.

Rogan wiped the tear away and bristled at the jolt to his heart. Her tears upset him, though more so the vulnerability he saw in her eyes. But then she was completely helpless, completely naked and having no choice but to trust him, more a stranger to her than friend and—her sister's future husband. Something he needed to keep reminding himself.

~~~

Rogan was grateful he stirred awake before Emma the next morning. He had warned himself not to sleep with her again, but she had become so restless that he had no choice but to climb in bed and soothe her. Once she stilled, he had tried to leave, but she had clung to him. He had to stay, or so he convinced himself, and they both had slept comfortably throughout the night.

She was warm this morning, though not as warm as yesterday and thankfully her fever had not spiked during the night. He was even more grateful that he had eased himself out of bed and finished dressing just before she called out to him.

He turned and saw that she had covered herself with the blanket and when he caught the look on her face, he hurried to her side. "What troubles you?"

"I need to go outside for a bit."

He realized her need, but worried she was too weak to walk. "There is a chill in the air, perhaps I
~~~

can find a bucket."

"No!" she all but screamed, her cheeks turning scarlet.

"The fever has left you weak."

Her chin went up. "I am strong enough."

"You are stubborn," he said with a smile.

She returned the smile, though it was a small one. "I am."

"Your garments are beyond repair."

She frowned, though brightened quickly enough. "My nightdress is in my sack."

He nodded and retrieved it, though warned as he approached. "You will go easy and lean on me while you gather your strength."

She nodded and waited for his help. Gently, he slipped his arm under her back and eased her up to sit. The room suddenly spun and she quickly latched onto his arm that had suddenly wrapped around the front of her waist.

He sat down beside her, and she immediately dropped her head on his chest.

"It will pass," he assured her.

His arms went tight around her, his chest comfortable, and the feeling she was safe more powerful than she would have imagined. The dizziness subsided, and she silently scolded herself. She had warned people, who had been ill and bed-ridden that she had tended, never to get up too fast and to expect some lightheadedness. She had not listened to her own advice. But then Rogan's arms seemed to work just as well.

The thought startled the last of the dizziness away. When it did, she realized that she was half-naked in front of him, the blanket having slipped down to her waist. And strangely enough, at the moment, she did not care. She was content in his arms and she did not want to move.

"Feeling better?" he asked, hoping she was, though not wanting her to leave his arms. He loved having her there.

"Yes," she said, telling herself to get her nightdress on and keep it on.

"Let me help you into this," he said, holding up her nightdress, and then easing her out of his arms.

She went slowly this time, though winced loudly when pain shot through her shoulder as he slipped her arm through the sleeve hole. She once again rested her head to his chest, this time fearing she might faint.

He mumbled several oaths and rested his cool hand on the back of her head.

"I am fine," she assured him, worried that he would stop her from going outside and seeing to her needs.

"Stubborn," he snapped.

She laughed softly. "We have already established that."

His finger slipped beneath her chin and he raised her head up slowly to look at him. "You will tell me immediately if you do not feel well or if you feel dizzy."

"That sounds like an order."

"It is," he said sternly.

She would have snapped at him if not for the worry she saw in his dark eyes, and it touched her heart.

"Lean on me as you stand, so that you give yourself time to gather some strength," he instructed and stood slowly, taking her with him as he went.

She held firm to his arm as she rose to her feet and the weakness in her legs forced her to rest against him. His arm quickly went around her waist, and she was grateful for the support.

"After I take a few steps, I should be fine," she assured him, or perhaps she was trying to reassure herself.

"Take your time," he said, keeping tight hold of her.

Emma was relieved to feel strength return to her limbs as she walked slowly to the door, though she made no mention of it. The more Rogan helped her now while her limbs grew stronger, the easier it would be once she had to stand on her own.

Once they stepped outside, the chill in the air sent a shiver through her.

"You need a cloak," he said, annoyed that he had not thought of it.

She shook her head. "No, the chilled air feels good against my heated skin, and I will not be staying out here long."

Rogan stopped a short distance into the woods and asked, "Are you sure you can do this on your own?"

Her warm cheeks flamed. "Even if we were wife and husband, I would not let you assist me in such a personal need."

Rogan took hold of her chin. "If you were my wife, I would not leave the choice to you."

"But I am not your wife and never will be," she said, hoping the sorrow that descended on her had not been reflected in her words.

It was good she had reminded him of that. He was growing much to use to touching her, holding her, and sleeping with her. "But as my future sister-in-law you are my responsibility and I will see you returned home safe, no matter how stubborn you are." He let go of her slowly, making certain she had enough strength to stand on her own.

Emma wanted so badly to step away from him, far away from him, but that was not possible. She needed his help until she healed and then... she would keep a good distance from her future brother-in-law.

Rogan had wisely left her to stand beside a tree, and she used the sturdy trunk to support herself. He had not gone far, a few feet away, and had turned his back to her. She saw to her needs, though far more slowly than she would have liked. And once done, she realized the simple chore had taken more from her than she had expected. But then fever still lingered with her and she had to be vigilant that it did not get worse. She could not push herself too much. Her body needed time to heal, time to fight the fever, and time to rest. Her brew would certainly help with that.

She walked over to Rogan, feeling the weakness in her limbs and realizing it would take days before she was strong enough to travel. The thought did not sit well with her.

Rogan turned at her approach and went to her

side, his arm coiling around her waist once again.

She wasted no time leaning against him, and he wasted no time scooping her up and carrying her back to the cottage. She did not protest. She needed to heal as fast as possible so that she could continue her search for Heather. The longer it took to find her, the more she feared they never would.

Rogan placed her on the bed, a pillow at her back and the blanket pulled up to her waist. It was good she wore the nightdress, at least now he would not be distracted by her lovely naked body. Or so he told himself.

"I will heat more of the brew for you, and you should eat something if you can," he said, walking over to the hearth. "We still have some of what Samuel gave us, and tomorrow I will hunt."

"Where are Samuel and your warriors?" she asked, blaming it on the fever that she had not taken note of their absence before now.

"You and I were the only ones left after the attack," he explained, setting the pot of brew in the hearth to heat. "My warriors and their horses were nowhere to be seen. As for Samuel," —he shook his head— "the place appeared deserted when we arrived. The hearth was cold, as if it had not been lit in weeks, no farm animals to be seen, and not a sign of Samuel. It was as if the place had not been occupied for some time."

A shiver ran through Emma and she hugged herself. "I do not understand any of this."

Rogan filled the goblet and brought it to her and gently moved her legs over some so that he would have enough room to sit on the bed beside her. "I agree, none of it makes sense. With the ghost warriors attacking us, it is reasonable to conclude that the Dark Dragon has taken your sister."

"But why?"

"That is my thought. Why take Heather? If he wanted her for a wife, then all he had to do was speak to King James and request her hand in marriage. With all he has done for the King, his request would have surely been granted. And the idea that he abducted her to sell her makes no sense either. He is a wealthy man. So why abduct her?"

"Perhaps he is not interested in a wife, but simply a woman to warm his bed," Emma said her heart filling with dread.

"From the tales that spread about him, it seems he does not lack for female companionship." Rogan shook his head. "No. There is more to this abduction and we need to find out what it is."

"We cannot stop searching for Heather," Emma said, worried that Rogan would halt the search.

"What search? It is obvious the Dark Dragon has taken Heather, and there is a good possibility that he may have Patience as well."

"But his men did not take me, and they certainly had the opportunity," she argued.

"I can make no rhythm or reason out of it, though I have come to realize since the last attack that it is no longer a search for Heather. To get her back, we will have to battle the Dark Dragon."

Chapter Eleven

Emma lay in bed resting, thinking over what Rogan had said and his reasoning troubled her, for it made sense. She still held hope that Patience had not been captured. If her sister had come to the same conclusion as them, then Patience would surely collect as much information as possible, before she returned home.

She had to get home. Patience could have returned home already or perhaps father had heard something. She turned to Rogan at the hearth stoking the fire. "I need to take a look at my wound."

He threw the stick he was using into the flames and walked over to her.

He seemed larger to her, his strides more powerful, but it was probably because she felt so vulnerable laying there, feeling much too helpless. She startled when he laid his hand to her brow, though calmed quickly enough, his hand cool against her warm skin.

"Can it not wait? It is better you rest. You grow warmer."

She was annoyed that the fever continued to not only linger, but to also vary in degrees. If it was not for that, she would be on her horse right now headed home. But fever could prove deadly, and it was not worth taking the risk.

"The morning then?" she asked, knowing his advice was wise.

"Aye, the morning," he confirmed with a nod.

Emma ate what Rogan gave her, though not all of it. She was not very hungry and she was not sure if it was the fever or worry that caused her lack of appetite. Either way, it was not a good sign and if she was to grow stronger she needed sustenance. So, she forced herself to eat.

She fell asleep with a prayer on her lips for a speedy recovery. A delicious smell woke her and she turned to see something roasting on a spit in the fireplace.

"You have slept the day away again," Rogan informed her as he approached. His hand went to her brow and he frowned, though made no comment.

He did not have to. Emma felt the heat in her body. The fever had risen instead of diminishing.

"Something smells good," she said, though she had no want for food.

"I decided to hunt today in hopes that roasted rabbit would tempt your appetite, but from the lack of a smile on your beautiful face, I would venture to guess I was wrong."

Beautiful face. No, he did not call her beautiful. It was the fever playing tricks on her.

"I am not hungry at the moment," she said.

"Perhaps you will be once the meat is done. In the meantime, you can enjoy some more of your brew."

He sat on the bed beside her, a commonplace action since their arrival, handed her the goblet, and waited until she finished taking a sip to ask, "Who is Daniel?"

Emma stared at him bewildered.

"The fever had you talking. From what I gathered, Daniel is a liar and he somehow hurt you."

"It was nothing," she said.

"I disagree. It was something. You ran to your sister Heather for comfort."

"It happened many years ago," Emma said, not wanting to recall the troubling memory.

"Tell me about it," he urged.

"Why?" He would probably find it amusing as most of the villagers had, though not once Patience had gotten done with Daniel. Not another word had been said about it then.

"I care about you. You are future family."

Her heart swelled with his first few words, then plunged with the ones that followed.

Whatever is the matter with you, Emma? She silently scolded herself. He belongs to your sister. How many times do you need reminding? Do not make a fool of yourself as you did with Daniel.

"I appreciate that you should care, but I would rather not discuss Daniel with you."

Perhaps she did not, but he wanted an answer to one particular question. "Did you love him?"

"As I said, I do not wish to discuss it with you," she reiterated.

He was not used to being denied an answer when he asked a question and her refusal irritated him. “It is a simple enough question. Why not answer me?”

“I do not want to,” she snapped.

“I am your sister’s future husband and—”

“Have no say over me,” she finished.

“But I do. With your father so ill, it will fall upon me to secure a good marriage for you. It is my duty and I will see it done.”

“You most certainly will not,” she said, biting back her anger.

“I most certainly will,” he insisted.

Emma went to sit up, but the pain forced her to stay as she was. She did, however, raise her chin a notch. “Listen well, Rogan MacClennan, you have no say over me now, nor will you ever. It is I who will decide who I wed or if I want to wed at all. I am finding I quite like life without a man and, at the moment, you are helping me to like it even more.”

He leaned forward to within an inch of her flushed face. “And I have no doubt I could change your mind easily enough.”

She closed her eyes against the tingling sensation that suddenly ran through her and seemed to refuse to subside. Her heart began to thump madly and her stomach fluttered at an alarming pace. “I am not feeling well.”

“Is there something I can do?”

“A wet cloth,” she said barely able to speak.

Rogan hurried to cut a strip of cloth from the blanket he had used to bandage her wound and dunked it in the bucket of water he had filled from the rain barrel. He rinsed it and took it to her, though he did not hand it to her.

He folded it and laid it across her brow, pressing it against her heated skin. He waited a moment, then turned it over and pressed it to her cheeks, chin, and then along her neck.

Emma sighed with relief, though worry remained. She was concerned that it was not merely the fever that had affected her. His remark left much to the imagination, and Emma had not been able to help but think what it would be like to make love with Rogan, for that was surely what he had implied. The thought had evoked an unexpected response from her body.

Rogan went and got the bucket of water and sat it by the bed, then returned to his position on the bed beside her. He continued to bathe her face and neck with the wet cloth, rinsing it after it became too warm.

These lusty feelings she was having toward him would not do. They had to stop and distance would be the one way to see to that. "I want to go home," she said, opening her eyes.

"When you are well enough to travel."

"My home, not yours," she clarified.

He did not answer immediately. It was as if he was weighing his words, and Emma knew she would not like what he had to say.

"In time you can go home, but—"

"No, once we return to your home, I will take my warriors and return to my home. I cannot help but wonder if Patience is already there waiting for me with news. She had to have reached the same conclusion as we did. She would know to battle the

Dark Dragon alone would be foolhardy. She would return home and devise a solid plan."

"Liam will let us know what goes on at your home upon his return," Rogan assured her.

"It matters not to me what you say. I am going home."

"I will not argue with you while you are in a feverish state, but know this—you go nowhere without my permission. And this time I will make certain of it."

"You have no right to—"

"Are we going to argue over what has already been established? Your father sent you along with your sisters to my home, knowing I would see to your care. I am responsible for you whether you like it or not."

"I do not need you—"

"You presently do need me and if we were sensible, we would realize we need each other. You know your sisters well and I know battle well. Together is the only way we will bring them home safely, God willing."

Her annoyance drained away. He was right and she had no trouble admitting it. "A wise observation and one I completely agree with. But I still think my home is where we may find some answers."

"You may be right, but first we return to MacClennan land."

She nodded a bit reluctantly. She may be feverish, but she was coherent enough to understand what he proposed was the best solution, presently, to their problem. If things should change, then plans could change. In the meantime, she would do what was necessary to bring her sisters home.

Unfortunately, that would require spending more time with Rogan than she thought was wise, but she had little choice. Somehow she would get through it, at least she hoped she would.

~~~

Emma was pleased to find she had grown hungry and ate a little of the meat, but as the night wore on she felt her skin prickle with heat. Having tended many ill clansmen, she had observed that illnesses and fevers always seemed to worsen as night approached. Some claimed it was that death liked to stalk in the shadows and darkness of night and toy with poor, sick souls. She did not know what caused it to be so. She only knew that it was wiser to be more vigilant of the ill at night. And so she spoke with Rogan about it.

"That is why I have slept with you since arriving here," he said after she finished explaining her concerns.

"You have been sleeping with me?"

"Aye, I have and you calm when I do. You also cling fiercely to me."

Emma was not sure how to respond. It was terribly improper of him and yet it was terribly thoughtful of him. "I want to thank you and admonish you at the same time."

He laughed. "You can do both if it pleases you. I think the truth of the situation is that we have no choice but to do what must be done. Though I must
~~~

admit, it is not a chore having you sleep in my arms."

His words shocked her and a tingle of heat ran through her, though this time she knew it had nothing to do with her fever. And that upset her all the more as did her own words. "I thank you and would not mind if you continued to calm me."

"As you wish, though you must know one thing."

"What is that?"

"I sleep naked with you to keep your fever down."

Emma was truly shocked silent. She could not respond if she wanted to. He was right to have done so and yet terribly wrong of him. No matter how hard she tried, she could not form a sensible response. She simply did not know how to reply to him.

"Since you voice no objections, I will assume the situation is acceptable to you."

Silence still had hold of Emma's tongue or did it? Could she actually want him to sleep naked with her? A yawn rose up within her to break the silence.

"Time to sleep," Rogan announced. "Do you want to stay in your nightdress?"

Emma nodded.

"Sleep well," he said, "I will join you later." He walked over to the hearth and returned to tending it.

She sighed softly, glad he would wait to join her. She had no idea how she would react to seeing him naked, and she preferred not to find out. She had no worry that sleep would be difficult, her weakened state would see to that, and it did. She was asleep in minutes.

Rogan waited until he was sure she was asleep and only then did he join her. He had seen worry cross her face when he had informed her that he had been sleeping with her naked. But she had no reason to worry. She was ill. It was unthinkable to even entertain the notion in her condition.

As he disrobed, he pushed a nagging thought aside, one that had been haunting him far too much lately. But it would not go away easily. It continued to poke its head up and torment him.

What if Emma was well and willing, would he deny a chance to bed her?

A muttered oath slipped out when he realized that the thought of such a possibility had turned him hard. Never had he expected to be attracted to Emma. Never had he thought he would find beauty in such a plain female. Never had he expected her to have such an exquisite body. And never had he expected his feelings to grow for his future sister-in-law in ways that were not at all proper.

He slipped into bed with her, though kept his distance. She would find him when she was ready. Until then, he would take the time to control his lust and to remember that she would never be his.

The thought did not set well with him and that troubled him all the more. In the short time they had been here, he had thought more about Emma then he had of Heather. Of course, Emma was ill and needed looking after. So, it was only natural for him to be more concerned about her. But when he did think of Heather, his concerns were more about rescue than how he felt about her. He actually felt nothing for her, but then he had never met her. Given a chance, perhaps they would get along well, maybe even fall in love. What did it truly matter? He had no choice. They had been promised to each other.

Emma no soon as stirred in her sleep, then she reached out to him and he eased her into his arms to rest against him. Though it had only been three nights, he had already grown accustomed to having her there beside him. He favored the way she clung so tightly to him, as if she never wanted to let him go. Truth be told, he did not want to let her go.

His arms tightened around her, holding on to her as strongly as she held to him, as if they both refused to be separated. But separate they must and like the previous days, he would wake before her and leave her reluctantly. It was the way of things. He was promised to her sister Heather, and it would Heather who he wed.

Sleep claimed him along with dreams, and it was not Heather who haunted them.

Chapter Twelve

Emma snuggled against solid warmth. It felt good since there was a chill in the air. She did not want to open her eyes and greet the day, at least not yet. She wanted to linger and enjoy this wonderful contentment.

Her eyes shot open as soon as she recalled where she was and who she was wrapped around. Her nightdress was up around her waist and her leg lay over his thigh, warm and hard between her two. Her arm was draped across his naked chest, and her head rested comfortably on his shoulder. Her cheeks stung red with embarrassment, and she was at a loss as to what to do.

"Your fever is gone," Rogan said.

Her hand went to her face. Her skin was cool, except for her glowing cheeks. She looked up at him with a smile. "You are right. The fever has broken."

"Let us have a look at your wound and see how it does."

"It does not pain me much," she said, trying to ease off him, but finding her one foot tangled in the blanket. She gave it a gentle yank. Her knee shot up and over, brushing against his enlarged manhood. She gasped and bolted up to get away from him, then winced, the sudden movement causing her pain.

Rogan's arm went around her waist. "Easy," he warned softly as he gently lowered her down on her back.

She lay staring up at him, a small voice insisting she tell him to leave the bed at once and another voice urging her to have him stay right where he was. She remained silent, refusing to give heed to either of them.

"The wound continues to heal," he reminded.

He was leaning over her and showed no signs of moving, and she did not want him to.

The wound... she would remain focused on the wound and not how her heart beat so wildly when he was close to her, or how her lips seemed to ache to be kissed when he was near.

"I have meant to ask you. Could you judge how deep the wound was?" she asked, forcing herself to remain focused on what was most important.

His fingers ever so gently pushed several strands of her hair off her cheek, tucking them behind her ear.

The faint brush of his warm fingers against her cooled skin sent it tingling. How could a touch make her flesh feel so alive?

"I do not think it is too deep. I recalled the warrior who struck you pulled the sword out quickly rather than shoving it through. "

"Perhaps he had a change of heart," she said.

"Or perhaps it was ordered that you not be harmed and he realized his mistake and withdrew his sword before any more damage could be done."

The thought lingered between them. It gave Emma hope that if she was not to be harmed, then neither would her sisters. Rogan thought the same, though he wondered why the sisters had not been harmed.

"Either way, I am lucky. It could have been far worse. I must take a look at it now and see how it heals."

"Let me dress and see to the horses first, then I will help you," he said and quickly took leave of the bed.

Emma felt a sadness twist at her heart as he moved away, not a good sign. She was caring more for this man than she had a right to. She warned herself to turn away and not look at his naked body, but she refused to listen to herself. And she was glad she did, though it only caused her heart to grow heavier.

She had seen naked men before, having tended her fair share of ill ones through the years, so a man's body was not unfamiliar to her. It was, however, the first time she was looking at a naked man who she had feelings for—and that made all the difference.

He was a beauty, all hard muscle and though he kept his back to her, she knew that hard muscle extended to every part of him. She turned her head away. This had to stop. Rogan did not belong to her... he belonged to her sister.

"I will not be long," Rogan said and hurried out the door.

Emma wondered over his hasty departure. She had been embarrassed at the lusty feelings she had felt toward him when finding them so intimately entwined, perhaps he had thought differently and was rushing to get away from her.

With that possibility troubling her, she carefully moved to the edge of the bed to sit. The pain in her shoulder was not unbearable, though it could stab at times. She so badly wanted to see to her wound before he returned, but it would be foolish of her to deny that she needed his help. She could, however, see if there was any way she could salvage her garments.

She slowly got to her feet and found herself steadier on them than she had expected. She was feeling much better. Three days of rest and tender care had worked well, and she was grateful to Rogan for being so attentive to her needs. He may be a mighty warrior, but he was also a considerate man.

Emma found her garments draped over one of the chairs, and it took only one look to see that she could salvage some of the material, but not all. At the moment, that would be of no help. She was grateful for her nightdress. She could fashion one of the plaids around it and that would suffice until she got home.

The door opened and Rogan entered, stopping abruptly when he saw her standing near the hearth.

"I am feeling much better," she explained.

Rogan shut the door. "That is good. Then we will be able to leave soon."

"Aye, we will," she agreed with a smile, but not feeling as happy as she had expected.

"Shall we have a look at your wound?"

Emma nodded and reached for her plaid, lying on the chair. She intended to keep as much of herself covered as possible.

Rogan felt as if she grabbed for a shield when she hurriedly went for her plaid, but perhaps that was wise of her. She was a much too tempting morsel that he ached to taste. When she had woken shortly after him this morning, he had hoped she would not move and discover how aroused he was. But then it seemed as if he was in a perpetual state of arousal around her, something he had never felt around any other woman. Of course, he could blame it on their situation. Circumstances had forced them to live here as husband and wife, and it had forced an intimacy between them that was becoming far too comfortable in one sense and far too uncomfortable in another.

"Let me get out of my nightdress and my plaid wrapped around me," she said. "Then you can help me."

Rogan walked over to stand in front of her. "Emma, I have seen every naked inch of you and have remained honorable in my actions. You have no reason to fear I would do otherwise."

He was right. He had remained honorable. She had nothing to fear from him. He was not at all attracted to her. She should be grateful, though she wondered why he was aroused this morning, too long without a woman more than likely.

"Perhaps, but it still is not proper," she found herself saying.

"But it is necessary at the moment and the

quicker we get you well enough to travel, the quicker we return home."

She could not argue with that and home was definitely where she needed to be.

"I will slip the plaid around you as I lift your nightdress."

She nodded, pleased that he had a solution to her misgivings. Before Emma knew it, he had her nightdress off her and her plaid wrapped around her just above her breasts. She held it there with one hand while he carefully removed the bandage.

One look at her wound had her smiling. It was healing well, there was only a slight redness and there were no signs of putridness settling in.

"How does your shoulder feel?" he asked.

"I cannot say it does not pain me, though my sisters claim I am more tolerant of pain than most. So to me it is a bearable pain. I also heal faster than most and I wish I knew why so that I could help others do the same."

"I believe you are stubborn enough to do just that," Rogan said with a smile.

"Call it stubborn if you like, but to me it is more a penchant for knowledge. The more I learn, the more I want to learn."

"Does that knowledge include all the things a woman learns to run a keep as well?"

"I can run a productive keep, but do not ask me to stitch a tapestry, though Heather is a true artist when it comes to stitching," she added quickly.

"What other talents does your sister have?" he asked, reaching for the bandage he had removed.

"No," she snapped and his brow shot up. She placed her hand on his arm as if it was the most common reaction, but then it had become so between them. "I will need a clean strip of cloth."

He nodded, though made no move to step away from her. He liked when she reached out and touched him without any thoughts to her actions. Her touch was always firm and confident, so full of courage.

"Heather's talents," he reminded as he finally stepped away to cut another swath of cloth from the blanket.

"She has many, though the way she coaxes plants to grow amazes me the most. I think it is her beauty and soft voice they respond to, for there is not a plant in her garden that does not flourish. But then people flourish around her as well."

"Does she handle a weapon as well as you do?"

Emma laughed. "She better or Patience would be relentless until she did."

"Patience is the warrior among you three?"

"And a fine one," Emma said proudly. "I wish father would realize that and let her lead the clan. She deserves the honor. The clan holds her in high regard as she does each and every one of them. She would make a great laird."

Rogan returned to her side with the strip of cloth. "It has healed remarkably well for such a short time."

"Time will heal the rest. We will see how things go today and if all is well, I believe we should leave tomorrow at first light."

"It will be several days before we reach my

home. Are you sure you do not need more time to rest and regain your strength?"

"I will do fine as long as the fever does not return," she said, though knew that rest would serve to help heal, while riding endlessly for days would not only delay healing, but cause her pain. But the latter would be preferable, since her sister Heather might be suffering far worse than she, and Emma could not live with that thought.

"We will find Heather," Rogan said, knowing her thought, for it was his own.

"If the Dark Dragon truly does have her, it will not be easy."

Rogan began to wrap the cloth around her shoulder, gently covering her wound. "No, it will not, which is why we need to make certain, leave no room for doubt, that the Dark Dragon has Heather. Or do we follow the wrong path?"

"Patience would know. She will not give up, not return home until she has found Heather or has found information that we help us rescue her. I cannot help but wonder if she is home now waiting on my return."

Rogan reached for her nightdress as soon as he finished wrapping her wound.

Emma was eager to slip back into it and just as eager to wrap her plaid around it, covering her body as much as possible. Wanting to be done with it quickly, she hastily raised both arms for Rogan to drop her nightdress over her head.

The pain shot through her shoulder with such force that her whole body went limp, and she knew she was about to faint. She managed to say Rogan's name just as her nightdress slipped past her face and everything turned dark.

Rogan felt her body sag before she called his name. His arm was around her waist in an instant and he had her up in his arms just as fast. He carried her to the bed and carefully laid her down. He felt her head; she was cool. The arm obviously still pained her and well it should. It had not been that long since the sword had plunged her shoulder. She should be in bed, continuing to rest and heal.

He rinsed a cloth in the bucket of fresh water, then sat on the bed and pressed it along her forehead and cheeks. She stirred and her eyes appeared as if they fought to open. This was one time he was glad she was so stubborn.

"You fainted," he said when her dazed eyes cleared. "You suffer more pain than you tell me."

"It is to be expected. I simply need to be more vigilant in my movements."

"And riding a horse all day will not prove painful?"

"It cannot be helped," she said. "Once home I can get plenty of rest."

"Why is it I believe otherwise?"

She smiled and laid her hand upon his chest. "Because you have gotten to know me too well."

Her simple touches were like magic, stirring his manhood and his mind with lusty thoughts. He stood, letting her hand fall away and it brushed his thigh as he stepped away from the bed. He silently muttered an oath, thinking what it would be like for her to touch him intimately.

He would be in serious trouble if he kept letting his thoughts turn so wicked and in worse trouble if they continued to remain here alone. Besides, she was recovering from a serious wound and it was not right of him to be thinking such improper thoughts. And how many times did he need to remind himself that he had no right to her?

"We should leave tomorrow," she said.

She knew his thoughts, but then there were times he knew hers. They were getting much too close. He had to put an end to it.

"We leave tomorrow," he said as he turned and faced her.

"Aye, at first light," she agreed.

"I need to hunt. Will you—"

"I will be fine," she assured him and waited until the door closed behind him to release the heavy sigh that had been locked in her chest. She had seen it. She was certain she had seen it—passion. It had sparked in his eyes. He desired her as much as she desired him, and there was no denying it. They could no longer be alone. They had to return home, preferably to separate ones.

"Get out of bed and see to your needs before he returns," she urged. "Whatever you do keep your plaid wrapped around your nightdress, and no more sleeping together."

She paid heed to her warnings and moved slowly so as not to cause herself any sharp pain.

A spring chill filled the air and a persistent wind rustled the new tree leaves yet in full bloom. The cool air felt good against her skin after having lingered with fever the last few days as did the sun that managed to reign over the sky. It was a beautiful day and once Emma finished seeing to her needs, she had no want to return to the cottage.

She wandered the woods, keeping in mind not to stray too far from the croft. She loved exploring forests, to her they were ripe with treasures and knowledge. She often got lost for hours, sometimes a whole day. That was when Heather and Patience would come searching for her. Patience would scold and lecture her on how she had not even heard them approach and what if it was someone besides her sisters who came upon her?

Her heart turned heavy at the thought of her sisters. They had never been separated. They might go their own way doing the day, but they always came together for the evening meal, where they would share news of their day. They never lacked for conversation or for things to do together. Father had cautioned that one day they would need to separate and go with their perspective husbands, but they had ignored him. Then arrangements had been made for Heather to wed, and his warnings proved true.

Emma shook her upsetting thoughts away, especially with how she found herself feeling about Rogan. It was something that she could not dwell on, something that could never be.

A patch of nettle caught her eye and diverted her attention. She was careful not to touch the plant and get stung by the sharp hairs. She always protected her hands when picking the prickly plant. She would look for the young pale leaves, since they were most tasty when cooked. Unfortunately, the plants had barely sprouted so she left them to grow.

She continued exploring, and it was not until her shoulder began to truly ache did she realize that she had been away from the cottage longer than she had intended. It would not be wise to tire herself today when she would be riding endlessly over the next few days. She headed back to the cottage and noted as she went that she had gone farther than she had thought.

Gray clouds had settled in overhead by the time she stepped out of the woods. The beautiful day was over, but she was grateful that she had had a chance to give her mind a rest while she had explored.

She entered the cottage with renewed strength, though she felt the weight of her limbs.

"Bloody hell, where have you been?" Rogan shouted.

Emma jumped, startled by his booming voice.

"Answer me," he demanded.

"I went for a walk in the woods," she said, wondering why he was so upset.

"A walk in the woods?" he said as if he did not quite believe her.

"The sun was bright, the air only slightly chilled, and I had the most persistent urge."

"Never again," he said his fist coming down on the table, sending a groan through the worn wood.

That did it. He had no right speaking to her as if she was a child. "I am not your wife to dictate to."

He reached her in two strides, grabbing both her

arms and holding her firmly. “Wife or not, never, ever frighten the hell out of me like that again.”

He was frightened? He had been that upset that she had been gone? She opened her mouth to offer an apology.

“Damn,” he muttered and captured her open mouth in a kiss.

Chapter Thirteen

Emma was so shocked that she froze, though his kiss thawed her fast enough. His lips were so strong and confident on hers that it made it easy to respond in kind, and it felt so natural to do so. A tingle permeated her body and turned to a jolt when his tongue slipped into her mouth to tease hers. The tingle grew as his kiss demanded more and strange sensations took hold of her and she thought... she thought that a kiss felt far more wonderful than she ever imagined it would.

Rogan felt as if he had lost control. He never wanted to kiss a woman as much as he had wanted to kiss Emma. When he had entered the cottage and discovered her gone, he had felt as if his heart had stopped beating. His thoughts had gone wild with possibilities of what might have happened to her, each worse than the previous one. His anger had mounted, and then she had entered the cottage and relief had flooded him. He had never been so happy to see someone and all he had wanted to do was grab her, hug her, and kiss her senseless. He had kept control of himself until... she had reminded him that she was not his wife. That had angered him even more and had made him want to claim her even more, and so he kissed her. And he did not want to stop kissing her. Never had a kiss twisted at his heart and gut like this kiss with Emma. And never did he ache to make love to a woman as much as he did to Emma.

The thought had him tearing his mouth away from hers and resting his brow against hers to catch his breath and calm his wildly beating heart, not to mention his thick, hard arousal. He wanted her like he had never wanted another woman, and it troubled him.

Emma tried to calm her breathing, but the kiss had somehow stolen much of her breath, leaving her feeling as if she gasped for air. And the tingles running through her body were relentless. They prickled her skin, turned her nipples hard, and tickled her senseless between her legs, and it was all quite delightful.

He is your sister's future husband.

The voice in her head was like a slap to her face and she quickly pulled away from him, not that he stopped her, and she wondered if he had remembered the same.

Emma pressed her fingers to her lips that never felt so alive, so wonderful, and she stood nearer the hearth, staring down at the flames.

Rogan thought to apologize for his improper action and yet he could not bring himself to do so. He had wanted to kiss her long before now and he could not deny it, would not deny it. He was attracted to her much more than he had realized. The kiss had made him understand just how much he cared for Emma and just how much of a problem it presented.

Emma felt her worries descend heavily on her and her already tired limbs grew heavier. She placed her hand on the worn wooden mantle for support and her head drooped, too tired to hold it up any longer.

In the next moment, she was swept up in Rogan's arms, tucked tight against his chest, and carried to the bed.

He laid her down with gentleness that touched her heart and she was ever so relieved when he sat beside her on the bed. She did not want him to leave her side. She had grown accustomed to him being there, and there, by her side, was exactly where she wanted him to stay.

"You need rest to heal. You should not have gone exploring the woods."

"Perhaps, but I needed time away from my troubling thoughts," she admitted.

"I would have accompanied you," he said, brushing her hair off her brow and feeling it to make certain her fever had not returned, and was relieved to discover it had not.

"I needed time alone," she said, wishing his cool hand would linger on her brow, a troubling thought, which had her saying, "We need to leave tomorrow."

"Aye, that we do," he agreed. "You feel well enough for it?"

"It does not matter if I do. We need to leave," she said with an urgency that startled her.

"We will leave at first light."

He turned, ready to leave her side, and she

wished she could reach out and stop him. She did not want him to go. She wanted him to remain there with her, never to leave her side, but that was not possible. And as he walked away from her, she felt as if her heart broke in two.

She turned on her side, fearing tears that threatened would fall and she would appear a fool. How had this happened? How and when had she lost her heart to Rogan? A tear slipped out and ran down her cheek. Was what she feeling love? Could she have truly fallen in love with her sister's intended?

Emma attempted to reason with herself. Surely, it was simply that Rogan had tended her in her time of need that had caused her to have such strong feelings for him. But it did not explain why he had feelings for her, for that could not be denied, especially after the kiss.

Another tear slipped out and down her cheek. She had never been kissed like that. Actually, she had been kissed only once when she was young and that had gone so badly that she had never wanted to be kissed again... until now.

Now she wished that Rogan would never stop kissing her.

"Emma, is something wrong?"

She choked back her tears to answer as calmly as possible, "No."

"I feel your tears, Emma," he said softly and his arms circled her, turning her and taking her gently in his arms to rest her against his chest. "I should not have kissed you, but I could not stop myself. The need to feel you, taste you, know that you were safe in my arms was too great to deny."

His truthful words made her tears fall all the harder.

"I have never known such a loving kiss," she said finally looking at him.

"You have known other kisses?" he asked, the idea annoying him.

"When I was young and barely eleven years, a lad who claimed to care for me, kissed me, though now I know it was nothing more than a peck on the lips."

"Claimed to care for you?"

Emma felt the embarrassment of that moment return to haunt her and heat her cheeks. "He laughed after he kissed me and told me that my lips tasted like mud and that no one would ever love someone as ugly as me. He had made me think he cared for me so that he could win a wager with his friends that I would let him kiss me."

"Daniel, the name you spoke when your fever raged. You said he never truly cared for you and you went to Heather for comfort," Rogan said with an anger that could not be denied.

"She cradled me in her arms while I cried and Patience went and beat Daniel until he cried for her to stop." She smiled. "She left him with two black eyes and a split lip."

Rogan could not help but laugh. "I like your sister Patience more and more."

"I believe she would also like you."

"So then I am the first to truly kiss you?" he asked, wiping away the last of her tears. "Is that why you cry?"

"I cry for many reasons," she said, not wanting to admit how much the kiss meant to her and how much she cared for him.

"You miss your sisters," he said.

Another tear trickled from her eye as she said, "So very much."

"Until I find them for you, I am here whenever you need me, and even afterwards if ever the need should arise."

"You will make a good husband for my sister," she said, though her heart ached at her own words.

Rogan did not respond. How could he when he believed he had made a mistake and would marry the wrong Macinnes sister.

"You should rest. You have had a busy day," he said, slipping her out of his arms and down on the bed. He pulled the blanket up over her. "I will see to getting things ready for our departure tomorrow."

Emma could do nothing but nod, tears once again flooding her eyes and she closed them tight to stop them from falling. Soon they would be home, whether it was his or her keep they went to, it did not matter. They would at least be able to keep their distance, no longer sharing a single room cottage, no longer sleeping with each other. The thought only managed to upset her more.

"Would you like me to fix more of your brew?" he asked.

"Yes, that would be nice," she said, keeping her teary-eyes closed. She forced herself to think on other things and soon her tears faded and by the time he brought her the brew, she had regained her composure.

He slipped his arm beneath her back and with a strong lift sat her up in bed, handing her the goblet. He did not linger by her side, to her disappointment and also to her relief.

Rogan was in and out of the cottage, making ready for their departure tomorrow. Nightfall saw them enjoying the fish Rogan had caught for supper and when it came time for sleep, Rogan told her he had more to see to and would join her later.

He was keeping his distance and she could not blame him. She was glad he did, for she did not know what she would do if he kissed her again.

With her thoughts chaotic, she worried sleep would not find her this night, but her busy day and tired limbs proved otherwise and she was soon asleep.

Rogan watched her from where he sat at the table. How long had it been since he first met her? A week? Two weeks? He had lost all sense of time in his quest for Heather or was it Emma who had stolen time from him? And what else had she robbed him of... his senses?

He was fighting the urge to go to her, crawl in bed, and wrap himself around her. Consequences stopped him from doing so. He knew if he did, there was a good possibility he would do more than kiss her and from the way she returned his kiss, he knew she would not stop him.

He rubbed his hands over his face, then shook his head. Once they returned home all would be different. It would no longer be necessary for them to spend time together. His gut squeezed tight at the thought of them rarely seeing each other. Not to kiss her again, not to hold her, not to have her stubbornness challenge him... his gut twisted ever tighter.

What was the matter with him? He was a warrior who would become laird of his clan. His future had been planned since his birth. His father had given him a chance to find love, but he had failed to find it, and so a marriage was arranged. He had had no objections to it. He had even agreed with his father when he had advised Rogan to choose the beautiful sister over the plain one. He had made the choice not to accept Emma as his wife and now... he regretted it.

A low growl rumbled in his chest and anger made its way slowly through his body until his hands formed into tight fists. Now Emma would marry another, and he might just have to be the one who chooses her husband. And that did not set well at all with him.

You have a duty.

How often had his father reminded him of that? But his da had also discussed his choice of a wife with him. His da had been fair about it and in the end Rogan had agreed to the arrangement. He had no one to blame but himself.

He got up and turned away from Emma. It would do him no good to stare at her, for it made it all the more difficult to accept his fate. He would never have her; she would never be his.

Pain jabbed at his heart and anger jabbed at his senses once again. He almost laughed aloud at the irony of his situation. The fault was all his that the woman who had stolen his heart would never be his.

"Rogan!"

He turned at the sound of her calling out his name in such desperation and hurried to her side. She was asleep, though caught in a troubling dream or was it a frightening nightmare?

"I am here," he said and went to take her in his arms. "Damn," he muttered. Her fever had returned.

"Rogan, where are you?" she pleaded, her body twisting and her hands reaching out as if searching for him.

He quickly shed his clothes and got in bed, taking her in his arms as he settled beside her. "I am here, Emma. You have nothing to fear."

She instantly curled in his arms, pressing her body hard against him and burying face against his naked chest. "Do not leave me. Do not ever lea..."

Her words drifted off as she stilled and fell into a contented slumber, and he tightened his arms around her. He wanted badly to tell her that he would never leave her that she belonged to him and always would, but that was not the truth. She did not belong to him.

He said the one thing that was the truth. "I love you, Emma, I will always love you."

Chapter Fourteen

"Rogan, wake up! Rogan! What the hell are you doing naked in bed with your future sister-in-law?"

Rogan fought to get out of the dream and away from Liam's accusing voice.

"Rogan!"

The shout had his eyes popping wide to see Liam standing over him and Emma clinging tightly to him, her eyes as wide as his.

Liam leaned down over Rogan. "MacClennan and Macinnes warriors wait outside."

Emma attempted to wiggle out of his arms, but he held her firm. He would not have her scurry away, as if proving they had done something wrong.

"What are you doing here?" Rogan demanded. "I gave you orders—"

"I met up with Macinnes warriors along the way and they had a message from Patience, sent to her father," Liam said.

"What?" Emma asked anxiously. "What did my sister say?"

"Send more men," Liam said.

"We must get home," Emma said, wiggling out of Rogan's arms, and wincing in pain as she went. "I must talk with my father."

Liam shot Rogan a questioning look.

Rogan sat up, helping Emma to do the same.

"We were attacked, the last of our warriors taken. Emma took a blade to her shoulder coming to my defense and has suffered a fever ever since."

"My fever is gone," Emma insisted, wanting nothing to stop her from going home.

"It returned last night," Rogan said, "though it seems to have faded again." He placed his hand on her brow to confirm and nodded when he felt her cool skin.

"We should leave right away," Emma said, remaining where she was since pain repeatedly stabbed at her shoulder.

Rogan took gentle hold of her chin. "Are you in pain? And do not bother to lie to me, since I can see it on your face."

"Then why bother to ask me?" she said, tugging her chin free. "My shoulder is going to pain me until it finally heals and probably beyond that. I want to go home *now*."

"Your father's orders were to find you and let you know that you are to follow whatever Rogan should decide," Liam said.

"No!" Emma all but shouted.

Both men looked at her shocked.

"I am going home," Emma said adamantly.

Rogan got out of bed and stood there stark naked as he pointed a finger at her. "No! You will do as your father orders and obey me."

"No," she repeated more adamantly than before.

"You do not have a choice," Rogan said, "and I will not hear another word about it."

Emma clamped her mouth firmly shut. She

would not waste words on him. She would not follow his dictate no matter what her father commanded. She needed to speak with her father. There had to be more to the message from Patience than she was being told. Father may not have realized it, but she would. She needed to know all of what was contained in the message so that she would know what to do.

"Leave us, Liam, and let the men have a rest. We leave for home within the hour. And say nothing of what you saw here."

"There will be talk," Liam cautioned, "though not our warriors."

Emma was ready to argue with him, and then realized what he meant. Her warriors would worry over her honor. And they would tell her father that she had been found in the cottage alone with Rogan. What then would her father do?

"I will deal with that when and if the time comes," Rogan assured him. "For now we return home and determine our next move in finding my intended."

His words cut through her heart like a sharp knife. She was reminded yet again that Rogan would wed Heather. The arrangement had been made and it would be kept. She had to accept it and put Rogan out of her mind for own good, and for her sanity.

Liam pointed to a cloth sack on the table. "Your father sent garments he thought might be more useful for you."

She smiled, grateful she would finally have clothes to wear.

"Leave us, Liam. We will join you soon enough," Rogan said.

Liam looked between the two, his curiosity obvious, but he held his tongue and with a nod took his leave.

"You can join your men," Emma said. "I will be done shortly."

"You will need help and do not bother to argue with me."

He could be a tyrant at times, though he was right. She wanted to check on her wound and hopefully find something among her garments to serve as a better bandage, and she would need help with that. It would also give her time to thank him for what he had done for her.

"I need to look at my wound," she said, letting the excuse serve as her capitulation.

Rogan grabbed her plaid off the back of the chair. "We will do as we did before, so that you do not have to stand naked before me, not that it is by any means a chore looking at your beautiful body."

Rogan could not take his words back, nor did he want to. He wanted her to know that he thought her beautiful, especially since no one had ever told her that. He was the first and the first to see her gorgeous body and to kiss her. In a way, he had laid claim to her and if anyone knew what they had shared, they would be considered wed. The startling thought did not disturb him in the least.

Emma stood speechless. This man had not only touched her heart, but had opened it as well. She had locked her feelings away after the incident with

Daniel, fearing to ever trust not only a man, but herself as well. Rogan had changed all that. He had barged past her defenses and into her heart, settling there before she could stop him.

He belongs to Heather.

She was grateful for the reminder and diverted her troubling thoughts by going through the sack of clothes. She found what she needed, an old worn skirt that would provide her with bandages. Looking through the garments, she knew that Maura, the woman who tended her father, had been the one who had gotten this bundle together for her. Maura had chosen the clothes Emma favored, and she could not wait to slip into them and feel her old self once again.

Rogan worked the plaid up beneath her nightdress to secure across her breasts, neither of them saying a word. It was better this way to have it done and over. If they had remained here any longer, the consequences would have been dire or would they have served as a solution?

The thought gave him a jolt and got him thinking as he removed the bandage. "It looks good," he said glad to see it was healing so well and so fast.

Emma glanced at it and smiled. "Yes, it heals well."

"Still, you should be careful," he cautioned.

Her tone turned serious. "I intend to be more than careful."

Rogan grew irritated, sensing that she had just erected a wall between them and he did not like it at all. He lowered his head until their brows almost touched. “And I intend to get what I want.”

“And what is that?” she asked, her breath catching.

“The woman who will be my wife.”

A stabbing pain struck her wound and she gasped and shut her eyes tight against it. She was never so grateful for the pain. It hid the devastating stab of pain to her heart that his words had brought.

“Easy, breathe easy, Emma.”

It took her a moment to realize that she had dropped her brow to rest on his chest and that his hand massaged the back of her neck. He was there for her as he said he would be, and she wondered what she would ever do without him.

“You need more rest and care with that shoulder,” he said calmly, though he felt anything but calm. His heart had slammed into his chest when she had gasped and shut her eyes against the pain. It had to have been bad for her to do that. She had born pain with such courage that to see her surrender to it meant it had to have hurt her tremendously. And he hated to see her suffer. “We should wait a few days before we travel.”

“No,” she was quick to say. The thought of spending a few days here in the presence of Macinnes and MacClennan warriors was not to her liking. It was time for them to return home. “I want to go home.”

“My home,” he reminded.

“For now,” she said and raised her head.

“Slowly,” he cautioned.

She listened, having no desire to give him any

more reason to delay their departure.

"Let me wrap your wound, then help you dress," he said with a look that told her not to bother to argue.

She had no intentions to. She wanted to leave here as soon as possible.

Her skirt went on without a problem, but when it came to her blouse it proved difficult, and it did not take long for Rogan to grow frustrated and rip the plaid away, leaving her naked from the waist up.

"As I have told you before, I have seen you naked and there is no undoing that and believe me I have tried, but your tempting body refuses to relinquish its hold."

For a sheer moment, Emma thought he would kiss her and she so very much wanted him to. God help her, ever since he had kissed her, she had wanted him to kiss her again and again.

Heather.

Her sister's name so strong in her mind was like a slap in the face, and Emma took a step away from Rogan. "We need to be done with this and be on our way."

Done with this. This was far from done between them, but they did need to be on their way before he did something very foolish.

He helped her into her blouse, tied the ties above her breasts, and then helped her on with her boots. After that she placed her garments in the sack, while he gathered their other items. When all was ready, he draped her cloak over her shoulders.

His fingers brushed her chin as he tied the strings and sent a soft stirring through her. Now was the time to thank him for all he had done and yet she could not find the words. She felt as if she was saying good-bye to him, and she had not expected such sorrow to grip her heart. It was as if life itself was being squeezed out of her and nothing—nothing—would ever be the same again.

Rogan saw the sorrow in her eyes and felt it in his heart, and he could not stop himself. He leaned down and kissed her, and not a soft kiss.

Emma's one arm went around his neck and one of his arms wound around her waist, and they drifted together, fitting to each other perfectly as their kiss deepened.

It was as if he was breathing life back into her, making her feel whole, making her feel more than she had ever felt. Time seemed to stop, though their kiss went on. Her body awakened, her flesh turned sensitive, and her desire soared. And she knew then and there that this was not lust—it was love.

God help her. She had fallen in love with her sister's intended.

She reluctantly eased away from Rogan, turning as she did and going to the door. There were no words to say, nothing that could be done. She opened the door and without looking back at him, walked out.

Chapter Fifteen

Rogan rode his horse behind Emma's warriors, making certain to keep her in view. The scene in the cottage continued to play vividly in his mind. When she had ended their kiss and turned to leave, he had ached to reach out and grab her and never let her go. He had felt as if part of him was being torn away, the pain had been so great, but he had stopped himself... for now at least. He had made a mistake—a serious one—and he needed to rectify it. He had to set things right and part of that was finding Heather.

He had been annoyed when he had followed her out and had seen that her warriors had surrounded her, as if shielding her from him. A big barrel-chested warrior with long red hair heavily streaked with gray had stood beside her, his head bent speaking with her. When her eyes had caught his, the big warrior's glance had followed as well. The look he had given Rogan had been meant to warn. Rogan had responded with a threatening look of his own. It had been Emma who had stepped in front of the man, her back to Rogan, and ended the standoff.

Rogan did not like that someone else now looked after Emma. She was his responsibility. Her father had decreed it when he had ordered her to obey him, and her warriors would soon find out that it was a decree Rogan intended to be obeyed by all.

Liam rode up beside him and kept his voice low. "I speak to you now as a friend. What went on between you and Emma?"

"It is no concern of yours," Rogan snapped.

"It is not a question I ask, but what her warriors are asking."

"Then let them ask me," Rogan said.

"The big one—James—will no doubt do that. From what I have learned he has been friends with her father since they were lads, like you and me."

Rogan turned to Liam. "If he asks, I will be truthful with him."

"I never doubted you would be."

"You are a true friend, Liam," Rogan said with a smile. "Now tell me what else you have learned from the Macinnes men and of this message from Patience."

"She was quick to get a message to her father," —Liam shook his head— "though I wonder why it went to him and not you. And I believe there is more to it than we have been told. Send more men where? There had to have been more to the message."

"I had the same thought and before we go rushing off blindly, we are going to return home and sought this whole thing out. After all that has happened, I have reached the conclusion that it is likely the Dark Dragon has taken Heather. Why, I have no idea, but I intend to find out."

"And get her back?" Liam asked.

"If I can."

Liam raised a curious brow. "What do you mean?"

"There is more to Heather's abduction than we see. And I cannot help but wonder if more powerful people are involved with it than we know. If that should prove true, nothing I do will get her back."

"Have you shared these thoughts with Emma?"

"Yes, except for the possibility that there may be no chance in seeing Heather returned. It is something that Emma would never accept. She and Patience will fight to the death to see her sister safe and that is something I would like to find out... that Heather is at least safe."

"How do we do that?" Liam asked.

"Find a way of getting in touch with the Dark Dragon."

Liam shook his head. "That will not prove an easy task."

"But a necessary one, for I fear Emma will take it upon herself to be caught by the Dark Dragon to see if it is true that he has abducted Heather."

"She is a brave one, coming to your defense with no regard to her own safety," Liam said.

"Braver than I ever thought possible, she is an exceptional woman."

"It is a good wife she will make some lucky man."

"A man of my choosing," Rogan said adamantly.

Liam's brow went up. "Her father—"

"Will agree," Rogan finished with such a sharp tone that Liam knew meant no more was to be said about it.

"What about our warriors who disappeared?" Liam asked.

"The attacks thus far have not proved deadly. I have a feeling they will show up either with minor injuries or unharmed."

"If not?"

"Another question that will be presented to the Dark Dragon," Rogan said.

"You do not take your eyes off Emma," Liam said with a grin.

Liam was much too perceptive at times, but then they were longtime friends and he knew Rogan all too well. "The fever, her wound, this has not been easy for her, and she would topple from her horse before she would complain."

"A female version of you," Liam said with a chuckle.

His remark had Rogan turning his head and sending him a threatening stare.

"I have seen that look all too often for it to have any effect on me," Liam said still chuckling. "But then I suppose the laird of a clan needs to be stubborn at times."

"Determined," Rogan corrected.

"Whatever way you put it, stubborn is stubborn," Liam said.

"Tell me more of the Macinnes warriors," Rogan said once again letting Liam know the matter was at an end.

Rogan kept an eye on Emma the whole time he and Liam talked. James, the big-chested warrior had taken his leave of Emma and was riding among his warriors, having a few words with each, and then moving on to the next. Rogan wondered over his action, though it caused him no concern. He had positioned his men so that they could easily surround the Macinnes warriors and easily disarm them if such a situation arose. But he doubted that Emma's father had given permission for them to battle MacClennan warriors. The big warrior's concern was probably more for Emma and seeing her protected—from him.

If that was the case, then James should be keeping a better eye on Emma. Rogan could tell by the slump of her body and the way her head sagged now and again that she was fighting to keep herself astride the horse. It was one thing lying in bed and allowing her wound to heal and another to ride a horse for hours on end and not expect to suffer the consequences.

Not a one of the warriors paid Emma heed, but then they had no need of her. They assumed her safe because they surrounded her, but paid no mind that she had yet to recover from her injury.

It was when Emma tilted precariously to the side and caught herself, straightening sharply, her shoulders drawing in from the pain that he urged his horse into a firm gallop, cutting through the Macinnes warriors surrounding her and scooping her off her horse and into his arms to set her across in front of him.

Her warriors descended on him, but his warriors blocked them before they could get near him. It gave him time to situate her comfortably against his chest and in his arms.

"Take your hands off her," James bellowed as he forced his way through the many warriors, though Rogan's men would not let him pass through to Rogan.

"She is in pain and exhausted, and you and your warriors would have realized that if you had paid her an ounce of attention. Since her father ordered her to obey me, I can only assume that you were instructed to do the same. From this point on, you follow my orders and as for Emma, she is my concern, not yours."

James' cheeks puffed red, his nostrils flared, and he looked about to spew fire from his mouth.

"I would mind my words," Rogan warned, "and obey what orders your laird commanded."

It took James a few moments to contain his anger and say, "Emma is good with this?"

That he defied Rogan and his own laird and was more concerned with how Emma felt had him respecting the man, though it did not stop him from responding with authority. "Good or not, the decision is mine."

Emma raised her head with some difficulty. "I am fine riding with Rogan MacClennan. If I was not," —she gave a light laugh— "neither of us would be astride this horse now."

James let loose with a mighty laugh and the other Macinnes warriors joined in.

The lethal look that surfaced on Rogan's face had his own men backing away from him and when the Macinnes warriors saw that, their laughter died abruptly and deep silence reigned.

Rogan's warriors circled him and Emma as they continued on. Rogan did not fail to notice the many stares from the Macinnes warriors when Emma settled comfortably in his arms, as if she had done so many times before.

"You will be riding with me from now on," Rogan said.

"I would argue with you, but there would be no point."

"Good," he said with a smile. "You are learning obedience."

She chuckled. "Actually, I am being sensible. I tire much too easily while riding. At least in your arms, I can rest comfortably."

"I knew the journey would be too much for you. We should have waited and given you more time to heal," he said annoyed that he had not listened to his own misgivings.

"No, it is imperative we return home. Patience could have sent more messages and we need to learn more about the Dark Dragon while we gather our men."

"Rescuing Heather is not going to be as easy as I first thought," Rogan said, wanting to prepare Emma for delays and, no doubt, disappointments.

"Aye, I will agree with you on that, though I am encouraged that Patience was able to send a message. It means she still follows Heather's trail, though the message seems incomplete."

"I thought the same myself," Rogan agreed. "She supplies no further information that might help in our search. Does she expect her warrior to lead others to her?"

"That troubles me as well, and when I told James I wished to speak with the warrior who delivered the message, he told me that he was not with them. That he had remained behind."

"That makes no sense. We need to speak with him and find out what happened and in what direction we must go."

"I voiced the same concern myself and James informed me that the warrior required rest after his strenuous journey and would arrive at the MacClennan keep with the second group of warriors my father was sending," Emma said, shaking her head. "I know there has to be more to my sister's message than what we were told, though I cannot understand why my father would keep it from me. Unless he thought it would upset me, but even so he would have confided in you, and James has made no effort to speak with you."

"The man does not like me," Rogan said.

"He believes you have taken advantage of me," Emma said bluntly. "I told him that was far from the truth."

Rogan lowered his voice. "Did you tell him we slept together?"

"No," she snapped, "and nor will I. No one would understand and they would believe us..."

Rogan said what she could not. "Wed."

"You are promised to Heather," she reminded him as well as herself. "And I will not take from my sister what belongs to her."

"So you are saying that she wished to wed me?"

Emma recalled Heather's response to their

father when he had informed her of the marriage arrangement. Heather had not objected nor had she smiled, she had—in a bare whisper—told their father that she would do her duty. And Emma related that to Rogan. "Heather wished to do her duty just like you, but then you requested my sister for a wife and rejected me. Heather will be your wife, not me."

Why did her heart have to ache at the thought? Documents had been signed and sealed and nothing could change that even if Rogan had kissed her with the intensity of someone who had fallen in love. Perhaps, though, it was what she wanted to believe.

"I will have who I want for a wife," Rogan said, as if the decision had already been settled.

"So you said once before. Determined to have your way, are you?"

Rogan leaned down close and for a moment she thought he would kiss her, but he would not dare. Her men were watching and already it did not look proper with his lips so close to hers.

"Always," he whispered, his warm breath brushing her lips as if in a faint kiss.

She tried to move away from him and winced from the discomfort it brought her shoulder.

Rogan adjusted her in his arms and ordered, "Do not be stubborn. Stay put, so your shoulder will suffer no pain."

She held her tongue, for she could not tell him that it was unexpectedly falling in love with him that caused her the most pain and being here in his arms did not help. When her father had first mentioned a possible union between Rogan and her... she had been hesitant. She had not believed he would agree and she had been right. He preferred the beautiful sister over the plain one. But her heart had not been set on the union, so she had not been as disappointed as others might have thought. Ever since the incident with Daniel, she had believed that she would never find love, and she had accepted her lot.

Then Rogan had to go and kiss her, hold her, care for her, and he had changed everything. And worse, she had seen the passion in his eyes for her, but where was the love?

"Sleep and get the rest you need," Rogan ordered. "You are safe in my arms."

She could not help but ask, "Am I?" His answer surprised her.

"For now."

A shiver raced through her, and he tucked her cloak more tightly around her, but it was not the chilled air that had caused her to quiver. It was what his words had implied. Would there come a time she was not safe in his arms? A time when they would do more than just sleep in bed together? The prospect frightened and excited her.

"We will camp early tonight and I will see you kept warm."

He could not mean that he intended to sleep beside her, not in front of her warriors. Already, they whispered among themselves about her being alone in the cottage with Rogan. If he slept beside her, surely they would think he was laying claim to her.

No, he would not do that. He was promised to another. He had a duty to see to. She was tired and not thinking clearly.

"Sleep, you are safe," he urged again.

Her eyes closed of their own accord. Aye, she was safe here in his arms and pleased to be there, until the time came she would be there no more.

Rogan felt her body grow limp as sleep took hold of her. He stared at her so content in sleep, but then she had slept contentedly in his arms the last few nights. It was almost as if she belonged there in his arms. That they had been waiting for her. She had driven him near to madness with her stubbornness and her courage had astounded him. She was a remarkable woman and an honorable one. She would not betray her sister and steal her intended away, and he admired her noble nature.

Was he as honorable as her?

The thought plagued him. He had a duty to his clan and he would see it fulfilled, though how was the question.

Rogan kept the pace steady, though not hard. He would not have Emma jolted about and plagued with pain. No one seemed to complain about their plodding pace, not his warriors or the Macinnes warriors. And while glances were cast their way, the warriors were busier keeping their eyes on the surrounding landscape. He knew they were concerned about the ghost warriors.

However, Rogan was not. They were headed home in defeat. Why bother to attack them now? No, the Dark Dragon had left his mark on them and he would leave them to return home with their tails tucked between their legs. Not something Rogan favored, but then how did one conquer a myth?

They rode several more hours and as Emma began to stir, Rogan ordered all to stop and make camp for the night. They had ridden farther than Rogan had expected, so he heard no mumbling complaints from anyone, though his warriors would know better than to do so.

"Emma," he said softly, giving her a light squeeze.

Emma opened her eyes. "Are we home yet?"

"Not nearly, though we are making camp for the night."

"I could use a stretch and some food," she said surprised by her grumbling stomach.

"Your stomach makes that quite clear," he said with a smile. "I am glad to see that you will eat because you are hungry, rather than force yourself to do so to stay strong."

He knew her too well. Had she truly failed to realize how close they had become over the last few days?

"A good sign that I heal," she said.

James was off his horse and over to them as soon as Rogan called a halt for camp to be set up. He reached up to help her off the horse.

Rogan did not object. He let the man take her, but when he saw how unsteady she was on her feet, he dismounted in a flash and had his arm around her just as quickly, leaving James a bit stunned.

"I will see to Emma. You see to your men," Rogan directed with an abrupt firmness that cautioned he would not be disobeyed.

James reluctantly took his leave, and Rogan could see that he was quickly making an enemy.

"James means only to help," Emma said.

"He can help by following my orders," Rogan said and with his arm around her waist and after snatching a rolled blanket off the back of the horse, he walked her over to a large pine tree. He pushed a bunch of fallen pine needles together with his foot and spread the blanket over them, then took her by the waist and helped her to sit.

Emma almost sighed aloud, the pallet so soft and welcoming after being on a horse all day.

"Stay put," he ordered something he found himself repeating often to her.

She yawned. "I am not going anywhere." How she could still be tired after sleeping a good part of the day away told her she had yet to recover sufficiently. While she had no want to rest, she knew it was necessary. She intended to be fully recovered and ready to join Patience in their search for Heather. Besides, she needed her full strength to keep her wits about her when it came to Rogan.

Warriors from both clans got busy setting up camp. She was surprised when after spying James speaking with Rogan, he came over to her and built a campfire not far from her.

"It will keep you warm on this chilly night," James informed her. "And if you need anything, you will let me know."

"You will be the first I confide in," she assured him and he took his leave, a wide smile deepening his many wrinkles.

Soon the camp was filled with delicious scents. Rabbits roasted on spits and the pungent smell of fish sizzled on fire stones. They would eat well tonight. Emma only hoped she could keep her eyes open long enough to eat.

It was as if Rogan heard her, for he was suddenly in front of her with a bowl of food.

She stared at the bowl, and then up at him.

He smiled. "I took a bowl or two and some goblets as well from the cottage. Take this and I will get you some ale the men have brought along. I would brew your leaves, but there are none left."

Emma took the bowl and Rogan left to fetch the ale. She had worried that her mixture would be spent, and she did not know if Rogan would have the plants she needed in his kitchen garden to mix more. If not she would have to search the woods near his home.

Rogan returned with another bowl in his hand and a goblet in the other. "We will share the drink."

He sat beside her and she was glad for his company, though she could have done without the questioning glances from her warriors.

They spoke little, both hungry from the day-long journey, and Rogan could see how fatigued Emma was. She needed rest, for they would leave with first light for another day's tedious journey.

"You will tell me if you grow too tired to travel," Rogan said.

"You know I will not, besides I will ride with you. Your arms are most comfortable and your chest, though hard, is pleasant to rest against."

While her remark was made innocently enough, she wondered if somehow it might be considered improper. She was glad no one was close enough to hear them.

Rogan did not think her words improper at all. He liked that she enjoyed being in his arms and he would see to keeping her there as long as possible. "I am glad you are comfortable there. You fit quite nicely."

He was right. His arms did seem a perfect fit, but she had no right to be in them. A yawn snuck up on her and her hand went to her mouth as if to catch it.

Rogan wanted to lie back with her on the blanket and wrap himself around her and sleep—in each other's arms—as they had done the last few nights. But that would be most improper to do in front of her warriors.

"I do not think my eyes will stay open much longer," Emma said.

"Then sleep, for we have an early start in the morning." Rogan collected the bowls and goblet. "You need more than that cloak to keep you warm. I will bring you a blanket."

Emma did not want another blanket. She wanted him sleeping wrapped around her. She would miss him tonight and the thought sent a shiver through her. She pulled her cloak more tightly around her before she lay back on the makeshift bed. She fought to keep her eyes open until Rogan returned, but exhaustion won the battle and she was soon asleep.

Rogan draped the wool blanket over her when

he returned, not surprised to find her asleep. He would be glad when they finally reached home where she would get the proper care and rest she needed. And where he could start setting things right.

James approached him with determined steps and Rogan was ready for him. Before the man could say a word, Rogan spread another blanket on the opposite side of the campfire from Emma.

"I will take guard of Emma now," James said and nodded at the spread blanket.

"Emma's father made her my responsibility," Rogan reminded. "You see to your men."

James appeared ready to argue.

"That is an order, not a request," Rogan said like a leader accustomed to commanding his warriors.

James stomped off, mumbling to himself and passing Liam as he went.

"Watch yourself with him," Liam cautioned once beside Rogan. "He will report all he sees to Donald Macinnes."

"Let him report what he wants," Rogan said. "How does the surrounding area look?"

"We have no company from what I can see, though it is what I cannot see that worries me. I would give anything to know how these warriors can materialize without warning."

"If they do follow, I believe it is to see their mission done."

"And won," Liam said, shaking his head.

"Not completely. They will expect us to retaliate

and will be ready when we do."

"Then what do we do?" Liam asked.

"The unexpected."

Chapter Sixteen

Emma woke with a start. Had she heard someone call her name or had she been dreaming? She laid there, the campfire having dwindled to embers and the camp itself eerily silent. Not a soul stirred, nor a sound could be heard. She knew that guards had been posted on the perimeters of the camp, so they were well protected, but somehow that did not settle her unease.

She sat up and saw that Rogan was sleeping soundly on the other side of the campfire, her stirring not having roused him. She looked over the camp and saw that all the warriors appeared to sleep as soundly as Rogan.

"Emma!"

"Patience?" She looked around, expecting to see her sister.

"Emma!"

She scrambled to her feet and called out, "Patience!"

When no one in the camp reacted to her shout, she knew something was wrong.

"Dreaming," she said softly. She had to be dreaming.

"Emma, hurry."

She did as Patience said and rushed off into the

woods. It was so dark that she could barely see anything, yet her feet seemed to know where to take her.

"Emma, stop!"

She halted and waited.

"Listen," Patience said, "we do not have much time. I did not send that message. Pay it no heed. Remember all I have taught you and follow your instincts. Do not—"

Footfalls turned Patience silent and Emma looked around, frightened by the heavy steps drawing ever closer.

"Do not trust anyone and stay brave. I am well and we will rescue Heather. Now hurry and go!"

Emma turned to run and nearly stumbled as she stopped abruptly. Before her stood a massive figure draped in black, the hood of his cloak drawn down over his head and face. His arms were spread out from his sides, making it appear as if he had massive wings. A black mist swirled at his feet and began to creep toward her. She looked around to run, but it was too late, the mist was licking at her legs and she could not move. He had her trapped. She trembled as the mist crawled up along her body. She had never seen anything so sinister or felt so frightened, and she reacted out of sheer instinct—she let out a blood-curdling scream.

Rogan jumped to his feet, taking his sword with him. He rushed to Emma's side when he saw her struggling in her sleep and hurried to rescue her from her nightmare.

He sat beside her and as he reached out for her, said gently, "You are safe, Emma, I am here.

Nothing can harm you."

Her eyes sprang open and it took her a moment for her to recognize Rogan and recall where she was, then she wrapped her arms around him and buried her face against his chest, tears falling to wet his shirt.

Rogan held her tight, felt her frightened shiver and her tears. He looked out at the camp, knowing her high-pitched scream had to have woken others, and saw James standing near the dwindling campfire along with several of his men, their swords in hand. Rogan's men surrounded them, ready to protect if necessary.

"A nightmare," Rogan informed the tense man. "Dawn is on the horizon. Have your men ready to go once the sun is strong in the sky."

"I will speak with Emma before we take our leave," James said and did not wait for a response. He turned and waved for his men to follow.

Rogan would deal with James later. Now he was more concerned with Emma and her nightmare. He blamed himself. Whenever her sleep had turned fitful, he had comforted her with soothing words and a gentle touch. She had calmed every time. This time, however, he had not been there to protect her and that angered him.

He wanted to know about her nightmare so that he could assuage her worries, but the tight grip she had on him told him she was not ready to talk. What she needed now was simply to be held and reassured.

Emma could not stop the shivers from racing

through her body, and she could not get the image of that sinister figure out of her head. She had never felt as threatened as she had in her dream. Then she recalled what had actually made her scream and her body was racked with more shivers. The black-garbed figure had raised its arms and reared its head and Emma could have sworn it had been a dragon.

"Those leaves you brew," Rogan said. "Do any grow around here? I could pick them and make you a brew. It might help."

She raised her head off his chest, shaking it. "There are too many plants that resemble each other and picking the wrong one could prove deadly. Besides, the leaves have to be dried before they can be used. Perhaps you will have what I need in your kitchen garden."

"Then the sooner we get home the better."

Was it? Would going to his home prove better than going to hers? At her home she could at least question the warrior that had brought the message. If she was to believe her dream—more a nightmare—then Patience had not sent the message, but if not her... who?

Rogan was eager to question her, but decided it could wait until she was on his horse with him. They could talk without interruption and he would make certain no one would be able to hear their conversation.

"I need to see to my men," he said. "Will you be all right until I return for you?"

"I will be fine," she assured him. "It was just a nightmare that frightened."

"A nightmare I want to hear all about." He

moved away from her reluctantly and stood, then offered his hand to her.

She took it, wanting to stand firmly on her feet in more ways than one.

"We can discuss it while you ride with me," he said and waited to see if she would object.

"As I told you yesterday, I will ride with you. I want to heal as fast as possible so that I may continue my search for my sisters."

"I will return shortly," he said and waved over Liam. "Liam will wait with you until I return." His hand went up as her mouth opened. "Have you not learned by now that it is senseless to protest my decisions?"

"I was going to thank you—"

Rogan laughed. "I am to believe that?"

"Of course, since spending a little time with Liam could very well prove advantageous. It is obvious he knows you well and with some gentle probing, I can learn more about you that could prove rather useful when dealing with you."

"That I believe," Rogan said and turned to Liam. "Tell her nothing about me."

Liam grinned. "I think she already knows a great deal about you."

"More than she should," Rogan said and walked off.

Emma wondered over his remark. She did not know him that well or had he allowed her to see more than most?

By the time Rogan returned, Emma felt as if she and Liam were old friends. He had allowed her extra time in the woods not only to see to her needs, but to linger over a few plants that had interested her. He had told her a tale or two about Rogan when they had been young and had her laughing at antics.

Rogan was pleased to see Emma smiling when he joined them. It was one of the reasons he had left Liam with her. He could spin a tale that would bring a smile to most anyone and because he knew Liam would protect her with his life just as he would Liam's wife Ina.

"I should speak with James before we leave," Emma said and hurried off, not letting Rogan stop her.

"She does not let her wound hamper her, though at times you can see it pains her," Liam said, watching how she turned a smile on a grumpy James.

"Which is why she will ride with me the remainder of the trip," Rogan said as if declaring an edict.

"You stir the pot to boiling," Liam warned.

"It can boil over for all I care." Rogan watched as Emma turned James' scowl into a smile. "Did she speak of her nightmare at all?"

"No, not a word, though when in the woods her every move seemed cautious. It was almost as if she expected something to pounce out at her."

"We are going to pick up our pace today," Rogan informed him. "I want to reach home as soon as possible."

"As you wish," Liam said with a nod. "I will go inform the men and Macinnes warriors as well."

Rogan walked off to get his horse, intending to

end Emma's conversation with James and have them on their way.

"You can ride with me or one of the other men," James said as soon as Emma informed him that she would be riding with Rogan today.

She almost blurted out that she would prefer riding with Rogan, his arms gentle and his chest quite comfortable, but caught herself. Instead, she said, "For some reason Father has entrusted me into Rogan's care and while I would prefer that he had not, I cannot do anything about it at this moment... but obey. As soon as I am able, I will see that changed. Until then, it would seem that you and our warriors as well as myself are to obey father's dictate."

"You are a good, obedient daughter," James said with a generous smile. "You do your father and clan proud."

"Time to leave," Liam announced, walking through the camp. He stopped next to her. "Rogan waits for you." He gave a nod and a look beyond her shoulder.

She turned and saw Rogan standing beside his horse.

"Your warriors are here should you need them," James said, "though I must admit, Rogan protects you well and for that I am grateful."

James walked away and Emma went to Rogan.

"Ready?" he asked, though did not wait for an answer. His hands went to her waist and the next thing she knew she was up on his horse. He mounted after her and adjusted her to rest comfortably against him. "We set a faster pace today."

"Then we get home sooner," she said with a smile, pleased to be in his arms again.

They were not traveling long when Rogan said, "Tell me about your dream."

Her sister's warning rang in her head like a tolling bell. *Do not trust anyone.* But she had also cautioned her to follow her instincts and instinct told her that it would do no harm to share her dream with Rogan.

"I woke to a strange stillness and my sister Patience calling out my name. It took me a moment to realize I was dreaming. She told me to hurry and so I ran into the woods. I never saw Patience, I only heard her. She told me that she did not send the message, though she did say she was well and that we would rescue Heather. We heard footfalls then and she told me to run. I turned to do just that and found myself facing the most menacing figure draped in black, blocking my path. It was when he spread his arms out, resembling a dragon that I screamed." She shivered. "It felt so real, not a dream at all."

"It would seem that all your worries took flight in a nightmare. We questioned Patience's message and so you dream she did not send it. You worry if she is well and she tells you she is fine, and she assures you that both of you will find Heather. And, of course, the Dark Dragon makes an appearance since you fear him having your sister the most," he said sensibly explaining the whole nightmare away. "Worry not, we will find our answers."

Emma nodded, as if accepting his explanation and perhaps she would have if she and her sisters had not reached out to each other in dreams before. And their strange connection had always proved beneficial. Rogan may think it nothing but a dream, but Emma believed that Patience had reached out to her. She intended to keep that thought private and she intended to find out who had actually sent the message.

~~~

The days wore on endlessly, the pace faster on some days more than others. Patience had not reached out to Emma in anymore dreams, though she had hoped she would, and she had hoped that Heather would do the same, but she had not.

She and Rogan talked often while they rode together and she grew more comfortable with him. It was strange since they seemed to be at ease with each other much like a husband and wife would be, at least her warriors believed so, for they grumbled about it amongst themselves, but not quite enough for her not to hear as she passed by.

It was with some relief that she saw Rogan's keep in the distance, though it also signaled that their time together was at an end. No more would she feel his arms around her and it saddened her heart and, once again as in the cottage, she felt as if she was saying good-bye to him for good.

They entered the keep together to find his father well into his cups.
~~~

"Good, you are home," Angus MacClennan said, waving his goblet at one of the servants, ale spilling over the sides. "Take the plain lass to a room and see to her. We have to talk, son, Ronald Macinnes sent me an important message."

"Then you will discuss it in front of me," Emma said, stepping forward, her hands on her hips and ignoring the pain in her shoulder.

"Nonsense, go do what women do and leave this to the men," Angus ordered, though none to clearly.

Rogan shook his head. He probably would have reacted the same as his father had he not gotten to know Emma. He almost cringed, recalling that he had reacted similarly upon first meeting her. Now, however, knowing her as he did, she was not a woman that could be discounted so easily. And her sharp intelligence could prove an asset to them.

Emma marched over to Angus and grabbed the goblet out of his hand.

The man stared at her in shock.

"What message did my father send?" she demanded.

Angus was so stunned by her actions that he answered her without thinking about it. "Donald says we are to do nothing until we hear from him."

Rogan stepped forward. "When did you receive this message?"

"Just this morning," Angus said.

"Who brought the message?" Emma asked.

"A Macinnes warrior," Angus said, reaching for the tankard of ale to fill another goblet. "Now, I want time with my son, so be off with you." He gave a yell for Bertha several times. "Blasted, where is that woman?"

"Right here," Bertha said her ample bulk swaying as she entered the Great Hall. "And your head will be planted on that table soon enough if you do not stop filling that goblet."

"Take her," —Angus waved in Emma's direction— "and both of you be gone."

"You cannot wave away women that easily." Bertha laughed and took Emma by the arm. "Come with me. You need some tending."

Rogan was surprised Emma did not protest, but then she had to be exhausted from the grueling journey, and since she heard her da's message there was no reason not to take her leave.

Before Bertha ushered her completely out of the hall, she turned her head and said, "We will talk later."

Rogan nodded. "After you rest." As soon as she disappeared up the stone staircase, he turned to his father. "What else did Donald Macinnes say?"

Angus raised his tankard and smiled. "You knew I did not tell her all, but then she does not need to know that her father has ordered his warriors home and we are to wait to hear from him, and," —his smile vanished—"he fears Heather may be lost to them."

"Why?" Rogan asked, though he knew the answer.

"He believes the Dark Dragon has taken Heather."

"How has he reached that conclusion?"

Angus took a generous gulp of ale before

answering. "His warrior told him about the ghost warriors and everyone knows who they belong to."

"So Donald Macinnes will give up and let the Dark Dragon have his daughter?" Rogan asked, anger rising up to choke him. "Do not bother to answer. It is not his choice to make. She is my intended and my responsibility."

"Not anymore," Angus said, staring down into his tankard.

"What do you mean?" Angus's hesitation had Rogan demanding, "Answer me, Father."

Again Angus hesitated.

"Father!" Rogan said firmly.

Angus finally looked up at his son, squaring his shoulders, though still swaying. "Donald and I have long wanted to join our clans. So to make certain that would happen, we agreed on inserting a clause into the marriage agreement."

"Without telling me?" Rogan snapped.

"Donald and I never believed for a moment it would see fruition," his father insisted.

"Tell me."

Angus did so with reluctance. "If for some reason your marriage to Heather did not take place when planned, then you were to wed Emma. I am sorry, son. I know she is plain to look upon, but Donald assures me she will make you a good wife."

Rogan stared at his father. His problem solved itself. He had planned on seeing the marriage agreement changed, and now it had been done for him. He was thrilled, though he did not let his father know that.

"One other thing," Angus said.

"Spit everything out, Da," Rogan ordered.

"Donald was worried that with his daughter's abduction and not knowing what happened to Patience that his clan could be in jeopardy if his illness should suddenly claim him. So he had you and Emma wed by proxy. I signed it this morning, sealing your marriage to Emma."

It actually filled him with relief and joy that Emma was his wife. Donald Macinnes had made a wise decision. He had been right to worry about his clan being left without a chieftain. Now with Emma and him wed, Macinnes land and its people would be protected.

The only problem was... how would Emma react to the news?

Chapter Seventeen

Emma liked Bertha. She was a jovial woman and a caring one, but at the moment she needed to get rid of her before she once again took her clothes and stranded her in the bedchamber.

"We will get you a nice hot tub to soak in and some good food in that grumbling stomach," Bertha said as they entered a bedchamber and she slipped off Emma's cloak.

"Food," Emma said, pressing her hand to her stomach. "I am so hungry. Could I eat first?"

"Of course you can, I will go get you something right away and tell the servants to wait with the tub." Bertha headed to the door. "You rest yourself in front of the hearth until I get back."

Emma sighed and nodded as she walked over to the chair and sat. As soon as the door closed, she sprang out of the chair, grabbed her cloak, and went to the door. She waited, giving Bertha time to clear the hall and head down the stairs. When she was satisfied enough time had passed, she peeked out and seeing no one about, she slipped out. She took the stairs slow, wanting to avoid anyone coming up or going down.

She had to find the warrior who had delivered her father's message. She had a feeling there was more to the message than Angus had shared with her. Besides, she wanted to hear it directly from the warrior himself, and she wanted to ask him about her father. She was worried about him and prayed that his illness had not worsened. The messenger could only be one place... with the other Macinnes warriors.

The shadows provided cover as she crept through the keep without being detected, and she breathed a sigh of relief when she finally slipped outside. The village surrounding the keep was busy with clansmen greeting the returning MacClennan warriors and consoling those whose warriors had failed to return. Emma was intent on no one seeing her, so her steps were slow and cautious. She stopped a few times when voices got too near her. It was those times she noticed that several of the cottages looked in need of repair and that many of the cottage gardens were much too small to provide an adequate supply of food.

She shook her head. Now was not the time to improve the MacClennan's lot. She had more important matters to attend to. She finally slipped unnoticed through the open, thick wood doors that enclosed part of the village and the keep and hastened her steps to the area were Rogan had directed James to join the camp where the injured Macinnes warriors had been set up. It lay beyond the village walls. James had scowled at the location, though he had been eager to see how the wounded warriors had fared.

Emma spotted James talking to a warrior and shaking his head adamantly. She hurried over to the pair.

James spoke up as she approached. "Your father has ordered us to return home."

"That is not what Angus MacClennan told me," she said, turning to the other warrior and recognizing him. His name was Thomas and she had fixed his arm when he had broken it, everyone thinking it was beyond repair. It had healed well and he had regained full use of it.

"He left out the part where your father said that Macinnes warriors are to return home and MacClennan is to do nothing until he hears from your father," Thomas said. "There were also sealed documents your father had me deliver that were meant for Angus MacClennan's eyes only."

"Do you have them?" Emma asked anxiously, curious of their content.

Thomas shook his head. "I gave them to Angus MacClennan."

Emma's stomach twisted in knots. What was her father up to? Why had he ordered the warriors home? What had happened that changed his mind so soon?

She turned to James. "Is there anyone not fit to travel?"

He shook his head. "The injured men you tended before going after your sister are doing well and will have no trouble traveling, but what of you? Do you feel up to another journey or do you need a few days rest?"

"Something tells me I should get home as fast as possible," Emma said, the urge to leave poking at her. "I would leave now, but the men need food and rest as do the animals. We will leave at first light."

James smiled and nodded. "And no one need know we leave so soon."

Could she leave Rogan without saying good-bye? But had she not already said her good-byes? And was it not better this way?

"Aye," she agreed, "no one need know."

~~~

Rogan stood in front of the hearth in his bedchambers, a towel wrapped around his slim hips and his skin still damp from his bath. He would let the heat from the fire's flames dry him the rest of the way. Right now, he wanted to do nothing but think of how to tell Emma that they were husband and wife.

He had made it clear to his father that he would be the one to tell Emma that they were wed, and nothing was to be said about it until then. His father had agreed, but had urged him to tell her before tonight, since he expected his son to consummate the marriage and seal their vows.

He wanted nothing more than to make love to Emma, but something told him that she might not feel the same way. Not after learning that she was his wife and that she now had a new home, and would return only to her old one to visit. She certainly would never believe that it had been his intention to see that they wed, and she definitely would not believe that he loved her. He hardly believed it himself.
~~~

Love had struck him hard, though when he did not know. He had realized it more and more while tending Emma in the cottage and when her warriors had arrived and their time together had come to an end, he felt as if he was losing her. The thought had torn at his gut and heart. He detested the idea that she would no longer sleep in his arms or that he would never have a chance to kiss her again. But he also disliked that this marriage had been forced upon her. He wanted her to love him, and he thought that she just might with the way she had...

He shook his head. He knew lust when he saw it in a woman's eyes, but love had overshadowed the lust in Emma's eyes. And the fact that he had been able to see the difference had made him realize that he had fallen in love himself.

There was also Heather to consider. He had promised Emma that he would find her, and he would not go back on his word. Somehow, he would see the Macinnes sisters reunited.

Presently, however, he needed to set things right with his wife.

Wife.

He smiled. He had a wife and he loved her. And tonight... he shook his head. He did not know exactly what tonight would bring, but he did know one thing for certain.

Emma would sleep in his arms tonight.

~~~

Emma sat by the hearth combing her hair. She had returned to the bedchamber earlier to find food,
~~~

a bath, and Bertha waiting. The woman had looked ready to question her, but Emma had simply announced that she was ready to bathe and eat. She had offered no explanation as to where she had been, and Bertha had not pursued the issue. Bertha had wrapped her shoulder with a clean bandage, and then suggested she rest. She had not argued and had slept several hours. She was now expected downstairs in the Great Hall for supper.

She would have preferred to spend the rest of the night alone and slip quietly away in the morning. Her heart was heavy with the thought of leaving Rogan, but it was time. She had to go. It would be better this way.

A knock on the door sounded and Bertha entered, a smile on her face and a dark red velvet dress draped over her arm. "Your safe return home deserves celebrating. Rogan's father sent this for you to wear this evening." She spread the gown out on the bed.

Emma stared at it. It was a beautiful dress, but not for her. "I am already dressed."

Bertha clucked her tongue and shook her head. "Nonsense. Why wear a simple skirt and blouse when you have this beautiful dress to wear?"

"That dress is not me," Emma said, pointing to it, "and this is no celebration. I have yet to return home. I will wear my own clothes."

Bertha spoke softly. "The celebration is not only for you, but for the warriors who fought and suffered along the way. Share this night with them so they know you appreciate their efforts."

Emma felt properly chastised. Bertha was right, though too much celebration could delay their departure tomorrow. But that would be for James to contend with.

"You are right, I will celebrate with them," Emma said, "though I will not wear the dress."

"Have it your way," Bertha said, "though I think you would look beautiful in it."

Another time her compliment would have delighted Emma, but at the moment she was more concerned with going home and finding out what exactly was going on.

"Hurry along now, the celebration has started," Bertha said.

"Go," Emma shooed her off. "I will be there shortly."

Bertha left and a few minutes later Emma dragged herself to the door. She did not want to attend this celebration, but her warriors would be there and so should she. She plastered a smile on her face before stepping out of the room and nearly collided with Rogan.

He grabbed her arms to steady her. "In a hurry?"

Yes, to see this done, but kept that thought to herself and said, "Hungry."

"Then we best get you fed, though there is an important matter we must discuss."

Emma did not want to discuss anything with him. The more she remained in his presence, the more her heart ached at the thought of him not being part of her life.

"Can it wait until later?" she asked.

He smiled. "That hungry?"

Hungry for what we have shared, she thought, so it was easy to answer, “Very.”

“We will talk after we have eaten.” He wrapped her arm around his and they walked to the stairs. He let her go before him, the stone staircase too narrow for two to pass.

He took her arm again when they reached the bottom and wound it around his, and she yanked it free.

“They will think us a couple,” she said and hurried ahead of him into the Great Hall.

He stared after her, debating whether it would be wiser to ease into the possibility of them marrying due to circumstances before coming right out with ‘we are wed.’

He saw that she had gone straight to her warriors and looked ready to join them at a table. He went to her side and took her arm, a bit more forcefully this time. “You sit at the dais with my father and me.”

She could tell by the way his brow knitted that it was not a request. He was even handsomer when angry and though his lips were set tight, she still had the urge to kiss them. It was good that she would be leaving in the morning. It was getting harder to resist what she felt, and she feared that she would eventually do something foolish, something she would regret.

Rogan leaned down and whispered for her ears only, “Wipe the passion from your eyes or I will see it satisfied.”

Emma caught the gasp before it escaped her

mouth, swallowing it hard. She did not know if she was more shocked that her desire for him was that obvious or that her body quivered, delighted with the thought.

Angus MacClennan had obviously slept off his inebriation, though he was doing his best to regain it. As soon as his tankard was empty, it was filled again. And for the first time since meeting him, she understood his plight. He loved his wife and found it too difficult to live without her. She would never have truly understood the possible consequences of losing such a strong love until she found herself falling in love with Rogan. But having treated the ill and dealt with death over and over, she knew that no matter what happened, good or bad, life continued for those left behind.

An abundance of food was spread out on all the tables and ale was plentiful. She sat next to Rogan, his father next to him and no one to her other side, which she did not mind. She did not have to worry about keeping conversation with someone. Instead, she surveyed the hall and found much that she would change about it. It definitely could use a cleaning, the tables needing scrubbing, the many tapestries a good beating and airing and improvement in the food since the scent was not that favorable.

She sniffed the air again and realized the unpleasant odor was coming from the fish on the platter in front of Rogan. She grabbed his arm as he reached for a piece. "That fish is bad and will turn your stomach."

"Nonsense," Angus said and reached for a large

piece and dropped it into his mouth. "See, nothing wrong with it."

"Your choice," she said to Rogan and turned her attention on her men, though hoped he would heed her advice. She did not wish to see him ill, for then she would have a difficult time leaving him in someone else's care. She smiled when she saw James shooing the servants away when they offered more ale. Bless him. The warriors would do well in the morning.

"For someone who claimed to be hungry, you eat little," Rogan said, his head bent close to hers. "Does our food not appeal to you?"

"Certainly not foul fish and stew that is so thick one wonders what lies buried in it."

Rogan laughed and waved to a servant. "Take the fish away and tell cook it is bad and to get rid of it."

Angus objected. "There is nothing wrong—"

Rogan interrupted his father. "We sent for Emma to help improve our lot. I trust her opinion. The fish goes." He waved at the servant to take it away and she did so with a look of surprise. He then turned to Emma. "I look forward to having you show me what can be done to help our clan prosper as well as your clan."

A warning rang in her head. It would take time to show him what not only needed to be done, but to implement the change. That meant he expected her to remain there for some time.

"That would take time I do not have," she said, intending to make it clear she would not be staying.

"You have plenty of time," Angus chimed in. "It was why you were sent here with your sister in the first place."

"All that has changed," she informed him. "I will be going home soon."

"Not until we hear from your father," Angus said, as if his remark settled it.

Emma held her tongue, anxious to tell him that she knew the truth of her father's message, but feeling it would be wiser to keep that knowledge to herself, along with the fact that she would be leaving at dawn.

"Besides, this is your home now," Angus said.

"Enough, Da," Rogan warned.

"Tell her and be done with it," Angus ordered.

Emma looked to Rogan. "Tell me what?"

He stood and held his hand out to her. "A matter we need to discuss privately." He took her hand in his since she seemed reluctant to give it to him.

Angus chuckled. "Aye, son, keep it private and do your duty to the clan."

"What is he talking about?" Emma demanded, feeling she was not going to like what Rogan had to tell her.

He led her to the staircase, but she yanked at his hand, forcing him to stop. "Where do you take me?"

"To my bedchamber," he said and did not like the sound of it himself.

"No, that is not proper. Say what you have to say, here and now, and be done with it." She tried to free her hand, but he refused to let go of her and that worried her all the more.

He moved away from the stairs and into the

shadows and down a hall to enter a room at the far end. "My father's solar," he said, closing the door behind them.

Emma went to the hearth, a sudden chill running through her.

"Do you care for me, Emma?" Rogan asked, walking over to her, though leaving a small distance between them.

His query surprised her as did the quick response she kept silent. *I more than care for you; I love you.* Her answer was far different. "You are a better man than I had first thought."

He took slow steps toward her. "But do you care for me."

She shook her head. "I do not understand what you ask. What does it matter if I care for you or not?"

"It matters a great deal." He stepped closer.

Emma stepped back, but Rogan stopped her, his arm going around her waist and drawing her gently against him.

"I am going to kiss you, Emma."

She stared at him, knowing she should stop him, but not wanting to. At least, she would have the memory of one last kiss with him to take with her.

"Your silence tells me much," he said and brought his lips down on hers.

Emma did not think she would taste or feel anything as wonderful as his kiss ever again in her life. It was filled with such strength and passion that she wanted to lose herself in it forever. Her own response grew eager as the kiss flamed her passion that had lain dormant far too long.

Her arms went around his neck and she pressed her body against his, but she could not seem to get close enough. She knew she wanted more from him. Her body cried out for it, ached for it.

His hands gripped her backside and yanked her hard against him, and there was no doubting how much he wanted her.

Emma instinctively rubbed herself against him and an urge to slip her hand down under his plaid and grasp the rock-hard strength of him, jolted her. This was not right. She could not do this.

She pulled away from him, hurrying to stand behind a chair. Her hands gripped the top, fearing her trembling legs might give out at any moment.

Rogan remained where he was. He took a deep breath, trying to contain the passion that raced through him and that had turned him as hard as stone. He wanted Emma with an urgency that was foreign to him, and knowing that she was his wife made it all the harder to keep his distance from her.

The passion hot and heavy in her eyes did not help either, though the confusion he saw there did. He wanted her to realize that they both cared for each other—no, it was love—they loved each other. He could feel it not only in himself, but in her as well. That was why it felt so different when he kissed her. He could only imagine how it would feel when he made love to her.

"Never kiss me again," she shouted at him.

He smiled. "I am going to kiss you again and again and again."

"What is wrong with you? You are promised to

my sister."

"Not any longer."

Emma scrunched her brow, and then recalled the sealed documents her father had sent to Angus MacClennan. "What has my father done?"

"He had us wed. We are husband and wife."

Chapter Eighteen

Emma gripped the back of the chair tighter, her legs having grown so weak from the shocking news that she thought she would collapse. How could her father do such a thing?

Rogan walked over to her and held out his hand. "Sit, while I explain."

She did not argue. She took his hand and allowed him to help her sit. She tried to keep her mind clear, but that was impossible. If she was truly wed to Rogan, it meant her life was forever changed, but what of her sisters?

"I can tell you have many questions," he said, sitting in the chair next to her. "Let me explain, and then we can discuss it."

She nodded, though one thought kept poking at her. *Go see your father.*

"There was a section in the marriage agreement that stated if for any reason Heather and my marriage could not take place, then you and I were to wed. So your father had us married by proxy. He feared for his clan if something should happen to him. With us wed, your clan is protected."

"Why not marry you and Heather by proxy?" Emma's eyes turned wide with fear. "Oh my God, he thinks we will never find Heather, that she is lost to us forever." Tears stung her eyes.

"I gave you my word we would find her and we will, Patience as well," he said.

"But what of my father?" she said. "Why does he give up on Heather?"

Go see your father. The words tolled like a warning bell in her head.

"He is not giving up on Heather," Rogan assured her, though he did wonder if the old man simply did not have the strength to see the task done.

"I am going to see my father," she announced, as if it was already decided.

"We will in a few weeks."

She stood. "No, now."

Rogan stood as well. "Emma, there are things that must be settled between us first."

"Nothing will be settled between us until I speak with my father."

"Speaking with your father will change nothing," Rogan said. "We are wed and we will stay wed. Your life is with me now. This is your home."

"And you expect me to simply accept this?"

He reached out to take her hand, and he did not like that she took an abrupt step away from him. "It is done and cannot be undone."

"It is not done for me until I speak with my father," she said.

He stepped toward her, and she scooted away from him. "I ask again, do you care for me, Emma?"

She stared at him, not sure how to answer and surprised herself when she said, "Do you care for me?"

"Very much," he said and took another step toward her.

Her heart nearly burst from her chest it beat so rapidly. He had not taken time to think. He had answered without hesitation. Could he have truly spoken from his heart?

Another step brought him in front of her and he eased his arm around her waist and drew her close to him. "I know this comes as a shock, but it is done and while I would like nothing more than to take you to my bedchamber and seal our vows, I know you may think differently. So, I will leave tonight up to you. Come to my bedchamber if you wish, if not I understand. But know one thing... I give you this night and this night alone. If our vows are not sealed tonight, tomorrow they will be."

"You would force me," she snapped.

Rogan smiled and shook his head. "You melt in my arms when I kiss you. I can feel your need, the ache of your body to join with mine. You want me as badly as I want you. It is not a bad start to a marriage when a husband and wife have the lusty passion that we have for each other. I have no doubt we will have many children."

Children. Husband. Family. She had never thought she would have any of that, though she had longed to. And to have it with a man she loved went beyond her dreams. But at what expense did she gain such happiness?

The loss of her sister? Would Patience return alone? Would Heather never be found? How then could she be happy with the man that had been

Heather's intended? As much as she wanted Rogan—felt she loved him—she could not help feeling as if she was betraying her sister.

"I know there is much that troubles you about this, but you have seen for yourself that we do well together and together we will find your sisters and bring them home. And then perhaps Heather will be as lucky as we are and she will find someone to wed who actually loves her."

The thought did bring some joy to Emma, though they would have to find Heather first for that to happen.

Rogan stepped away from her. "I have a few things to discuss with Liam, and then I am going to my bedchamber. You can be there waiting for me or come later if you prefer. If not, I will see you in the morning and we will spend the day together... and the night, and all nights from then on."

He kissed her gently, and then walked out of the solar, leaving the door open.

The decision now was hers and she hurried out of the room and took flight up the stairs to her bedchamber. Once inside, she paced the floor in front of the hearth, her mind jumbled with thoughts. How could she start a new life and be happy with her sisters still missing? The answer was simple—she could not. She would feel forever guilty for deserting them when they needed her the most. She could never do that.

She had to get home and speak with her father. She worried that someone could be manipulating him or that his illness had somehow made him irrational. Until she could make sense of it all, she had no intentions of consummating their union. That meant one thing... she had to leave for home right away. She also had to keep her distance from Rogan, for if she did not, she might never leave.

He was right about her wanting him, and it did her heart good to know he wanted her as well. He was right when he said that she melted in his arms, to his touch, to his kiss. She would not have the strength to stop herself from making love with him, especially now being his wife, and it her duty, though duty would have nothing to do with it.

Her whole body suddenly came alive, imagining what it would be like to make love with him. And the desire to find out almost had her racing to the door, but a sudden thought of Heather being held captive, possibly hurt and suffering somewhere quelled it fast enough.

Before she had any right to happiness, she had to find her sisters.

It was a full day's ride to get home, sooner if she traveled faster. She stretched her shoulder back and winced at the pain. Though the pain lingered, she was healing nicely and she had no worry it would continue so.

She sat in the chair near the hearth to rest while she still could. She had no doubt that Rogan would have her men watched and possibly her as well, since she had taken off on him once before. She would need to get to James and work something out that would give her a chance to get away before dawn tomorrow. She was not sure what Rogan would do when she failed to be waiting for him in his bedchambers. Would he come see for himself that she was in her room or would he send Bertha?

She needed a plan and her mind got busy with one.

~~~

Rogan walked to his bedchambers hoping Emma would be there, but somehow doubting she would. He was concerned that she might take off as she had done the last time when she had not seen things his way. He had informed Liam that the Macinnes warriors were not to leave before speaking with him. And he had extra guards stationed near them, though not visible, in case trouble should erupt.

Now if only Emma was waiting for him. He smiled at the thought and grew aroused when only a few feet from his door. He was more than eager to make love to her, to have them start a life together as husband and wife. He loved her strength, her courage, her determination. He laughed. Stubbornness was more like it, though it somehow suited her intelligent nature, and then there was that gorgeous body of hers.

The thought of her naked in his arms turned him rock-hard and had him taking quicker steps to his door. He did not hesitate. He grabbed the latch, swung the door open, and stepped in.

The room was empty, and he let a string of oaths fly and slammed the door behind him. He had to force himself not to go after her and carry her
~~~

back to his room. He had—foolish as it was—given her this night to absorb the startling news that they were wed. He had believed that once she gave it thought she would understand that nothing could undo what had been done and she...

Bloody hell, he had hoped she would have surrendered to her passion and be waiting there as eager as he was to make love. Or was she stubborn enough to...

He ran out of his bedchambers and up the stairs to her room. He did not bother to knock. He swung the door open and stopped abruptly when he caught sight of her asleep in the chair. He walked as quietly as he could over to her and silently berated himself for not considering how tired she must be. She was still healing and she needed rest.

Rogan reached down and carefully lifted her into his arms. He had to smile at her reaction. She cuddled against his chest and his name fell in a soft whisper from her lips. Even in sleep she knew whose arms held her. He carried her to her bed and gently placed her on it, draping a blanket over her.

He kissed her cheek and whispered, "Tomorrow, wife."

He shut the door quietly behind him and returned to his bedchamber, stripping out of his clothes and getting into bed. He would sleep well and so would Emma. They would need a good rest in preparation for tomorrow night. He fell asleep with a smile on his face.

~~~
~~~

Emma waited several minutes after the door shut before she sat up in bed. His arms had felt so good, his scent so enticing, and his chest much too comfortable. Then she had realized that she had actually been in his arms, it had not been a dream. How she managed to pretend she was asleep, she did not know. But it was over and done and she was certain he would not return to check on her. The thought hurt, for he trusted her and she was about to break that trust.

She grabbed her pouch of herbs and tied it around her waist, and then draped her cloak over her shoulders. It would not be easy traveling at night, but it was necessary. She had to get as much of a head start as she could, for she had no doubt that Rogan would come after her.

She was his wife and his responsibility.

Emma did not think it would be hard to sneak out of the keep. The MacClennan warriors had celebrated hard and many, if not most, would be passed out from drink by now. Still, she kept to the shadows, knowing Rogan was no fool and had probably made sure that there were warriors who had not touched a drop of ale last night.

She made it out of the keep with ease and stuck to the night shadows where almost nothing could be detected. She did not enter the Macinnes camp. She went to where the horses were being kept and got the attention of the one warrior guarding them. She ordered him to bring James to her, but warned him to make it appear as if he woke James to take his shift, since she feared they were being watched.

James yawned, stretched, and scratched his belly as he approached the horses, making it seem that he was slowly and reluctantly doing his duty.

Once among the shadows of the horses, Emma approached him.

"What is wrong?" James asked.

"I do not have time to explain," she said. "I need to leave for home tonight—alone."

"I cannot let you go alone, at least take one warrior with you."

One warrior would not be missed, so she agreed.

"Thomas will go with you. He waits in the woods with two horses."

She shook her head. "How could you possibly know I would—"

"I did not know, but I thought it might be wise just in case."

Emma hugged the burly man. "Bless you, James, and tomorrow you may hear news that—"

"Will matter little to me as long as you are safe," he said. "Now be off with you before we are caught and your plan foiled."

He told her where Thomas would be and she hurried off, wanting desperately to be gone from here, and yet wanting desperately to stay. She found Thomas and they walked the horses a distance away before mounting them and taking off.

~~~

I want to go home and see my father.

Rogan woke with a start, jolting up in bed, the words echoing in his head. He threw the blanket off
~~~

and hurried into his clothes. He took the stairs two at a time as he made his way up to Emma's room. He flung the door open. Her room was empty. He was down the steps and into the Great Hall. Emma was not there. He went to the kitchen and found Bertha there.

"Where is Emma?" he demanded.

"In her room the last I saw," she said.

"When was that?"

"Last night before you retired yourself," Bertha said.

"Damn," he muttered and stormed out of the kitchen.

Dawn was barely cresting on the horizon, the village just stirring to life. The few who were up and about quickly moved out of Rogan's path, seeing the anger on his face.

He called out to his warriors as he approached the Macinnes camp and they hurried out of the shadows to follow behind him.

James was awake, had been for some time, waiting for this moment.

"Where is she?" Rogan demanded when he was a few feet from the man.

"Who?" James asked.

"Do not dare play games with me," Rogan warned, coming to stand directly in front of the man, his warriors spreading out behind him and Macinnes warriors waking and hurrying to their feet ready to aid James. "Tell me where Emma is."

"I do not know."

"I am going to ask one more time, and then I am

going to beat it out of you," Rogan warned with such fierceness that James took a step back. "Where is my wife?"

Shock rippled through all the warriors.

"Wife?" James asked, as if he did not believe him.

"Your own chieftain, Donald Macinnes had us wed by proxy. Your messenger delivered the sealed document to my father. Emma and I are wed. It is done. She is my wife. Now where is my wife."

James understood now and did what he had to, safe with the knowledge that Emma probably was not far from home. "Your wife is on her way home."

"I may still beat you if you tell me you let her go off on her own," Rogan said, trying to contain the anger rising in him.

"A warrior went with her." James could not help but add, "If you knew your wife, you would know that no amount of reasoning would stop her."

"Careful with your words, old man," Rogan snapped, annoyed that James was right. He should have realized Emma would do something like this. But he had taken precautions, and he intended to find out how his wife could have snuck past his warriors undetected. "When did she leave? And I caution you to tell the truth or pay the consequences."

"She took her leave last night when all were asleep or passed out from drink."

Rogan wanted to roar to the heavens, he was so angry. The thought of the danger she had placed herself in tore at his gut. "Ready your men," he ordered. “We leave shortly.”

“Where do we go?” James asked, though knew.

“To bring my wife home,” Rogan snarled and jabbed a finger toward James. “And God help her when I get my hands on her, and God help you if anything has happened to her.”

Chapter Nineteen

Emma was exhausted, but she would not let that stop her. She did not care that her body ached from the long night's hard ride, sleep would wait. She wanted to see her father and since it was well passed dawn, she did not worry he would be sleeping, resting perhaps, but awake.

When she had entered the village, shouts of welcome home had greeted her and the same now in the keep. All who saw her were happy she had returned. She had not realized how very much she had missed home and family until now.

Tears stung her eyes, wishing her sisters were here to welcome her as well, though she could not shake the ache in her heart for having left Rogan. She had not expected the separation to disturb her as much as it had. It was quite foolish of her, since he would no doubt follow after her. Yet, here she was missing him.

She shook her head. She had no time to ache for her husband—ache—was that what she was doing? Is that what love did? Make your heart ache and your soul feel empty when the one you loved was not close by? She had much to learn about love and oddly enough, she was looking forward to it.

Emma shook her head again as she stopped in front of her father's bedchamber and knocked.

"Father, it is Emma. I am home."

"One moment," he called out.

That struck her as odd. He had always bid her enter right away when she would knock at his door.

The door opened and Emma was relieved to see Maura. She was a few years younger than Emma's father, tall and slim, with soft features and an equally soft voice. She kept her long pure white hair braided and thankfully had the patience of a saint, which was why she had been the perfect choice to tend her father.

"How is he?" Emma asked anxiously.

"Some days better than others, but today is a good day," Maura said. "I will leave you to talk with him, and it is good to have you home."

"It is good to be home," Emma said and entered the room, relieved to see her father looking much better than when she had left. She had worried over being away from him, fearing he would not eat properly. He had always been a robust man, larger than life, so it was good to see that he had regained some of his stamina. It appeared Maura had taken good care of him and her own herb mixtures appeared to have worked well. Emma was hopeful that he would continue to improve and be his old self in no time.

She approached his bed with a smile.

"What are you doing here?"

Emma halted in her steps, surprised that he sounded as if he reprimanded her. Another time she would have lowered her head and apologized for what she did not know, but not this time. Things were different, much different.

With determined strides, she walked over to him with her hands planted on her hips. "I have questions that need answers and we will start with... why did you marry me to Rogan MacClennan?"

His shoulders slumped and his strength seemed to deflate with his heavy sigh. "I had no choice. I did it to protect the clan. The message I got was not from your sister."

Emma felt her breath catch.

"A peasant delivered a message and told me he was paid handsomely to do so. The sealed message warned me to do as told or I would never see Heather or Patience again. I was to say that I received a message from Patience requesting more men. Shortly after the contingent of Macinnes warriors left with Liam, I received another message. I was to tell Angus MacClennan to do nothing until he heard from me, which I did. The message also warned that I was to do the same, say nothing, until I heard from this unknown person." Donald turned tear-filled eyes on Emma. "The signature was that of a Dragon's claw."

Emma felt as if she could not breathe. It was true. The Dark Dragon had Heather and possibly Patience as well.

"I recalled the amendment I had placed in the marriage document and decided it was time to make use of it." A tear ran done his cheek. "I am so sorry, Emma, but our warriors alone cannot protect us from the Dark Dragon. At least with MacClennan warriors, we have a chance. So I signed the proxy marrying you to Rogan MacClennan."

Emma had to sit, her legs feeling as if they would no longer hold her. She lowered herself to the chair beside her father's bed and asked a question she feared she knew the answer to. "What does the Dark Dragon want from us?"

Donald shuddered. "I think he wants Heather as his wife."

This was a nightmare and Emma wished she could wake and find it gone. She could not imagine, sweet, thoughtful Heather wife to a cold-hearted bastard, or that she would never see her sister again. That could not happen. She could not let it.

"I see that stubborn look on your face and it will do you no good to think that you can rescue Heather. I will not lose the only daughter I presently have. You will stay put and do as I or your husband tells you until we can sort this out. I intend to send a message to King James requesting his help."

Emma laughed, though it sounded more like a strangled cry. "The King even fears the Dark Dragon."

"And well he should," Donald said. "The Dark Dragon rescued him from a siege the King thought lost. The King owes him his life."

"Then if the Dark Dragon wants Heather, he will have her," Emma said her words turning her blood cold. She suddenly felt defeated, though more likely it was exhaustion that weighed heavily on her.

"I am fatigued beyond words, Da," she said, slowly pushing herself up out of the chair. "I must sleep."

"Your husband—"

"Is not with me, though I suspect he will be arriving later today or tomorrow." She bent down and kissed her father's cheek.

"I will see you after you have rested?" he asked and took hold of her hand. "I have missed you. I have missed all three of my daughters."

"And I you, Da. We will talk later," she assured him, needing to leave, not wanting him to see that his tears were bringing on her own.

She gave his hand a squeeze and hurried out of the room. She was not surprised to see a tub of steaming water in her room and food on the table by the window. The servants were well aware she preferred privacy, so no one waited to help her.

She let her tears fall as she washed. How could this have happened? Why did the Dark Dragon want Heather? Why not? Heather was beautiful. She shook her head, her heart much too filled with sorrow to think on it anymore. She would finish up, eat, and rest, then she would be able to think more clearly. She would not give up on her sisters. Never, ever would she give up.

Emma surrendered to sleep as soon as she pulled the blanket over her, grateful to slip away from all her worries, if only for a few hours.

~~~

Emma woke with a start, sitting up, and half expecting someone to be in her room, but she was alone. The fire had dwindled down and shadows hugged more than the corners, which meant she had
~~~

slept into the evening.

Her skin prickled with gooseflesh, the room having taken on a chill and she shivered, though not from the cold. Something was amiss, she could feel it. She hurried out of bed and slipped on her robe. She opened the door and peered around the edge. The hall was empty and the silence deafening.

She hurried to the end of the hall and pushed the tapestry aside to look out of the slim opening. Her eyes could barely believe what she saw. Numerous campfires and glowing torches surrounded the village and a hundred or more warriors occupied the encircling camp.

Her husband had arrived, and he had brought an army with him. She was about to face the consequences of her actions, though she was not sure what those consequences would be.

She turned and froze. There at the far end of the hall, near her bedchamber door stood Rogan. The breadth of him seemed to consume the narrow hallway and the flicking torch light highlighted his handsome, though angry face.

He stared at her, his brow wrinkling, and then as if realizing it was her, he started toward her with heavy and determined strides.

Emma felt her heart swell and suddenly all she wanted was to be in his arms. Instinct took over and she ran toward him.

As soon as he caught the startled look in her eye, Rogan prepared himself for an altercation with his wife. She shocked him when her expression suddenly changed to one of longing, as if she had actually missed him. When she started running toward him, his heart slammed against his chest. He rushed toward her and when she flung herself into his arms, he grabbed her around the waist, lifted her, and settled his mouth on hers. His kiss was hungry and he feed like a starving man, needing to taste deeply of her, needing to know she was real, here with him and safe.

His kiss robbed her breath and woke her passion, sending it soaring. What was it about this man's kisses that turned her senseless and made her melt in his arms?

He kept his arms firm around her waist, her feet dangling several inches off the floor as he walked to her bedchamber. With a shove of his shoulder at the door, they entered and a forceful kick sent it closed.

The feel of her there in his arms made him hungrier for her. It was as if he had been deprived of her for far too long and all he wanted was to strip her bare and make love to her. And from her eager response, it appeared she felt the same.

He lowered her feet to the floor, his hands roaming down over her backside to give her full cheeks a squeeze as he pressed her hard against him. He wanted her, good God, how he wanted her. He groaned when she rubbed herself against him. She wanted him just as much, but...

With reluctance he tore his mouth away from hers, released her, and walked over to the hearth. He busied himself by adding logs to the fire while he tried to control the overpowering need to turn, grab her, and make love to her.

Emma felt her legs go weak as soon as he

deserted her and she collapsed to the bed, grateful it was behind her and wishing that was where they both were right now—in bed making love. There was no worry, no pretense with Rogan, he truly wanted her. And to know that he wanted to make love to her as much as she did with him made her all the more eager to do so. She had always feared that an arranged marriage would bring a disappointed wedding night. Not so with Rogan. She had been fortunate to get to know him, care for him, fall in love with him and that made bedding him all the more appealing.

So, it disturbed her that he should stop when it seemed apparent that they both were fully agreeable to consummating their vows.

She refused to sit there in worry, so she spoke up. "Why stop?"

He dusted his hands before pointing a finger at her. "You disobeyed me."

"So you punish me by making me want you, yet not satisfying me, though I daresay you punish yourself as well, for I felt your hard need for me."

"And satisfying your hunger for me would be a good deterrent?" he asked with a shake of his head.

"It would be a start," she said softly. "I knew if I came to you last night and we made love that I would never want to leave you—not ever. And I had to speak with my father."

"I told you I would bring you here."

"At your leisure," she reminded. "I could not wait."

"Stubborn!"

"Aye, you are," she said with a smile.

He walked over to her, his anger having faded, though not his desire. He reached up and stroked her cheek. "You frightened me half to death. You could have been attacked and taken like your sister."

"Is that why you brought an army of warriors with you?" she asked, resting her hand on his chest.

"No ghost warriors would stop me this time." He lowered his lips near hers. "I will not lose you, Emma, not when I have just found you." He brushed his lips over hers. "And not when I have realized just how much I love you."

Emma's mouth dropped open, though no words came out.

Rogan whispered, "Perfect." He settled his open mouth on hers and turned her senseless once again.

She ended the kiss this time and shook her head as she asked, "You truly love me?"

"With all my heart, and then some," he said encircling her waist with his arms. "You stole my heart and I do not ever want it back. It belongs to you now."

"That is only fair," she said smiling.

"Why is that?"

"You stole my heart as well. No matter how hard I tried to keep it from you, knew I had no right to it, you managed to take all of it, even the broken part. I love you, Rogan."

He kissed her again, soft and easy.

A knock sounded at the door and Emma shouted, "Go away."

Rogan laughed, turned, and settled at her side,

keeping his one arm firm around her waist. "Enter," he called out.

A servant stuck her head around the door, as if fearful to obey his command.

"Enter," Rogan reaffirmed with a wave of his hand.

"Sorry to disturb you, my lord, but I was told to see if my lady was awake and hungry."

Emma blushed when her stomach answered loud enough for all to hear.

Rogan laughed again. "You have your answer."

The servant nodded with a smile. "I will return shortly."

Rogan pulled Emma into his arms. "Wise servant, she lets us know we have only a short time before her return." He kissed her quick, and then stepped away. "Not enough time to make love to you. Besides, you have rested and now you need to be well fed so that you will have enough stamina for us to make love."

Emma laughed this time. "And have you rested or eaten since arriving here?"

He walked over to her and ran his finger down along her slim nose, tapping the tip as he said, "Whether I did or not, I will always have the stamina to make love to you. You on the other hand..." He smiled, purposely letting his words trail off.

She poked him in the chest. "Is that a challenge?"

"One you could never hope to win."

She walked her fingers up and down his chest.

"Perhaps, but you forget that you have lain with other women, while I have never known a man." Her hand slowly made its way down the length of him. "And I hear that once a woman tastes a man," —she grabbed his covered manhood—"she hungers for more."

He took hold of her chin. "Feel me growing larger? Keep squeezing me like that and when the servant returns she will find me poking you good and hard."

Emma let go of him and stepped away with a wide smile. She loved knowing she could turn him so hard.

"So you want to taste me before I make love to you?" he asked with a sly grin.

Her brow wrinkled. Had she somehow misunderstood the women she had overheard talking.

"I thought so," he said with a sly grin. "Would you like to know what the women meant?"

Knowledge was important to Emma, so she quickly nodded.

He stepped closer to her, though not close enough that she could touch him. "You would stroke my swollen member with your tongue, and then take it into your mouth and suck most greedily on it." He thought to tease her, though truly he wanted to see her reaction and if she would be adverse to the idea. What he did, however, was grow himself even harder at the thought.

She looked at him and licked her lips slowly as if getting ready to taste him, and his loins tightened to an unbearable ache.

Emma stepped closer, though left a small space between them. “Tell me, would you taste me as well?”

That did it, Rogan let out a groan and reached out to grab her just as a knock sounded at the door. “Go away,” he yelled.

Emma laughed and bid the servant to enter, though she was no longer hungry for food.

Chapter Twenty

The one servant hurried the two other servants along, then shooed them out of the room and gave a quick bob of her head before closing the door behind her.

"Eat!" Rogan ordered, walking away from her and fighting the desire to pull her into his arms and feel her body surrender to his kisses.

"It is not the food I want to taste," Emma said, feeling more bold than she ever thought possible and terribly eager to make love with her husband.

"You need to eat," he said firmly, her stomach having protested several times since they had entered the room.

She took a step toward him. "I need you more."

He reached out and yanked her into his arms. "I am going to make love to you, and then you are going to eat, and then I am going to make love to you again—"

"And again and again," she whispered and pressed her lips to his.

Rogan did not waste a moment, fearful someone would interrupt them again, though this time he intended to beat anyone who dared try.

He carried her to the bed and set her on her feet to undress her as fast as he could, but Emma's hands were on his garments first.

He reluctantly tore his mouth away from her eager one. "In a hurry?"

"Aye, I am," she said and finished unwrapping his plaid, letting it drop to the floor. His shirt followed, though he saw to getting rid of his boots.

"My turn," he said, though there was little to take off her, a robe and her nightdress. His brow scrunched when he saw the bandage. "Your wound."

"Does well," she assured him.

"We go easy," he said as if it was a command. His finger went to her lips when he saw her ready to protest. "I will stop here and now if you do not agree. I will not have you suffer any pain or jeopardize your healing." He moved his finger off her lips slowly.

She smiled. "You truly do love me."

"More than you will ever know," he said and scooped her up in his arms. He laid her on the bed, stretching out next to her. "You will tell me if you feel any pain."

"I am in pain right now."

He sat up silently cursing and spit out the words before he could change his mind. "We stop." He forced himself to continue. "We will not make love until your shoulder pains you no more."

Emma ran her hand down along his muscled arm, loving the feel of him, so soft and yet so hard. "It is not my shoulder that pains me. It is my need for you that goes unsatisfied that pains me."

He lay back down relieved and turned on his side, his hand settling on her breast to cup it gently.

"I will make sure that I turn that pain to pleasure." He cradled her breast in his hand while his mouth took hold of her nipple.

Passion shot through her body with every lick and nip and to think this was just the beginning. She gasped and sighed when he finished feasting on both breasts, then he moved slowly down along her body. It was as if he was branding every inch of her with his lips, and delicate nips. He was making certain there was no doubt that she belonged to him and him alone, and the feeling thrilled her and made her ache for him even more.

He raised his head and looked at her with such love that tears threatened her eyes.

"Good God, you are so beautiful," he whispered. "I cannot believe you are mine. I am a lucky man."

She wanted him to know how lucky she was to have found him, but instead she gasped, his tongue licking a spot that had her fisting the bedding in her hands. Sensations rushed through her, tingles and prickles that had her moaning and tossing about.

His hands grabbed hold of her bottom and held it firm while he continued to pleasure her, a deliciously tormenting pleasure that she did not want to end.

When he moved off her, she cried out, "No, do not stop!"

He spread her legs apart slowly. "I am just getting started."

She smiled and it widened when she saw his engorged member jutting out so big and thick and without hesitation she reached for it.

He grabbed her hand before she could capture it. “Not now, or we will finish sooner than I want.”

She kept her hand to herself when he released it. “Another time?”

“Many other times,” with that said, he leaned over and kissed her, his hands braced on the bed on either side of her head, keeping his body suspended over hers.

He brushed his hard chest over her nipples, sending wave after wave of tingles rushing through her, all coming to rest between her legs and turning her ache unbearable.

“I need you,” she said on a harsh whisper, her hands grabbing hold of his taut arms.

“Soon,” he said and rubbed the hard length of him against her.

She gasped and squeezed at his arms, feeling as if she was about to burst in two.

He brushed his lips over hers. “I love you.”

Her gasp captured the response, hovering on her lips as he entered her, though not all the way. He tempted and tormented and, good lord, but she wanted more. Instinct, need, desire, she did not know what it was that made her do it, but she suddenly and quite forcefully swung her hips and bottom up to greedily take more of him.

He slid in so easily, and then he gave an extra push and went deeper. She gasped at the light pain that assaulted her. Then there was nothing but exquisite pleasure as he drove in and out of her gently at first, then harder and harder, and she welcomed every delicious thrust.

Rogan had held back, not wanting to hurt her, giving her time to accept the size and width of him, but when she thrust herself up, taking almost all of him into her, he burst with an overwhelming need for her. She was warm and wet and so damn welcoming that he knew at that moment he would never get enough of her, and he would never stop trying to.

"No pain?" he asked after realizing he had met a slight resistance when he had plunged deeper.

She smiled. "You are teasing me, are you not?"

He had to smile and give her a quick kiss. "Hold tight, I am going to make you explode."

"Yes, yes, please do," she begged and squeezed his muscled arms.

Rogan loved the way her brow creased and how she squeezed her eyes shut, and how her moans grew along with his mighty thrusts. He had ignited a passion in her and set it burning. Now it was time to set it ablaze before letting it burn out.

With his own desire near to erupting, he quickened his rhythm.

Emma slammed her hips against him, over and over, feeling an incredible sensation take hold, run through her, turning her moans louder and louder until...

"Rogan!" she screamed as she exploded in a fiery climax that she wanted to go on forever. Tingles rushed to every part of her body, shivering her senseless, and continuing to assault her in a never ending wave of pleasure.

Rogan quickly followed, not able to contain himself once she yelled out his name and tightened around him. He groaned aloud as he too burst in a fiery climax and let himself fall more helplessly in love with her.

The tingles had yet to fade completely when Rogan eased out of her and stretched out on his back beside her. They lay quiet for a few moments, their breathing still labored. But Rogan could not go long without her in his arms, and he turned to slip his arm under her back and ease her to rest against him.

She sighed, burrowing against his warmth, being more content than she had ever been.

"Are you satisfied, wife," he asked with a chuckle.

"Aye, though I think it would be wise to do it again to make certain," she said with a touch of laughter.

"You have my word that we will do it again," —he turned, the strength of his body forcing her on her back— "and again." He kissed her. "And again."

Her stomach's loud protest stopped him.

Emma felt herself blush.

"At least I will always be able to tell when you are hungry."

"And I you," she said with a smile, her hand moving down to gently cup his soft member.

He pulled her hand away. "First you feast and then—"

"I feast again," she said, her smile growing.

He kissed her quick. "Up and out of bed before you do not get to eat at all." He turned on his back, bringing her with him, intending to swing her over him and off the bed. But somehow she landed on top of him.

After a moment of silence, Emma spoke. "I love being naked in your arms. I love how you make love to me. I love that fate made us husband and wife."

He grabbed the back of her neck and raised his head up so that their lips would meet. The kiss bordered on danger, for he felt himself growing aroused and that was unusual so soon after having a woman. But Emma was not just any woman. She was his wife and he loved her.

Her stomach rumbled and he reluctantly ended their kiss. "You have to satisfy your hungry stomach or it will give us no peace tonight."

She laughed and slipped off him and the bed, not that she wanted to, but he was right. She needed to eat, not having eaten since the previous night. She bent to grab her nightdress off the floor when a pain ripped through her shoulder, stunning her and causing her to stumble.

Rogan had her in his arms in seconds.

She shut her eyes and took a couple of deep breaths to help deal with the stinging pain.

He sat on the bed, keeping her close against him. "Your shoulder?"

She nodded, the pain beginning to subside.

"You are not giving yourself time to heal," he scolded with concern. "We are going to remain here at your home until I am sure you are well enough to travel."

Joy filled her heart, though she contained the

smile fighting to surface. She did not want him to know how happy she was that she would not be leaving her home just yet. She wanted time with her father, and she hoped during that time another message would arrive from the mysterious person sending them.

Rogan set her gently on her feet and helped her into her nightdress and robe. He would have preferred she remain naked, but that would not be wise. He already felt a stirring for her, but then his loins seemed to be perpetually aroused around her. And with her being as eager to bed him as he was to bed her, he expected they would spend much time in the bedchamber, though he could think of more interesting places they could make love.

"Have you eaten since your arrival?" she asked, walking over to the table and reaching for a bowl of venison stew.

"I came to find you posthaste," he said, wrapping his plaid around his waist.

She handed him the bowl and a spoon once he was at her side. "Then enjoy. You will find Macinnes food preferable to MacClennan."

"Ours is not that bad," he said and tried a spoonful. His eyes turned wide. "This is beyond delicious. It is magical. Is your cook a witch?" He laughed before taking another spoonful.

"It is in the handling and preparation of the food and the spices added that make the difference," Emma said proudly and took a bowl for herself after taking a seat at the table.

Rogan was quick to join her and just as quick to

tear a hunk of bread off the large loaf in front of him. He took one bite and the rest of the piece was soon gone. "More spices?" he asked, tearing a larger piece off the delicious bread.

"That and the preparation of the grain," she explained. "Try the bramble jelly. It truly is exceptional."

He eagerly reached for the small crock and grabbed a knife to spread a generous amount on his bread.

Emma smiled as he grinned from ear to ear.

"I thought I was a lucky man before, but now I realize that I am also blessed to have a wife of many talents. We will have a good life together, Emma." He reached out and gave her hand a squeeze, his smile fading and sincerity filling his eyes. "This I promise you."

Her appetite waned along with her smile. "I have no right to happiness with my sisters missing." She shook her head when he went to reassure her. "I know you tell me you will find them, and I believe finding Patience will not be a problem. She may even return on her own before we can find her. Heather, however, presents a far more difficult problem. It is not so much about finding her as it is seeing her returned home that may prove impossible."

"What have you learned?" Rogan asked.

She could see and hear his eagerness for what she had to say, and so she told him all that her father had related to her. Sorrow filled her heart and worry weighed on her shoulders after she finished. Heather's situation sounded all the more direr hearing it once again.

"I cannot help but think what she must be going through at the hands of such a cruel and evil man," Emma said.

"If Heather has only a small amount of your courage and strength, she will fare well against the Dark Dragon. And if she possesses only an ounce of your mule-headedness then I would worry more for the Dark Dragon, for she will defeat him in no time."

"Heather is sweet and kind—"

Rogan shook his head. "You cannot tell me that she does not possess some of yours and Patience's courage. Did not Patience worry leaving you on your own when she went off after Heather, and did you not survive and do well?"

"Aye, but—"

"But what? The three of you are strong women more than capable of surviving separate from one another, no matter the circumstances. Pray for Heather's well-being, but know that she is strong enough to survive this, for she knows those who love her will not fail to rescue her."

A slow smile spread over Emma's face. "Heather has more strength than Patience and I combined. She raised us and managed the keep after our mother died when she was just a child herself. Father relied heavily on her for years. It was only when Patience and I were older and could help that her burden was lifted. She is a remarkable sister and woman."

"Then do not assume she suffers, assume she

survives. And know that we will somehow bring her home."

Emma felt her worries lessen with his words. "I am glad you feel that way, husband, for my thoughts are the same."

"One thing, Emma," he said, though sounded more like he warned, "you will give me your word here and now that you will not go off on your own in pursuit of your sister for any reason."

Emma chewed on the inside of her lower lip as she gave it thought.

"You must think about it?" he asked annoyed.

"Aye, I do," she admitted with her own annoyance. "There may be circumstances that warrant my leaving on my own and I would not want to give my word and have to break it."

"So you are telling me that you would once again take off without telling me if you thought it prudent?"

"Aye, I would," Emma said with a firm nod.

Rogan shook his head. "I do not know whether to be angry that you refuse to give your word or pleased that you are honest about not giving it."

"Honor means much to me. I could not give my word falsely."

"Another fine quality I discovered about my wife and one that makes me love her even more."

Emma felt her heart quicken. Never had she thought she would have a husband who even saw qualities in her, let alone admire them.

"My words surprise you?" he asked, pushing his chair back and standing.

"I never expected to be loved with such—"

"Resolve?"

"So you are resolute in your love for me?" she asked as he approached her.

He leaned down and gave her a gentle kiss. "I will have it no other way. I love you and that is all there is to it and nothing on God's earth or in His heavens will say otherwise."

"How? When? Why?" she asked, finding it difficult to believe that a man could love her that strongly.

He hunched down beside her. "How I fell in love with you, I have no idea. I only know that one day I realized that my heart belonged to you, and there was no denying it. When?" He shrugged. "I honestly think it was the first moment I met you. Something about you standing there, soaking wet, alone, and yet so determined had me wondering about you. And as for why I fell in love with you... that is the easiest to answer. You are beautiful, intelligent, courageous, honest, and passionate." He grinned. "And you kiss better than any woman I have ever kissed."

A smile sprang across her face. "Truly? I kiss better than other women you have known?"

Rogan laughed. "All those qualities I love about you and the kiss interests you the most?"

"With no experience, I worried I might disappoint you."

"You definitely did not disappoint me, though," —he stood— "we could practice if you would like." He reached down and with an arm around her waist scooped her out of the chair.

"I believe I need lots of kissing practice, though there are some other things I need to practice," she said, her hand slipping under his plaid.

He sucked in a heavy breath, the teasing play of her hand on him growing him hard much too fast. He grabbed her chin. "And there are things I intend to teach you."

"Then let the lessons begin," she whispered.

It was hours before they fell asleep, Emma having very much enjoyed the lesson and looking forward to more.

Emma woke first only a few hours later and with her husband sleeping soundly and knowing his journey here had not been the only thing that had exhausted him—the thought bringing a smile to her face—she left him to sleep, quietly leaving the room.

Chapter Twenty-one

Rogan woke with a smile and ready to make love to his wife again. He turned and sat up with a jolt when he saw that Emma was not there. She was nowhere in the room. She had disappeared yet again.

He threw the blankets off, got out of bed, and dressed. He was not worried that she had gone far. He knew she was where she wanted to be—home—at least for now. He wanted to give her time to accept the fact that she now had a new home and she would no longer be living here. He had, however, planned on waking up beside her this morning and giving her another lesson, not that she needed it. The woman learned quickly.

He grinned as he slipped on his boots and headed to the door. Now if he could just teach her to stop disappearing.

As soon as he entered the Great Hall, Maura approached him about meeting with Donald Macinnes. He had met her yesterday upon his arrival. She had been gracious and appeared to be in charge, the servants paying heed to her words. She had not denied him Emma's whereabouts, telling him she was resting in her bedchamber. She had also requested that he wait until today to pay his respects to Donald Macinnes, and Rogan had agreed. He had been more interested in seeing his wife than meeting with his father-in-law, which was how he felt now, but it would be disrespectful to delay the meeting any longer.

He followed Maura, thinking that it had been about a year since he had last seen Donald Macinnes. Donald had visited with his father from time to time or Angus would visit with Donald. He wondered now if both men had spoken about a marriage arrangement between the two families on those visits. It certainly was a wise move and, if anything, both men were wise when it came to protecting their land and clans.

He noticed that Maura did not knock before entering Donald's bedchamber, but then he was expecting Rogan.

"Come in. Come in," Donald called out from a chair by the hearth.

Rogan was surprised that the man did not appear as ill as he had expected. A wool blanket lay across his legs, covering him from the waist down, but his face was not gaunt or did it lack color. His shoulders were as broad as he had remembered and his chest just as powerful beneath his linen shirt. His hair was mostly gray now, though he saw no more wrinkles on his face than the last time he had seen him.

"Welcome, son-in-law," Donald said with a cheerful smile and extended his hand.

Rogan took it and again was surprised by his strength. "I am pleased to see you looking well."

"I always feel my old-self in the morning. It is

as the day wears on that my strength wanes."
Donald pointed to the chair next to his. "Sit and please tell me you are not upset that you had to wed Emma instead of Heather. Emma may not possess her sister's beauty but—"

"Emma is more beautiful than either of her sisters," Rogan said, annoyed that Donald did not recognize his daughter's exceptional features.

Donald nodded. "I am glad you see what others have failed to see. Emma is a distinct woman. There are few like her."

Rogan smiled. "There is no other like her. She is unique."

"She belongs to you now and you must take her home or I fear she may never leave here. She is far too attached to this place."

"We will be staying for a while yet," Rogan said firmly, as if giving the man no option. "Emma's shoulder has yet to fully heal and I will not have her traveling until I am sure she is well."

A look of alarm crossed Donald's face as he sprang forward in his chair. "What is wrong with her shoulder?"

"She took a sword to it, coming to my defense. She was lucky it was a clear slice and though the wound appears to heal fast, it still pains her. So, she will take time to rest whether she favors it or not."

Donald laughed and settled back in his seat. "You will never get Emma to rest. She is like a whirlwind that never settles, always doing something, trying something, learning something."

Her father was right about one thing. She was

learning something. Rogan had to stop himself from grinning at the thought. He also had to stop recalling the images of his wife's first taste of him, since the memory of her eager tongue aroused him.

"Your stay will not be long," Donald said. "Emma has always healed fast. When she was young and took ill, it was all Heather could do to keep her in bed. She would also drive Heather mad with her healing mixtures, trying this and that, and poor Heather worried that Emma would accidently poison herself."

Curious to learn all he could about his wife, Rogan asked. "How did she learn so much about plants and their properties?"

"An ill monk wandered into our village one day. He was wild with fever, claiming he needed plants mixed and brewed in the broth of a cabbage. No one wanted him here for fear he would pass his illness onto others, not so Emma. She took him to an empty cottage in the woods and followed his instructions." Donald shook his head, smiling. "No more than a week later he walked into the village a well man. He asked for my permission to remain at the isolated cottage for a while. Little did I know when I granted him permission that Emma had asked him to stay and teach her what he knew about healing plants."

"He taught her well."

"Emma learns as she heals... exceptionally fast."

Another image struck Rogan, Emma pleading with him not to stop as he drove in and out of her since she was about to have another orgasm on top of the one she already had. Then afterwards she had asked him about multiple orgasms, wondering if she had done something wrong the first time, since she had only come once. That had led to a very interesting and most unexpected discussion.

"The monk died about eight months after arriving here," Donald said. "I think he knew he was dying, and I believe Emma knew as well, though she never said. She did, however, spend as much time with him as possible, to her sisters' worry. My Emma is a determined one."

"That she is and from what I hear Heather is kind and sweet. What of Patience?"

"Patience is not at all patient. She could not wait to be born. Not only did she birth early, but my wife almost delivered on the steps of the keep." Donald smiled at the memory. "She has the heart of a warrior, though she does not always think before she leaps."

"Emma has confidence that Patience will return on her own. What of you?"

"I have no doubt that Patience will return soon enough, though I fear it will be without Heather. I am sure Emma has told you about the messages from the Dark Dragon."

"Are you sure it is him?"

"He is infamous for his claw signature, and since my daughters and you and your warriors were attacked by ghost warriors, who else could it possibly be. I am preparing a missive for the King to see if he is aware of the situation and what help he can offer."

A soft knock sounded at the door.

"That would be Maura," Donald said. "She is as bad as Emma, watching out for me. She is here to advise I need rest."

"We will have time to talk more before your daughter and I take our leave," Rogan said, standing.

"I am glad Emma has a good and honorable husband to look after her, and I am pleased that our families are finally united."

"Until later," Rogan said and walked over and opened the door to Maura waiting patiently. "He is expecting you."

Maura bobbed her head, smiled, and stepped aside. "He knows me well, my lord."

Rogan turned once out the door to ask, "By any chance have you seen Emma?"

"No, my lord, and I must warn you," she said, her smile spreading, "she is not always an easy one to keep track of."

Rogan walked off silently agreeing with her. A servant hurried over to him as soon as he entered the Great Hall.

"Food, my lord?" she asked with a bob of her head. "Cook makes a fine porridge and there is flowered honey for the warm bread just baked."

Recalling how delicious last night's meal was, Rogan could not resist. He planned on eating quickly, but the food was so good that he lingered a bit, savoring the taste. He also took the opportunity to ask any servant who passed by if they had seen Emma.

He got nearly the same response from all four. "She is out and about by sunrise, though to where I could not say."

Once he finished, he was eager to go find his wife. He wanted to spend the day with her, have her show him all she had accomplished here and perhaps find a secluded spot where he could make love to her.

After asking a few people if they had seen Emma and being told by most that she was around somewhere, he grew annoyed. Did everyone simply ignore her?

He stopped a plump woman with a broad smile. "Does anyone pay heed to where Emma is?"

She laughed and bobbed her head. "That, my lord, would be impossible. She is here, there, and everywhere." Her smile broadened as her look turned more sincere. "Emma is the heart that keeps our clan beating. We are blessed to have her and will sorely miss her when she leaves us."

He was pleased to know that her clan cared for her more than she realized. "By chance, would you know where I could find her?"

"There are so many places she could be," the woman said, shaking her head. Then her smile burst wide. "But it is morning, and she can usually be seen carrying a basket to the woods to collect plants."

"Alone?" he snapped.

"Possibly, my lord, though Patience has insisted many times that she take one of the warriors with her, Emma usually sneaks off on her own more often than not. With Patience not here, I would imagine she went alone."

“Where in the woods might she be?” he asked, anxious to find her and throttle her for going off by herself.

“That I do not know, my lord. Emma knows the woods around here as well as the trackers, since she spends so much time there.”

With a quick thank you to the woman, he hurried off with determined strides. He thought to ask James if he would know where to start looking, but since the man did not seem fond of sharing any information when it came to Emma, Rogan decided differently.

He had left Liam home to look after the keep and Angus, but he had brought another one of his trackers with him. So he was sure he would find Emma in no time.

~~~

Emma sat on the stump staring at the empty cottage while memories danced in her head. She had planned on collecting a few plants and returning to the keep when she found herself growing more and more melancholy as she saw to her familiar task, until she had finally found herself here.

How could she leave her family and home, the people and place she trusted the most? She loved Rogan, but did she truly know him? And here—at home—she came and went as she pleased. Patience would order her to take a warrior with her when she went in the woods, but she had rarely listened to her sister. She preferred her time alone in the woods. And there had been no repercussions if she did not
~~~

obey her sister.

No one had stopped her, though her sisters had argued most strenuously with her when she had brought the monk here and tended him. Duncan had taught her so much and not only about herbs, but about herself. He understood her penchant for knowledge, for knowledge had been his endeavor his entire life. He had encouraged questions and debates, and she missed that. He had challenged her and in so doing had taught her more than she had thought possible.

She wondered what Duncan would think of her unexpected marriage.

A new experience. Learn all you can.

His voice was quite clear in her head. He had believed that every new experience was a lesson to be learned. Death was even a lesson to him. She had been so upset when he had told her that he was very ill and would die in a few months. But he was thrilled that the good Lord had seen fit to send him someone he could pass his vast knowledge onto before he left this place. And he had encouraged her to learn all she could in the short time they had together. He was a remarkable man and she missed him. Tears pooled in her eyes, and she could almost hear Duncan tell her not to cry that he was deep in a learning experience, and was exactly where he wanted to be.

"Do you know how long it has taken me to find you?"

She jumped, startled by her husband's angry voice.

"You did not hear me approach. You were too lost in your thoughts," Rogan scolded, coming to stand in front of her.

Emma stood, her chin going up and a tear falling.

"What is wrong?' he demanded, reaching up to wipe her teardrop away.

She pushed his hand aside. "Nothing."

That she rejected his touch and denied that something troubled her, annoyed him. "I expect honesty from my wife."

"And I expect my husband not to anger so easily," she snapped.

He turned away from her, ran his fingers through his hair, and turned back around to face her. "My heart races, my stomach clenches, and my mind goes mad with worry whenever I cannot find you. I fear you have taken off again or worse have been abducted or God knows what. I only know you are not with me and, therefore, not protected. I am insanely in love with you, and there would be no life without you."

She stared at him a moment, and then hurried to his side. "Your words melt my heart and my anger."

His arm coiled around her waist. "You cannot keep disappearing like you do. You will worry me to death." He kissed her before she could respond, having wanted to do so since he had spotted her sitting on the stump.

He had dismissed his tracker as soon as he had seen her. He had all he could do not to rush over, grab her, and kiss her senseless. He had been so relieved to see her. Unfortunately, his anger preceded him. Now nothing mattered but the taste of her and how good she felt in his arms.

He brought the kiss to an end with a light brush of his lips across hers. He was about to ask about her tears when suddenly warriors dropped from trees and emerged from bushes.

This time there was no question that they were the Dark Dragon's infamous ghost warriors. Their faces were painted pure white, the way they looked when riding into battle or raiding areas. The way they looked when ready to kill.

Rogan pushed Emma behind him and drew his sword.

Chapter Twenty-two

"Stay behind me," Rogan ordered Emma, his hand clenching his sword ready to fight. He would see them all dead, and die himself if he must, before he would let them take his wife. There were eight warriors, a substantial amount against one, though he was a superior swordsman, but then so were they from what he had experienced.

That they made no move toward them worried Rogan. What were they waiting for?

Anger gripped Emma, squeezing so tight she thought she would never be able to breathe again. With courage born of fortitude, she hurried around in front of her husband, keeping a wide birth so he could not reach out and stop her. She halted not far from one of the warriors. Her arm shot out and she pointed a finger in his face.

"I demand that the Dark Dragon return my sister?" she said with a ferocity that quivered her voice.

Silence so chilling seemed to freeze everyone where they stood, except Rogan. He moved to stand behind Emma, protecting her back and ready to defend.

Suddenly, one warrior tossed something to Emma. Her eyes followed the small pouch as it sailed through the air and she caught it with one hand. She gripped it tight and looked up at the warrior, but he was gone along with the others.

Rogan stepped around her. “You will be the death of me with your foolish actions.”

“If they had come to kill us, they would have been on top of us in an instant. They were here to deliver a message,” Emma said.

“Then why the painted faces?”

“A warning,” she said and opened the pouch, dropping the contents in her hand. She gasped, all color fading from her face.

Rogan wrapped his arms quickly around her. “What is it?”

“A ring.”

“So this ring confirms that the Dark Dragon has Heather and the face paint warns they are ready to battle if we attempt to rescue her,” he said with a heavy heart, knowing how painful this must be for Emma.

Emma pulled out of his embrace, shaking her head. “No, the Dark Dragon may have intended that message, but Heather did not.”

“What do you mean?”

“Patience was always concerned for our safety so she made us agree that if there should ever come a time or situation where one of us needed help we would send a message that only we would understand. Patience would send the silver clasp that ties her hair. I would send my healing pouch and Heather would send,” —Emma paused a moment— “our mother’s pin she always wears.”

“But she sent a ring,” Rogan said.

Emma held the small ring up. “Heather wore this on a string around her neck. The lad she had been in love with since they were children had forged it for her and declared his love when he had given it to her. She never parted with it. Her sending this means—” Tears choked her words and her heart hurt so badly that she surely thought it would break. “It means she begs for help.”

Rogan caught her in his arms as her sobs caused her to stumble. He held her tight, her pain his pain. “I swear to you and the heavens that I will do whatever it takes to bring Heather home.”

She let her tears fall, seeking solace in her husband’s strong arms. Some of her pain faded with her tears and left her more determined than ever to help Heather.

“We should return to the castle and inform my father,” she said, having no intentions of telling him the significance of the ring. She did not want to weigh him down with any more worry.

As soon as they entered the keep, Emma left her basket of plants and cloak on one of the tables in the Great Hall before hurrying up the stairs to her father’s bedchamber, Rogan keeping pace behind her.

To Emma’s relief, the door sat open. She entered and was pleased to see him sitting in the chair by the hearth, with color in his cheeks that she had not seen in some time.

“What is wrong?” Donald Macinnes asked as soon as he saw Emma.

“I never could hide anything from you,” Emma said, recalling how when she was young she felt her father was this magical creature who knew her every thought and could solve every problem. For a moment, she wished she was that little girl again.

"Heather was the only one who could do that, though I feared it cost her dearly. Now what is wrong?" he said in a father's no nonsense voice as he stretched his hand out to her.

Emma grabbed his hand greedily, needing the love and support only a father could give his daughter. She no soon as hunched down in front of him then words spilled from her lips, though the true purpose of the ring went left unsaid.

Rogan remained near, hearing desperation in his wife's voice and seeing concern shadow Donald's face.

Donald held his daughter's hand firmly and when she finished, he took her hand in both of his. "We know now, without a doubt, the Dark Dragon has our Heather. Now we must find out what he wants. I will change what I was going to inquire of the King and demand the Dark Dragon be called to task for this. We will have answers and we will get our Heather back."

Donald coughed and reached for his tankard on the table beside him. He coughed again, and then shook his head. "I forgot. Maura went to make more of your brew. Could you—"

Emma jumped up. "I will brew you enough to last the day." She turned to Rogan. "You will stay with him until I return?"

"Of course," Rogan said and as soon as the door closed behind her, he turned to Donald. "What is it you want to tell me that you did not want your daughter to hear?"

"You are observant," Donald praised, "that is good. My Emma will be safe with you."

"If she does not drive me completely insane first," Rogan said with a laugh. "But then I do love a challenge."

Donald smiled and chuckled softly. "Emma can be challenging, though not half as much as Patience. The man Patience weds," —Donald sighed— "will be in my prayers every day." His expression turned serious. "I fear the longer Emma remains here, the more likely she will be to makes plans to go find the Dark Dragon and demand her sister's return. She would be much better off acclimating herself to her new home and family."

"Emma would worry and plan no matter where she was," Rogan said.

Donald's smile returned. "Not when she sees what she could do to improve your keep and land. She will not be able to help but take on the task of making all the improvements she feels is necessary, giving her less time to dwell on her sisters. Nothing can be done until we hear from the King and see if he is aware of this problem, and if he will help to resolve it."

He could not fault Donald for being truthful or for being right. Nothing could be done until they heard from the King and being here, being reminded of what her life had been rather than living her life as it was now, could make it all the more difficult for Emma.

"I have told her that we would be staying a

while and she does need rest," Rogan reminded.

"If my daughter can walk the woods in search of her plants, then she can ride to her new home in a pace suitable to her condition."

"You are persistent about Emma leaving," Rogan said with a curious tone.

"I am determined to see Emma safe and a chance at a good life. If I felt she could do something, make a difference in finding her sisters, then I would demand that my daughter remain here until things were settled. I may not be well, but my mind is as clear as it has always been. And I do what is right and good for Emma. You are a good man and will do the same someday for your own daughter if necessary." Donald smiled. "I expect many grandchildren, another task that can keep her busy." His smile faded. "I need to know Emma is safe and with someone who will prevent her from doing anything that could cause her irreparable harm."

"Now that we are family, it is not necessary that you take the burden of this situation and your clan all on yourself. Let me help," Rogan offered, seeing not only the concern, but fear for Emma in Donald's aging eyes.

"You have helped much already and you will help much more when the time comes, that I promise you."

"Then I will see that we leave here in the next couple of days," Rogan agreed.

Donald's whole body seemed to slump in relief. "You have lifted some of my burden already."

"You should rest," Rogan said, seeing how weary the man suddenly appeared.

"Aye, the day wears on and so do I."

"Let me help you to bed," Rogan offered.

As he reached for Donald, the door swung open and Emma entered along with Maura.

"What is wrong?" Emma demanded, rushing to her father.

"Nothing. Nothing," Donald insisted with a wave of his hand, chasing away her concerned fussing. "I grow tired that is all."

Maura reached him before Emma could. She placed the pitcher of Emma's special brew on the table beside Donald, then turned to Emma. "I will see to your father, go and see to some rest yourself."

Rogan settled his hands on his wife's shoulders. "Maura is right. You have had quite a morning and could use some rest."

"We will talk more later," Donald said.

"Before supper I will come visit with you," Emma said, wanting to tend her father, but seeing he had become quite comfortable having Maura look after him.

Rogan took her hand and was not surprised when she tugged him to a stop once outside the bedchamber.

"I have no need for rest. There are things I must see to," she said quite empathically.

"I will accompany you." Before she could object, he took her in his arms. "You know you have a husband now, do you not?" He grinned. "And, to his surprise, he very much wants to spend time with his wife, and not only in the bedchamber.

Of course, if you wanted to go there now, I would most certainly oblige you." He nuzzled his face in her neck, kissing and nipping her soft skin, needing to taste her.

A tingle raced through her and she shivered. *Husband.* She had a husband and the thought brought her both tremendous joy and absolute fear. She was much too accustomed to spending her time on her own or with her sisters. She was not accustomed to being answerable to anyone. Her father had given her much freedom, though truth be told she had taken the freedom for herself, and she was not about to surrender it. However, she had to admit that a stop in her bedchamber with him sounded mighty appealing.

His lips found hers and she returned his kiss with vigor and a need that tingled her senseless.

His lips left hers to urge, "To the bedchamber, all else can wait."

His words tempted far too much. "I have things that I must see to."

He took her hand and placed it on his rock-hard arousal. "Aye, you have something that needs your immediate attention."

She laughed softly and gave him a squeeze. "Did I do that?"

"Aye," he said again, "and I would be most grateful if you would relieve his suffering."

"And will you relieve mine," she asked on a whisper, then brushed her lips over his.

"Many times, you have my word on it."

"Then let us not delay, for we have much to do."

He took her hand and hurried her down the hall, their smiles growing with every step.

They were brought to an abrupt halt at the top of the stairs, almost colliding with a servant hurrying up them.

"My lady, George says you must hurry there is a problem at the mill."

Emma did not even acknowledge Rogan, she shooed the servant down the steps and hurried down behind her.

Rogan watched her disappear down the curved staircase, shook his head, and followed down after her. He was annoyed that she would take her leave of him without a word, or that it seemed it did not matter to her whether he joined her or not. And it also annoyed him that the miller's message was a demand not a request. Or was it that Emma had not hesitated to do as the miller asked, leaving her husband behind without thought?

Rogan shook his head as he entered the Great Hall and saw that his wife did not grab her cloak off the table where she had left it earlier. He snatched it up as he hurried his pace.

He was glad he had. A slight crispness lingered in the spring air today. Of course, clouds hiding the sun did not help any. As far as his pace, he had to double it to keep up with her, since his wife moved with remarkable speed. An image of her naked popped into his head, and he now understood why her legs, arms, and just about all of her had retained such firmness. She was forever active, and he had no doubt she was involved with far more strenuous work than most noble women.

He saw then that villagers started running in the direction Emma had taken and he rushed along with them. The crowd stopped on a slight rise, a few feet from the mill. It was an impressive structure with a sizeable wheel that was not moving. He made his way through the crowd, though everyone parted quickly enough when they saw it was him.

The sight that caught his eye had him running full speed. Men were yelling, an older woman held a young woman in her arms and they were both crying. Then he saw the problem. The large mill wheel sat immobile. A man appeared to have gotten jammed in it. The man's head was being held up above the water by another man. His expression was one of pain mixed with fear as he relied on the other man to keep his head tilted back, the water resting at his chin.

Before he could join his wife, he saw her remove her boots, blouse, and skirt, leaving her in her shift, and then she jumped into the stream, the water covering her to her shoulders. When she got her footing, the water settled just beneath her breasts, her soaked shift clinging greedily to her two firm mounds and hard nipples. Next thing he knew, she disappeared beneath the water.

Rogan dropped her cloak on the ground, ripped off his boots, and hurried into the water to find his wife.

She broke the surface as he reached the spot where he saw her go under.

"What are you doing?" he demanded, his worry sounding more like anger.

"Daniel is wedged in the wheel.

"Is the wheel secure?" Rogan asked.

Emma gave a nod to the burly man holding Daniel. "George would not be where he is if it was not secure."

"Is it George?" Rogan snapped, fearing that his wife could get swallowed up by the churning wheel.

"Aye, it is secure, and I have two men making sure it stays that way."

"Order two more men on it," Rogan said in a commanding tone that had the man shouting out Rogan's exact order. He wanted to ask how the hell this accident happened, but now was not the time, though he damn well would find out later. He turned to his wife. "Leave. I will see to this."

"I will not," she said defiantly.

He was ready to drag her out of there when she disappeared beneath the water again. He swore aloud, not caring who heard.

"Emma knows well what to do, my lord. She has done this many times before," —George looked down at Daniel— "for fools who do not obey orders."

Rogan shot Daniel a murderous look. "Anything happens to my wife because of your stupidity and you will pay dearly." He was about to duck beneath the water and retrieve his wife when she surfaced.

"Stop disappearing on me," he scolded, wanting to haul her out of there and plant her safely on the ground. But she would only jump right back in the water and the delay could prove costly. Instead, he did what was best to see the situation resolved as quickly as possible and with no harm to his wife.

"What do you need me to do?"

Emma wanted to hug her husband for not making the situation worse by ordering her to leave, for she would not have obeyed him, and for his help. "He is wedged good and hard."

Daniel moaned and tears began to gather in his eyes. "I do not want to die, please, Emma, help me. I am sorry for what I did to you when we were young, but please, please, do not let me die." He began to sob. "Helen! I love you, Helen."

The young lass the old woman held as they stood waiting on the bank of the stream slipped out of her arms and hurried to the edge of the water. "I am right here, Daniel. I love you so much. Please, Emma, do not let my husband die."

"Bloody hell," Rogan shouted. "Emma would never let anyone intentionally die and you should be ashamed to even think it. If it were up to me I would let the bloody bastard die for his cruelty to Emma, but my wife has a more generous heart. And it is glad I will be to take her away from the lot of you." He looked to Emma. "Let us see this done, wife." He lowered his voice. "And do not dare climb out of the water until I can wrap your cloak around you."

She had to smile, for never had a man spoken up in her defense and never had her body felt so alive since meeting Rogan. And most importantly, never had a man loved her as Rogan did.

Emma turned to George. "The wheel will need to be moved some to free him and as soon as it is he must be pulled away from it."

"If your man is not strong enough for such a grueling task, that wheel can slip and take more than just Daniel with it," Rogan said to George, though turned to his wife as he finished.

"I have done it before," George said, "I can do it again."

"And I will pull Daniel away as you do, just make sure you hold that wheel. And you, wife," he said, turning to her, "will wait on land." Rogan did not fail to catch the look that George and Emma exchanged as the man handed the task of dealing with Daniel over to Rogan.

"I am afraid that is not possible," she said.

A dreadful feeling gripped Rogan's heart.

"Daniel's arm should free easily enough, but his foot is wedged beneath a large stone that can only be moved once the wheel moves."

"Do not dare tell me that you intend to do that," Rogan said anger and fear stirring in his voice. He did not give her time to respond. "Go get someone right now to help Daniel while I move the stone."

"I have done this before. No worries," she assured him and before he could protest she shouted out to a man on the bank to release the wheel and he shouted to another and another.

Rogan wanted to strangle her as he heard the wheel creak and watched as his wife disappeared beneath the water. From the way Daniel dropped in his arms, Rogan knew his arm was free.

Emma bounced up out of the water to shout to the man on shore again for the wheel to be released one more time, and then she disappeared once again.

The wheel creaked again and when he felt no change in Daniel's body, he silently cursed. He should have never let his wife have her way. Suddenly, Daniel gave a yell and Rogan felt his body give. He immediately pulled him away from the wheel and watched for Emma to surface.

His heart slammed against his chest in relief when her head cleared the water. He was even more relieved when she remained in the water as he got Daniel to land.

"I will get your cloak," he said to her after leaving Daniel in his wife and mother's care."

Rogan snatched up the cloak and turned just as the wheel sprang loose and water gushed forward, the force knocking Emma off her feet and dragging her under the rushing water.

Chapter Twenty-three

The water rushed up like greedy arms, pulling Emma down. This was not the first time the stream had caught her unaware, and she had learned from it. She let it have its way, knowing it would tire out soon enough and she would be able to make her way to shore.

What she did not count on was the pain in her shoulder from being tumbled all around or the toll her body had taken helping Daniel. Fortunately, she felt the water slowing and knew she would soon be able to reach the bank.

She was suddenly jolted out of the water and she knew full well whose arms held her.

"Damn it, wife, I will not have an ounce of sanity left being wed to you," Rogan said with more relief than anger as he hugged Emma tightly to him and walked out of the stream.

He set her on her feet only long enough to wrap her cloak around her, then he had her up in his arms again. "I am taking you to our bedchamber, getting you dry, and tucking you in bed where you will stay for the rest of the day and night."

"I have no objections to that, though—" A cough did not allow her to finish, and she turned her head away as she coughed up some of the water she had swallowed.

Rogan took a seat on a large rock with Emma on his lap. He bent her over at the waist and rubbed her back. She coughed up more water before settling back in his arms.

"That will have to wait," she finally finished. "Daniel's arm and especially his foot will need tending."

"Let one of the other healers see to him," Rogan said, more concerned with his wife's well-being than Daniel's.

"I would if his foot was not so badly damaged," she admitted, preferring to retire to their bedchamber as Rogan suggested.

"You saved his life. He deserves no more of your help."

"If I do not help him, he may never be able to walk on that foot again and I would never be able to live with that thought."

Rogan grumbled beneath his breath. "I do not care what happens to Daniel, but I do care very much about my wife. If you must do this, I will not stop you." He felt her tense in his arms and took gentle hold of her chin. "Like it or not, *wife*, you now have a husband you are answerable to."

Emma thought to ask if he was answerable to her as well, but she did not have the strength or the desire to debate the issue at the moment. Let him think as he will, and she would live as she wished.

"Excuse me, my lady," an older woman said, catching both their attentions.

"Marianne, how is your son?" Emma asked with concern.

“Alive thanks to your bravery and your husband’s help. Helen and I are most grateful, but he is in much pain and his foot...” She shook her head and tears ran from her eyes.

“And what of your mistress?” Rogan snapped. “She almost drowned saving your foolish son, yet you have no kind words for her?”

Marianne paled. “I am so sorry, my lord. My lady, please forgive my ill manners—”

“It is all right, Marianne,” Emma said softly. “My husband is not aware that this has happened before and that I know how to handle the rushing stream. You owe me no apology. As soon as I change out of these wet garments, I will come have a look at Daniel and see what needs to be done.”

“I cannot thank you enough, and I do not know what the clan will do without you when you leave for your new home, though I am happy for you.” She turned and walked away, her gait slow from age and no doubt worry.

Emma slipped off Rogan’s lap. He stood slowly and for some reason she felt thwarted by the breadth of him and wrapped her cloak more tightly around her.

He leaned down, planting his face close to hers. “Know this well, wife. If I desired to put you on a horse right now and leave for home, no one could stop me. I give you leave to tend this fool. So be done with it, for when I come to fetch you, I will brook no argument from you. But first,” —he scooped her up in his arms— “I will make certain you get to the keep safely.”

His words stirred anger in her, but she did not

bother to argue with him. He would learn that she would do as she wished.

Emma was surprised when he carried her up the stairs to their bedchamber, thinking he would simply deposit her in the keep.

Their bedchamber.

How easily it had become *their bedchamber*. The thought sent a flourish of tingles racing through her. It continued to amaze her that this man could stir her passion so easily?

Love.

She did love him, though she had tried not to. After all, he had been intended for her sister, but the attraction had always been there. To her surprise, it had grown over the time they had spent together. Until, she had finally realized that she was madly in love with him.

"I love you," she said softly, snuggling her face in the crook of his neck as they entered the bedchamber.

"And I am a blessed man that you do, for though you drive me quite mad, I cannot think of life without you."

Her breath caught at the intensity of his words and she turned her face up in search of his lips.

He captured her mouth in a hungry kiss. She shivered in his arms, and he ended the kiss sooner than he would have liked. She was soaking wet and needed out of her clothes and that took precedence over appeasing his passion. However, he could not remain in the room while she disrobed, for he would rush her into bed and make love to her for the rest of the day.

It would take great effort to step away from her, though he reminded himself they would have tonight.

"I will fetch a servant to help you," he said, sitting her on the chair near the hearth and moving away from her.

She thought he was taking his leave, but he walked over to the bed and stripped off his wet garments. She had forgotten he was as soaked as she was and allowed herself to enjoy the view of him naked. She wished he would not hurry to dress. She loved looking at his chiseled body, hard in all the right places. And she was growing wet in just the right place. Good Lord, her body ached from what she had been through, and it ached even more for him.

Rogan could feel her eyes on him and he knew if he turned and looked at her all would be lost. He would have her in bed in seconds, and she did not need him slamming repeatedly into her at the moment. She had been through enough, her body probably already feeling the consequences of her ordeal. He would not add to it, no matter how much he wanted to make love to her.

He never dressed so fast or ran from a woman's bedchamber so fast. He hurried past her without looking at her, yanked the door open, and cringed when she called out to him.

"I will see you later?"

He did not turn around. "Aye, that you will, wife. You can count on it."

The door slammed behind him and Emma shook

her head and shivered. One moment he stirred anger in her and the next passion. How did she go from being annoyed with him to wanting him so badly? It made no sense, but then Patience often claimed that love had no rhythm or reason to it. She had warned that anyone who attempted to understand love was a fool. Emma had not understood what her sister had meant then, but she certainly did now.

She shook her head again. Now was not the time to question love. She hurried out of her wet garments and toweled herself dry, making sure to ring her hair dry as well. She slipped on a shift, adding a plain brown skirt and tan blouse over it, securing the ties on both. She did not bother putting on stockings. They itched and scratched and she hated wearing them. She grabbed her sandals and tied them around her legs, having left her boots by the stream.

After braiding her damp hair, she hurried to the door, yanking it open. She and the servant on the other side of the door both drew back startled.

"You need help, my lady?" the servant asked concerned.

Emma smiled and shook her head. "My husband has yet to learn that I prefer to tend myself."

The servant nodded and stepped aside.

Emma stopped after taking only a few steps and turned. "Please see that cook sends some food to Daniel's cottage."

"Aye, my lady," the servant said with a bob of her head. "You will be sorely missed, my lady."

She was the second one to tell Emma that today

and it surprised her just as the first one had.

"You tend the clan well. We never want for food, shelter, or tending when ill. And you rescue even the most foolish among us. While we are happy for you, we are also sad to see you go. The MacClennan clan is lucky to have you join them."

Emma stared as the servant bobbed her head once again and rushed off. She was certain she had seen tears in the young girl's eyes, and she felt her own heart grow heavy with the thought of leaving her family.

Maura was in the Great Hall and greeted her with, "Finally I find you, your father is frantic to speak with you and know you are well."

"I have no time to spare for him right now. Please tell him I am fine and, if time permits, I will visit with him after I see to Daniel's care."

Maura nodded and Emma hurried off.

Emma heard Daniel's cries of pain long before she reached his cottage. Marianne waited outside the cottage door with Emma's healing pouch in hand.

"I knew you would need this," Marianne said tears in her eyes as she handed it to Emma. "Please. Please, help him."

Emma placed a comforting hand on the old woman's shoulder. "I will do all I can."

Marianne nodded. "Then my son will do well."

Emma entered the cottage, wondering if what she did would be enough to save Daniel's foot.

~~~
~~~

Rogan had not expected Donald Macinnes to provide food for his large troop of warriors. His men had seen to their own needs, though he had been surprised to see that Donald had generously provided his men with bread and ale. And they were all looking quite pleased.

He grabbed a tankard of ale himself, needing it. He walked among his men talking with them to get his mind off his wife. He wanted her like no other woman, and he could not wait to get her home where she would be all his.

He spoke with his lead warriors, ordering them to be ready to leave at daybreak in three days' time. One of his trackers would be sent out ahead to scout, though he doubted ghost warriors would attack them. The message had been delivered, the warning received, and returning home to MacClennan land would surely appear a retreat to the ghost warriors that probably watched undetected.

Having promised his wife time to tend Daniel, he decided to go to the mill and find out what exactly had happened that lead to his wife placing herself in danger. He heard the screams before he saw the villagers gathered in groups in front of a cottage. He did not have to ask to know who screeched like a banshee.

He dismissed the thought of going to his wife as soon as it entered his head. She would think he came to collect her, a tempting idea, but he had seen the worry on her face and he had told her he would allow her time to do what she must.

He made his way around the crowd, hearing snatches of chatter.

"She will heal him."

"He will lose the foot and his life along with it."

"Emma will not let death take him."

"Sad day when she leaves us."

"Who will take care of us?"

"Patience and Heather gone."

"Emma will find them."

"Emma will make things right."

Rogan could not fault the villagers for worrying. He was, however, annoyed that they were more concerned with themselves than Emma's happiness. They should be pleased that she made such a strong match and that they now had the MacClennan clan to rely on.

That they believed she could keep death at bay also worried him. Surely, she had not saved everyone she had tended. His strides grew more determined as he approached the mill. He intended to get some answers about the accident and learn some things about his wife along the way.

~~~

Rogan left the mill pleased that he had learned much more than he had anticipated. He even had a better understanding about the working of the mill. But it was the things he had learned about Emma that had pleased him the most. She was a superior woman in so many ways. He could learn much from his wife and she could learn much from him. He looked forward to the life they would share
~~~

together. There was one thing that troubled him though. He was well aware of Emma's willfulness, but to hear George say that once Emma set her mind to something there was no changing it made him realize the possible problems her stubbornness could present.

George had made it clear that he was grateful for all Emma had taught him and pleased that she had been eager to learn from him as well.

"A kind heart and quick wit," George had said about her.

That was his Emma and he was eager to collect her so they could spend the rest of the day together. He had not realized how much time he had spent at the mill, several hours if he read the sun right.

He hurried his pace and seeing no one lingering around Daniel's cottage had him thinking and hoping that Emma was done with Daniel and already gone.

He knocked on the door and the old woman answered. She bobbed her head and stepped to the side. "My lord, you are most welcome in our home."

Rogan stepped in. Helen sat in a chair next to the bed, though jumped up and bobbed her head at Rogan. Daniel lay with his injured foot resting atop two pillows and partially covered with what resembled a poultice.

"Forgive me, my lord, for not rising, Emma will have my head if I dare move this foot."

"More frightened of my wife than me?" Rogan asked sternly.

Daniel bowed his head. "Aye, my lord, I am."

Rogan smiled. "Wise man."

Daniel sighed in relief. "Thank you, my lord."

"It is Emma you should be thanking most heartily," Rogan said.

"I have, my lord, repeatedly. She saved my life and my foot. My injury is not as bad as first thought. Emma says the water saved it from being crushed beyond repair. She has ordered me to stay off it completely for a week, and then I am to use a crutch for several weeks."

"And I am to apply the poultice for several hours a day for the next three days," Helen added.

"And your arm?" Rogan asked.

"Bruised and sore, that is all," Daniel said with relief.

"Emma has returned to the keep?" Rogan asked.

"No, my lord, just as she finished with Daniel, she was called to Nessa's cottage. She has gone into labor with her first child," Helen said.

That his wife was off tending yet another clan member irritated him. "Is there no one else who can deliver the babe?"

"Other women will help Emma," Emma said, "but we all prefer to have her attend our births. We feel safer with her there. She is knowledgeable about so much."

"But she has also been through an ordeal herself today and needs rest," Rogan said annoyed and waved his hand at the two women. "Go, I wish to speak to your husband alone.

Helen looked hesitant to leave her husband, but she did as ordered, taking her mother-in-law's hand

and hurrying out of the cottage.

All color left Daniel's face as Rogan leaned over the man. "I would have let you drowned without a qualm after learning how cruel you were to my wife when she was young. Make certain you extend a proper and heartfelt apology to her before we take our leave, and make certain others hear it or you will wish you had drowned."

"I will, my lord, I will," Daniel said with an emphatic nod of his head.

Rogan stood straight, squaring his broad shoulders and once again Daniel paled. "You would never make a good warrior."

"I am a simple farmer, my lord, though I would raise a weapon to protect my clan and the Macinnes sisters."

"That is good to know and it redeems you some in my eyes. Now tell me how I find Nessa's cottage."

Rogan gave the two women a nod when he walked out of the cottage. "Daniel is fine and will remain so as long as he does what he has been told."

He heard Daniel's mother, Marianne say as soon as she entered the cottage, "You will obey Lord Rogan's command as an honorable man would do."

Rogan had no doubt Daniel would. Now it was time to find his wife and have her all to himself.

Several women stood talking outside the cottage Daniel had directed him to. They bowed their heads as he approached, one stepping forward.

"If you look for Emma, my lord, she is no longer here," the young red-haired lass said. "Just as she finished delivering Nessa's babe, a fine strapping son," —the young lass smiled— "word came that she was needed at Anna's. One of her young lads has a sick stomach."

Rogan followed the direction the young lass gave him to Anna's home only to find that Emma had been summoned someplace else. So, he followed from one place to another until he was told that Emma had been called to the keep, her father needing her.

At least now she was in the keep and he would see that she remained there. Dusk was near to claiming the land and he worried that she was bone-tired from her long day of helping others. After seeing that her clan demanded far too much of her, he swore that life would be different for her once home. She would have time for herself and time for him.

Rogan entered Donald's bedchamber, the door open. He stopped and watched Emma fuss with the blankets around her father. There was concern in her eyes and he wished he could ease her worries. She had been through enough for one day. She did not need to end the day fearful for her father's well-being.

"I told you not to exert yourself. Now you tell me you are much too exhausted to eat. You must eat to retain your strength," Emma scolded softly.

"I will eat a little if you will stop fussing," Donald said. "I am more concerned about you and the incident at the mill, and why has it taken you so long to come tell me about it?"

"Half your clan summoned Emma for help,"

Rogan said, approaching the bed.

Emma turned and smiled at Rogan, happy to see him. "Not half, but close."

Her soft laughter rippled across him like a gentle touch and damn if it did not arouse him.

She turned to her father, once again fussing with his blanket. "Nessa delivered a hardy son, Anna's youngest ate too much porridge, Terence was worried about his mare, but she is fine and will birth any day now. Flora's stomach ailment is finally the child she and Peter have been waiting for and Robert was worried about a section of the crop, which has refused to accept the seedlings, but then I let him plant as he wished so he would learn that the crops must be moved each year and some plots left unplanted. No worries, though, I am having extra seedlings planted elsewhere. The clan will not lack for food this coming winter."

"You do too much, daughter," her father scolded with concern. "I order you to go rest."

"I will, Da, as soon as I wrap the heated stone and place it by your feet to chase your chill." She turned with a flourish, feeling a light spin in her head as she did and had to steady herself.

"Emma?" Rogan and Donald said simultaneously.

She went to speak, to tell them she was fine when she realized she was not. All light was dimming and she knew she was about to faint.

Instinctively, she reached out toward Rogan. She tried to call his name but darkness claimed her before it could reach her lips, though she thought she heard someone yell his name.

Chapter Twenty-four

"Rogan, grab her!" Donald yelled.

Rogan was moving before Donald finished calling out to him and he had Emma up in his arms before she could hit the floor. He held her firmly against his chest and turned to Donald. "My wife will not be lifting a finger to help anyone else before we leave. See that everyone in your clan knows that or I will make it known."

It sounded like a threat and Donald was certain it was meant as a threat, but he could not fault his son-in-law for protecting Emma. While he was glad that he did, Donald was not sure how Emma would respond to her husband's warning. That, however, would be for them to determine.

"I will see that Maura is summoned when a healer is required," Donald said to appease the imposing warrior. "And Maura tends me well enough. Emma need not worry about me."

"She will worry anyway. Now I will see to my wife and talk with you on the morrow."

Donald nodded, concern weighing heavily on him as he watched Rogan leave with Emma tucked lovingly in his arms. He prayed she would do well with Rogan and that Patience and Heather would return home soon. He dropped his head back on the pillow, a litany of prayers falling in whispers from his lips.

~~~

Rogan felt his wife stir as he entered their bedchamber, and he placed her gently on the bed after shoving the door closed with his shoulder. He pushed a few strands of stray hair off her face that was much too pale as he watched her eyes flutter open. She had felt so limp in his arms that he had feared she had suffered far worse than a swoon.

Emma sighed as she fought to chase the grogginess away, to wake from the dream that weighed so heavily on her or was it a dream? When had she fallen asleep? She raised her hand to touch her husband and make certain it was actually him that she saw sitting by her and not just an image in her dream.

Rogan caught her hand in his and pressed it to his chest. "You will never frighten me like that again."

She smiled, though she was not sure if it reached her lips, every movement proving to be an effort. She could tell it was truly Rogan and she was not in a dream since he scolded her. But what had she done? She could not recall.

"How are you feeling?" he asked more calmly.

"Like I have battled a hundred warriors and lost," she said with a soft laugh as her eyes fluttered closed again.

"Leave the battles to me, you are to rest," he said sternly.
~~~

"Is that a command?" She did not give him a chance to answer. Her eyes flew wide open and she tugged her hand free of his, suddenly recalling what had happened. "I swooned. I never swoon."

"Proof that you have pushed yourself too hard this day."

Emma sighed and nodded her head. "You are right."

"What is that you say?" Rogan asked with feigned surprise. "Are you admitting that your husband is right?"

Emma caught the playful glint in his eyes and smiled. "You are right—this time." Her smile suddenly faded. "My father," she said ready to rise and go see to him.

Rogan stilled her with a gentle hand to her shoulder. "He is fine. Maura is seeing to him, and he wishes for you to rest. You did far too much today."

"No more than I usually do."

"You save that imbecile Daniel every day?"

Emma smiled again. "I do not know how I ever thought I cared for him."

"Young, foolish love."

She reached out and took Rogan's hand, lacing her fingers with his. The strength of him as he gripped her hand sent a warm thrill racing through her. "No, it was not love. It was a need to be favored by a suitor like my sisters. The lads would be after them every chance they got, but they ignored me. And I so wanted to be like my sisters."

"I am glad that you had no bevy of suitors,"

Rogan said his words stinging Emma. "You were meant for me and only me, and I am relieved that no man saw the beautiful gem you truly are, for if anyone had your father would have tired of chasing them off at every turn." He leaned down and kissed her softly, then whispered, "Besides, no one could ever love you as strongly as I love you."

Emma captured his lips for a hardier kiss. She loved kissing him, the taste of him so vibrant and virile. It made her feel so much more alive, so much more aware of her own body and the sensations that ran through it. And that he truly loved her made it all the more wonderful.

Rogan raised his head and the pinched look she sent him made him realize that she was not happy he had ended their kiss. "If we keep that up, I will hoist your skirts and take you fast and hard."

"What do you wait for?" she challenged, feeling the need for him to do just that.

"For you to regain your strength," he said and stood away from the bed, much too tempted to do as he threatened, though it was no threat. It was pure wicked passion that had him wanting to plunge into her and take her like a man deprived too long of a woman.

"What is there for me to do but lie here? I need no strength for that," she said with a sweet innocence that was anything but innocent.

"You play with fire, wife. You know full well you will not just lie there. You will throw your hips up against me time and again until you have taken me as far deep into you as I will go, and then you will match me plunge for plunge, greedily demanding more than one climax." He walked further away from the bed.

Emma felt her whole body blush with excitement, and she could not stop herself from voicing how she felt. "I have always wondered if intimacy with my husband would prove difficult or enjoyable, and it has proven to be both." She continued as Rogan's brow knitted. "It is difficult having such a greedy hunger for you that I feel like a harlot, and it is enjoyable because making love with you goes far beyond all expectations."

"Damn it, Emma," he growled and stepped further away from her. "Your hunger for me makes you no harlot. It fills me with joy and it bloody hell turns me hard knowing that you want me as much as I want you and that I pleasure you beyond what you thought possible, for you do the same to me, but..." He turned away from her for a moment, squaring his shoulders as he turned around to look at her. "Whether you admit it or not, you have exhausted yourself today and I will not add to that by making love to you. Rest, eat, and rest some more and perhaps—"

"Later we will make love?" she asked eagerly.

"We shall see," he said, not wanting to promise and then disappoint her.

She turned away from him.

"Emma?" he said, though did not approach her.

She turned back with a sigh. "Am I too forward about wanting you, about voicing my enjoyment in making love with you? I truly do not know what is proper and what is not. Heather told me that she would speak to me of wifely duties when the time came. I wonder now was it because she did not know herself and once wed would know what to tell me. The village women would not talk of such things in front of us, though I caught bits of chatter about it when they did not know I could hear them. The only thing I understood from the little I heard was that some women enjoyed their wifely duties and others did not. And it made me wonder why and which one would I be."

"I am most pleased you are the one who enjoys her husband," Rogan said with a grin.

Emma chuckled. "So am I."

"Let me have food brought to us and we can eat and talk more. In the meantime, change into your nightdress so you can rest more comfortably."

"Will you help me?" she asked, making it sound like an invitation.

"No, I will not," he said more abruptly than he intended. "I will go see to our supper while you see to the task." He walked to the door, fighting not to turn around and do as she requested, and then do... He groaned silently at the lusty thought that grabbed hold of him in too many vulnerable places.

"Rogan," she called out anxiously and had him turning.

"What?" he asked worried that something was wrong.

"Instead of helping me put my nightdress on now, later, you can help take it off."

"Careful, wife, I may just rip it off you." With that said he hurried out of the room, slamming the door behind him.

Emma smiled and hugged herself. Where had she gotten the boldness to tell her husband how much she wanted him, she did not know, but she liked it. And Rogan found no fault with it. He actually seemed to favor her forthrightness. She felt blessed that fate saw fit to bring them together.

Her happiness, though, was overshadowed by Heather's horrible fate.

Emma rolled out of bed, her body reminding her of the truth of her husband's words—she had done too much. But the pain she felt was nothing to the heartache she suffered thinking of Heather. How did she allow herself to be happy when her sister was held captive by a monster?

Pain rolled through her shoulders and down her back as she slipped out of her clothes and into her nightdress. And why shouldn't she suffer when she had failed not only Heather, but Patience as well. Patience had expected her to return with help, so that they could rescue Heather together.

A single tear pooled in her eye, then fell to roll down her cheek. Her sisters would not stop hunting for her if she had been the one taken. How could she think of her own happiness at a time like this? Heather had reached out to her sisters for help when she had sent that ring. She needed help now, and this was one time Patience's impatience could prove useful.

Emma went and sat in the chair by the hearth, stretching her chilled feet out to the flames while working to unbraid her hair. She understood that her father wanted to send a missive to the King, but that would take time. Time Heather would continue to spend in the clutches of the Dark Dragon. And what horrors would she suffer during that duration? And what if the King refused to help or, worse, what if he ordered her father to do nothing?

Emma could not live with that thought. To find the Dark Dragon's lair would be almost impossible, but not so to find Patience. If she could find Patience, then they could work together to find Heather. And Patience may already have information that could make their task easier.

A sudden thought disturbed her. Her father assumed Patience would return home, he did not worry about her, and she was guilty of the same thought. What if Patience was being held captive herself? There was no denying she was an exceptionally skilled warrior, an unlikely trait for a woman. And men, thinking her no threat at all, left her with an advantage. But recalling the attack when Heather was abducted, the ghost warriors did not hesitate to battle Patience. It was almost as if they were well acquainted with her skills.

She eased out of the chair, ignoring the aches and pains that assaulted her and began to pace in front of the hearth. What if Patience was being held captive by the Dark Dragon as well? Surely, if she was continuing to pursue Heather, she would have sent a message by now to let them know she was all right. And there was that dream she had of Patience telling her she was well, but there had been approaching footsteps and that dark, winged figure. Had the Dark Dragon been closer than Patience had been aware of?

She had always thought Patience invincible, having seen her best many a man larger than herself without much effort. But Patience had taught her and Heather to never underestimate your opponent, to do so could prove fatal.

The ghost warriors were opponents of unmeasurable skill. Had Patience finally faced a foe that she could not best? Had they captured her as well as Heather?

Emma groaned with frustration. Too many questions and not enough answers. What she did know was that the Dark Dragon had Heather. What she did not know was what had happened to Patience. And that was where she felt she should start in her effort to find Heather and rescue her.

The knock preceded the door flinging open and Rogan entering, followed by a bevy of servants with platters of food and drink and fresh bedding.

Emma quickly turned away from them, not wanting them to see her distress, and moved to tuck herself and her troubled thoughts in shadowed corner.

Rogan followed her, slipping his arm around her waist and whispering, "You have been thinking of your sisters."

Emma let her weight and worries fall against her husband's solid body. He did not ask, he simply knew and for some reason it offered her some comfort.

"We will talk," he said and hugged her closer against him.

She felt so safe, so protected and yet what right

did she have to this security and love when her sisters had none? It did not seem fair.

As soon as the door closed on the last servant, Rogan walked her over to the table that had been moved in front of the hearth and eased her down into one of the chairs. He moved the chair from the other end of the table around to the side so that he could sit closer to her and once he did, he reached out and took her hand. "Feeling guilty over your happiness will not help your sisters."

She frowned and held tight to his hand. "How did you know?"

"It is a reasonable assumption, since I know how much you love your sisters. I gave you my word and I will give it again and again to you. We will find Patience and Heather," —he smiled— "though it seems most believe Patience will find her own way home."

"But what if she cannot?"

Rogan filled her tankard with wine and handed her a piece of bread. "You worry that something may keep her from returning home?"

Emma nodded, taking the bread from him. "What if she has been taken captive?" She took a bite and realizing how hungry she truly was reached for more food.

Rogan was relieved to see her eating. "The Dark Dragon does not have her or he would have sent something of hers along with Heather's ring."

"You are right," she said excited at the thought.

"Can you repeat that?" he asked with a grin. Her smile returned and it warmed Rogan's heart.

Pleased that he had alleviated some of her

worry, she appeased him. "You are right."

He held up two fingers and wiggled them. "Twice in one night."

"You need not remind me. I am well aware of your brilliance," —she leaned over and kissed his lips gently— "in all things."

He was tempted to deepen her tender kiss, but he knew where it would lead them, and she needed to fortify herself with food and rest before he would touch her, and not stop touching her.

He turned talk once again to her sisters. "Patience could still be following Heather's trail."

"True," Emma admitted. "Patience is not one to give up easily."

"A trait you both share, and does Heather share it as well?"

Emma shook her head. "I do not believe so. Heather is a kind and gentle soul. She could ease anyone's anger with her soft voice and thoughtful words."

"Then perhaps she can tame the Dark Dragon or at least keep herself safe from him."

Emma's brow knitted. "I never thought of that. I have seen her calm angry men and ease disagreements between women. All she has to do is lift a crying babe in her arms and the child cries no more. I have never heard her raise her voice to anyone and, though I have seen her upset, I have never seen her angry."

"Then I would say that she has the strength and courage to survive this ordeal, and you should keep that in mind, for your worrying will not help her."

Emma realized that she had continued to grip his hand this whole time and she released it and brought her hand to rest upon his cheek. "Thank you for reminding me how strong my sisters are."

"It would seem it is a trait all three of you possess, and I suspect that Heather and Patience have no doubt that the three of you will be reunited soon. You would be wise to feel the same. And know that I am here and will do all I can to see that that comes to pass very soon."

His words gave her strength and that he shared her burden eased her worry. She was not alone in this. Her husband was here to help her. "I am grateful to have you as my husband."

"As I am to have you as my wife. We will do well together, Emma, I promise." He pressed his hand atop of hers and brought it to his mouth to kiss her palm.

It sent a shiver through her and set off a rash of tingles that she quite enjoyed. But that was for later, after she rested.

They returned to enjoying the food and drink and conversation turned less worrisome.

"Over the next week or so, I will show you all that I have implemented here so that the clan and land prospers. It will give you a good indication of what I wish to do once we return to your home," Emma said.

Rogan did not want to disturb their talk by telling her they would be leaving in two days, but he also did not want her to think that he purposely kept the decision from her. So he had no choice but to say, "We are going to be leaving sooner than planned."

"When and why?" she asked, placing the tankard of wine she was about to drink down on the table.

"There is not much to be done here and the sooner we leave, the sooner you will grow more accustomed to your new home."

Emma sat up straight, not caring for his explanation. "When?"

"Two days, and your father agrees it would be the wisest thing to do."

He was letting her know that it would do her no good to run to her father for help. They had decided this together, thinking they knew what was best for her, and leaving her no recourse, or so they thought.

Rogan had expected her to object immediately and when she did not, he wondered what thoughts spun in her head. He was not fool enough to believe that she would accept this decision without protest and that she said nothing made him wonder what she was plotting.

"We will leave early in the morning and ride at a brisk pace. I want to reach home before dusk," he said curious if she would argue.

"As you wish," she said and raised her tankard of wine to take a drink.

"You are not upset that we leave sooner than planned?"

"Would it matter if I was?"

"I do not do this to upset. I do what is best for you."

"And you know this is best for me... how?"

Rogan stretched his arms out from his sides and grinned. "As you say, I am brilliant."

A smile surfaced before Emma could stop it. "I shall choose my words more carefully next time."

Rogan leaned closer to her. "I do not do this to hurt you, Emma. Nothing more can be accomplished by remaining here. And while we wait to hear from the King, we can determine what other options may be possible."

"What if Patience returns?"

"We would return here immediately."

His explanation made sense, though she still felt reluctant to leave. How did she bid farewell to the only home she had ever known? How did she leave her ill father in someone else's care? How did she get through a day without seeing her sisters? It was difficult enough already without them. How would it be when they returned and she was no longer home to enjoy their companionship, their support, their love?

Her heavy thoughts and long day took its toll and she never felt more battered and bruised from both than she did at that moment. She did not want to think anymore or feel the burden of her sisters' absence. She wanted to forget, if only for a while.

She reached out to her husband. "Make love to me."

Chapter Twenty-five

Rogan took her hand. "You are exhausted and need rest."

"I need peace, if only for a while, and I have that when we make love."

How did he deny her an escape from her burdens? And how did he deny himself, since he wanted so desperately to make love to her? "You will do nothing but lie there," he commanded.

"I will try," she said with a soft smile.

He stood and scooped her up off the chair and into his arms. "You are beyond stubborn, wife."

"Aye, I am," Emma said, nibbling at his neck as he carried her to the bed. "Stubbornly in love with you."

He set her on her feet and when her hands went to remove her nightdress, he grabbed them. "You will do nothing," he reminded.

She let her hands drop to her sides after he released them and waited as he quickly disrobed. She loved looking at him naked, though she loved touching him even more. He had warned her, but she could not help herself. He was so hard, yet she knew he would feel like velvet to the touch and she reached out.

He grabbed her wrist.

She opened her mouth to protest and his lips claimed hers before a word could escape. He kissed her senseless like he always did and, oh how, she welcomed it. Passion hot and strong chased away her aches and pains and troubled thoughts. There was only this moment with her husband, nothing else mattered.

She felt him tug her nightdress up along her legs and over her hips. Soon she would be as naked as he was, and she would feel the heat and strength of his body against hers. The thought sent a sensual shiver through her.

He stopped and his lips left hers to ask, “Are you cold?”

She shook her head. “Needy for you.”

He brought her nightdress up and over her head in one swift motion, tossing it aside. Then he lifted her and laid her gently on the bed, coming down beside her. “I am going to touch and taste every part of you, beginning here.”

His fingers teased her one nipple and she was soon lost in a cloud of pure passion. He licked, nibbled and kissed his way down her body, and she sighed and moaned, quite loud, with pleasure.

Her excited cries turned him harder and the way her body so eagerly responded to his touch made it difficult not to slip over and into her just yet. He wanted to bring her endless pleasure and in so doing he would bring himself the same.

“Enough,” Emma finally begged. “I must have you inside me now.”

And he damn well wanted to be there himself. He moved over her and slipped inside her with ease, she was so wet. He set a fast pace, knowing it would not take long. They both were too close to the edge, ready to topple off.

Emma came first, screaming his name, and he followed soon after, though he kept driving into her, knowing she would climax again, and she did. Her moan of sheer satisfaction sent a ripple through him, driving hard the last of his climax.

He moved off her, grabbing the soft wool blanket up from the end of the bed to pull over them. Then he collapsed next to her and she quickly wrapped herself around him. His arm circled her, nestling her closer and only after she fell asleep, which took only a few minutes, did he allow himself to drift off.

~~~

Rogan woke with a start and knew why without looking. His wife was absent from their bed and their bedchamber. He did not know how she could wake and slip away without him hearing or sensing her. He would much prefer to wake up and find her in his arms, and he was going to let her know that as soon as he found her.

Warriors were entering the Great Hall, the morning meal just being served when Rogan stepped into the room. He gave a quick glance around, assuming he would find his wife there, but after a thorough search, she was not to be found. He grabbed a hunk of bread off a nearby table and stopped a servant to inquire if she had seen Emma.
~~~

"No, my lord, but she usually rises before most and is well gone before the morning meal is served."

He shook his head and spotting Maura approached her. "Has Emma been to visit her father this morning?"

"Emma never visits with him in the morning, my lord. She rises much earlier than her father and does not wish to disturb him."

"Would you know where she might be?"

Maura smiled. "Emma is not an easy one to keep track of, my lord. Patience got to the point where she assigned a warrior to follow her, since she would disappear for hours, sometimes half the day, and worry her sisters senseless. Somehow Emma would lose the warrior and he would return to face Patience's wrath. Finally, Patience gave up, and let Emma have her way. Emma can be fearless."

"Fearless or foolish?" Rogan said with a shake of his head.

"Does it not take foolishness to be fearless?" Maura said with a smile, though did not wait for a response. "You might try the monk's cottage in the woods. She goes there sometimes in the morning."

"Thank you, Maura," he said and after retrieving his cloak from his bedchamber left the keep and inquired directions to the monk's cottage. Though he had been there, he could not recall the way. Besides, he was too annoyed that she would take the chance and return there by herself after the ghost warriors had shown up there.

He could not wait to leave here and get her

home. At least, there he had the advantage of knowing the area. Besides she would have enough to keep her busy with tending to the many changes needed to his keep, which he had only realized ran far too inefficiently compared to how efficiently the Macinnes keep ran.

The quiet of the woods settled around him as he made his way to the cottage. New leaves rustled overhead and soon the trees would be bursting with them. The sky was overcast and the scent of rain was in the air. He shook his head, thinking of Emma walking this path alone. The woods held beauty, but it also held danger. He hurried his pace, anxious to see that his wife was safe.

Rogan was relieved when he finally came upon the forlorn cottage. Emma was nowhere to be seen outside, so he marched straight to the door, his heart beating a bit faster with concern. He did not knock. He opened the door and entered with a quick step.

He was shocked, though also pleased to see her standing there, a dirk drawn, prepared to defend herself.

She shook her head and scolded him as she went to return the dirk to the sheath at her waist. "I could have hurt you."

He laughed. "I think not."

Rogan felt the wisp of air against his ear as the dirk flew past and landed in the frame of the door behind him. He glared at his wife. "Patience taught you?" He closed the door and retrieved the dirk, handing it to her.

Emma nodded, taking the weapon from him and

slipping it back in the sheath. "She did, insisted on it, since I spent so much time alone."

"That is changed now," Rogan said and stepped forward. The space was so small that it took only one step to reach the opposite side of the table from Emma.

Her brow scrunched, as if she did not quite understand him.

"You will not be spending so much time alone."

"But I will not surrender it entirely," she said, as if declaring an edict.

"You do not want to spend time with me?" he asked and stepped slowly around the table to her side.

She was quick to smile and to settle her hand on his chest. "I love being with you."

He rested his hand over hers. "Then why do you leave our bed so early."

"I love the morning when sunrise peaks on the horizon and the mist is just beginning to lift off the land. It is so quiet, so peaceful, and so beautiful. I cannot resist being part of it."

"And I cannot resist the desire to find my wife naked in my arms in the morning, so I can show her how much I love her." He kissed her, a soft, lingering kiss that had her slipping her arms around his neck and had his arms coiling around her waist.

Emma sighed and rested her brow against his when it finally ended. "Then my desire to make love with you in the morning is proper?"

He kissed her quick. "Passion does not always wait for a proper time or place. When you have a need for me, tell me."

"And you will do the same?"

"Aye, wife, I will."

"And what if I need you often?" she asked quite guilelessly.

"Have me as often as you like."

"You will not grow tired of me?"

"Never," he whispered and kissed her again.

"I want you now," she said and reached down, her hand disappearing beneath his plaid. She loved holding him and stroking him and having him grow hard in her hand.

"Keep that up and it will be a fast joining," he warned and felt himself swell with each stroke and tug.

"Oh, yes, please," she said on a heavy sigh, "I am so wet and wanting."

Damn, if she did not torment with words as well as her hand.

Her touch turned more ardent and he would not last if...

He shoved her hand off him and lifted her, intending to order her to wrap her legs around his waist, but it was not necessary. She did so on her own as he carried her around the table to brace her back against the door. He held her firm with one arm, while he hoisted her skirt, pushed his plaid aside, and found his way between her legs to plunge into her.

Emma cried out, which fired his blood even more, and he held her waist tight as he drove in and out of her fast and hard.

Emma kept her legs secured around her

husband's waist and her arms around his neck, never believing that being slammed hard against a door could feel so good. She tried to hold back her climax, wanting the titillating sensations consuming her body to last a while longer, but it was impossible. She burst in such a fiery explosion, screaming her pleasure aloud, over and over.

Her passion-filled cries sent Rogan crashing into his own climax and surging when Emma gave a sharp shout, another climax having hit her. He came so damn hard that he had to brace his one hand against the door for support while he kept his one arm firm around her.

Her head dropped on his shoulder as she fought to control her ragged breathing. She was glad Rogan was not in a hurry to slip out of her, since she was continuing to enjoy the last ripples of her climax as they faded from her body.

It was several moments before they separated and Rogan eased her to her feet, their respective garments falling in place as he did.

Rogan curled a stray strand of her hair behind her ear. "Was I too rough? I did not hurt you, do I?"

Emma smiled from ear to ear. "It was perfect and I feel wonderful. I believe I have found a cure for anything that ails me."

"I will tend you anytime you feel the need," he said with a grin.

"Then it is good you have such stamina, for I am very needy."

"I never thought I would be happy to have a needy wife," he said with a laugh.

She grabbed his hand. "Come—"

"I already have." He laughed again and Emma playfully punched him in the arm.

"I came here to collect some things that I would like to take *home* with me."

"I will help," he said glad that she was thinking of what she wanted to take home with her and even more pleased that she had referred to his home as home. He knew it was not easy for her and that she was making the effort to accept it, made him love her all the more.

It did not take them long to collect what Emma wanted. She explained to Rogan that after the monk had died she had moved most of the things she wanted to retain to the keep. What they gathered now, she felt she could make good use of at home.

The more she mentioned *home*, the more eager he was to be on his way there.

Once they finished, they stepped outside to see that the sky was awash with dark clouds and rain was imminent.

"We best hurry," Rogan said, turning to his wife to see that she was frozen in place, staring at the cottage. His heart went out to her when he saw the sadness on her face.

"Duncan taught me so much. I would race here every morning and he would be waiting to teach me. I had so wished that I had more time with him. His knowledge was so vast, though he told me that he gave me a good foundation and I was to build on it. I miss him so much."

"I am sure such a learned monk is grateful for having had the time he had with you, someone who truly wished to receive his knowledge and carry it on."

Emma sighed. "He told me that the heavens brought him here to me and that he was grateful to have known me."

"We will visit with your father and your sisters, and you will come here again," he assured her.

Emma shook her head. "No, there is nothing here for me any longer." She closed the door and turned, taking Rogan's hand. "My life is with you now, and Duncan would be the first to tell me that."

"I would have liked this Duncan," Rogan said. "Tell me about him."

And Emma did as they walked back to the keep.

They no sooner entered the village than someone approached Emma about an ailing elder.

"Go," Rogan said when she looked to him. "I will take these things to the keep and see you when you finish."

Emma smiled and kissed his cheek before running off.

There was not much Emma could do for one as aged as Agnes. A soothing brew and conversation was the most help she could offer.

"I will miss you, Emma," Agnes said, her gnarled fingers gripping the goblet as best she could. "You are such a kind and loving soul." Agnes lowered her voice as if not wanting anyone else but Emma to hear, though there was no one in the cottage but the two of them. "And you are the most beautiful of your sisters."

Emma was stunned.

Agnes nodded slowly. "It is true. Your beauty is

rare and not visible to everyone, but those lucky enough to see it are granted the privilege of seeing beauty at its finest."

A knock at the door interrupted Emma's shocked silence.

Marianna entered. "I am sorry to disturb, but when you finish, my lady, my son wishes to see you."

"Is he all right?" Emma asked with concern.

"In pain, but as I told him, he is alive, so he has no reason to complain."

"Wise words," Agnes said and turned to Emma. "Go, you are needed. And know I wish you a long life, many children and enduring love."

Emma was hesitant to leave her, knowing in her heart she would never see Agnes again.

"Marianna, will you join me for one of Emma's healing brews?" Agnes asked.

Marianna nodded with a smile. "These old, complaining bones could use some healing." She turned to Emma. "Go, with our blessings, your time here is done."

Emma tearfully hugged the two women, giving Agnes a longer hug and bid them good-bye. She hurried out the door, her eyes brimming with tears.

She was only a few steps away from the cottage when she was grabbed and wrapped in strong arms. She sunk into their strength, knowing they belonged to her husband.

"What is wrong?" Rogan asked, holding her tight.

"Good-byes are much too difficult," she said not

able to stop her tears from falling.

"I am sorry, Emma, I do not wish our leaving to cause you pain."

"I know and it is not your fault," she assured him, wiping her tears away. "And what are you doing here? You said you would wait at the keep."

"I intended to, until I recalled what happened yesterday and decided I would remain your shadow today so that you do not exhaust yourself again." He released her, though took her hand. "Now where are you off to?"

"Daniel's cottage, and, Rogan," —she stared at him unable to find words as a teardrop hung from her one eyelash.

Rogan wiped it away with his thumb. "I am here for you, wife, and I always will be."

His words touched her heart and she held firm to his hand as they walked through the village together. When they reached the cottage, Rogan told her he would wait outside. After giving her a light kiss, he walked over to a worn bench and sat, stretching his long legs out in front of him.

Emma smiled when he settled himself comfortably, letting her know he would wait for her as long as it took. She entered the cottage, eager to be done with Daniel so that she could spend time with her husband. She was surprised when Helen excused herself and stepped outside. She approached Daniel who appeared to be doing well, of which she was glad.

"What can I do for you, Daniel?" she asked with a warm smile, stopping next to the bed.

"I am fine, Emma, thanks to your bravery and

knowledge." He coughed lightly, then spoke up. "I want to apologize for what I did to you when we were young. It was wrong of me and I regret it most profoundly. I do hope you can find it in your heart to forgive a fool like me."

Emma stared at him, not quite sure it was Daniel who had spoken. Where had this sudden heartfelt apology come from? He had already apologized when he thought he would not survive the mill accident. So why do so again and with such sincerity?

It dawned on her then. "Did my husband force you to apologize?"

"I had all intentions of apologizing for my horrid behavior."

"That is not what I asked, Daniel," she said. "Did my husband force you to apologize?"

"He persuaded me to do the honorable thing," Daniel said and lowered his voice. "And I would be grateful if you would express your appreciation that I did so and in a most sincere manner, for I am truly sorry, Emma. And let him also know that I will tell everyone how I apologized to you."

He wore his worry for all to see and fear quivered his voice, and Emma felt sorry for him. "My husband frightens you."

"Aye, he does," Daniel admitted without hesitation. "He is a mighty warrior who could do me great harm with the mere swat of his hand. And that he loves you makes it all the more possible that he would have his revenge. But I will say it again regardless of that... I truly am sorry."

"You do not have to keep apologizing. I was just as foolish for thinking myself in love with you when all I wanted was a lad to pay me the attention that was paid to my sisters."

"You did not love me?" he asked, sounding disappointed.

"At the time I thought I did, but looking back on it," —she laughed— "I was jealous of my sisters and you were sniffing after me, so you were—convenient. Now if all is well with you, I will be on my way."

Daniel nodded. "I am fine."

"Good, then do as I told you and you should continue to heal." Emma left the cottage, talking briefly with Helen before going to her husband who was already headed her way.

His arm no sooner went around her, then one of Rogan's warriors approached with a shout. "Stay here," he said to Emma and went to the warrior who hurried toward him.

Emma's stomach clenched, watching the exchange. It was obvious something was wrong.

Rogan returned to her in quick strides. "My father has taken ill. We need to return home now."

Chapter Twenty-six

"We travel fast, so take only what is necessary," Rogan instructed as he walked her to the keep. "Have your servants packed what you wish to take from here and I will leave a few warriors behind to bring your belongings as soon as they are made ready."

"Do you know how ill your father is?" Emma asked with concern for Rogan and for her own father since she would have to leave him, and his illness still lingered.

"No, but the message is from Liam and he would not summon me if he did not think it serious. Now hurry, we leave shortly."

Emma went straight to her father and was pleased to see him up, standing by the hearth, his cheeks flushed and a hardy smile on his face. It faded when he took one look at her.

"What is wrong?" her father asked, opening his arms to her.

She ran into them and he closed them tightly around her. It was as if she was a young lass again and all was right, her worries fading with her father's generous and loving hug. For a moment, she allowed herself to believe that her father's arms could dissolve her problems and all would be well.

But the truth was that she was leaving him and would no longer be able to seek his reassuring arms or even speak to him every day.

"Emma?" he questioned with worry.

She raised her head off his strong chest. "Rogan and I must leave now." She went on to explain what had happened.

"Of course, you must go and see to Rogan's father," he said when she finished. "You are not to worry about me. I am doing well, and Maura will continue to tend me when needed. You will return to visit and celebrate when your sisters come home."

He sounded so confident that Patience and Heather would return home that it gave her own belief a boost, though she asked, "You will let me know the King's response to your letter?"

"As soon as I hear," he said. "Now you must hurry. I am sure Rogan is impatient to leave." He hugged Emma tightly. "I believe Rogan will be a good husband to you, Emma, so be an obedient wife." He grinned. "Or at least try to obey him."

She laughed softly. "I will do my best, Da."

"Then Rogan will have no complaints."

Emma's eyes filled with tears and her heart pounded in her chest as she gave her father one last hug. When he kissed her cheek and told her he loved her, she had to run from the room, not wanting to cry in front of him and upset him.

Servants were waiting in her room to help her, but she left the decision of what garments she should take to them. She was more concerned with what herbs she would require to help Angus

MacClennan. She made certain to speak with Maura before she left, the woman assuring her that she was not to worry about her da, that she would look after him and he would be fine.

In no time, Emma found herself on her mare ready to leave.

Rogan approached her on his steed, the horse prancing hard, as anxious as his master to leave. "We will ride hard and fast, Emma. If you tire, let me know and you can ride with me and rest. I do not plan on stopping until we are home."

Emma nodded and watched her husband take the lead and his warriors surround her as they rode off. She did not dare look back at her home or she thought for certain her heart would rip from her chest. She may have gained a loving husband throughout this whole debacle, but she had lost so much.

She longed for the days when worry was limited to minor problems and the evening was shared with her father and sisters. And she had time to pursue her interests and learn all she could. But then Rogan would be lost to her, and she found that she quite liked having him around. Life would not be bad with him. Actually, she could not see a day without him. She had grown accustomed to him and found that she favored sleeping with him. She had not thought she would want to share her bed with any man, but Rogan was not any man... he was exceptional, and he belonged to her.

A roll of thunder had her glancing up at the cloudy sky. Rain seemed likely and if it proved a downpour, then it could slow their pace.

An hour later they were forced to take whatever shelter they could find against the pouring rain. She snuggled in Rogan's arms beneath a pine tree, the thick growth of branches preventing them from getting completely soaked.

Emma suffered little from the rain, Rogan having wrapped his cloak around her, tucking her close against him.

"This will delay us," he said annoyed.

"I am sure your healers have matters well in hand," Emma said, trying to reassure him.

"Matters cannot be good if Liam sent for me."

She tried to ease his worries. "Once the rain slows we will be on our way home soon enough."

"You will make him well," Rogan said, though it sounded more a command.

"I will do all I can," Emma assured him.

"Then he will get well soon enough," Rogan said with confidence. He hugged her close and shook his head. "I sometimes think I lost my da along with my mum the day she died. And I often wish the Da I knew would return home, but I think he would prefer to join my mum."

"He stopped living, he needs to start again."

"He refuses."

"He needs a push," Emma said.

"I have tried, but it is useless. He has turned all the duties of running the clan over to me and no doubt will soon relinquish the title of laird to me. He does nothing, but drink and drown in his sorrows."

"He has not drowned yet. There is still hope."

"It would take a miracle to set him right, but enough of my father. How are you?"

"I am fine."

"Truthfully?" Rogan asked. "I yanked you away from your father so fast that you barely had time to bid him good-bye."

"It was not easy, but when I gave it thought the prospect of not having you in my life every day outweighed the sorrow I felt about leaving my da. I will see him again. You, I want to see every day." She kissed him softly. "I want to do that often. I want to be in your arms whenever possible, and I want," —she slipped her hand beneath his plaid— "to touch you and feel you grow hard in my hand." She stroked him to life.

"Bloody hell, woman," he grumbled, squeezing his eyes shut against the delectable feel of her determined touch.

"I love the feel of you swelling in my hand," she whispered and gripped him firmer, eager to bring some joy to him and herself.

"Emma, you must stop," he groaned quietly.

"Why? Do you not enjoy it? I do."

Her innocent remark flamed his already heated passion.

"No one is near. No one can see what we do. And I want to chase your worries if only for a while as you did mine."

"And what of your pleasure?"

She smiled. "You can see to it later," —she released him and cupped his thick sac in her hand— "though the delicious feel of you just may have me climaxing."

He jerked when her hand returned to grab the long hard length of him and he had no want to stop her. He could think of nothing but how good she was making him feel in the middle of a downpour under a towering pine. He had planned to show her that making love knew no specific time or place and here she was showing him that she instinctively understood that.

She turned her lips on his neck, though it was light, loving nips she settled upon him. He caught himself before he groaned aloud, fearful that it would drift off on the wind and become a roar.

"Emma," he ground through clamped teeth, feeling himself ready to explode.

"Good lord, how I want you," she murmured and hoisted her skirt just far enough so that she could rub him against that tiny spot that brought her so much pleasure.

Rogan exploded in a blinding fury and it magnified when he heard Emma sigh her release as she continued to tug and stroke until he was completely spent and her ripples had faded.

She wished she could linger in the moment with him, but that would not be prudent. She almost laughed. What she had just done had not been prudent, but it had been extremely enjoyable and so very satisfying. She reluctantly tucked his plaid back over him, straightened her garments, and then dropped her head on his chest. "That left me spent." His chest shook against her cheek as a chuckle rumbled through it, and she smiled.

"Not half as much as me," he said his hand

slipping up to the back of her head, grabbing a handful of hair and gently tugging her head back. "I owe you for that, wife," he said playfully and kissed her quick.

She smiled. "I shall make certain you pay your debt."

He laughed. "I have a feeling I will be indebted to you often."

"A distinct possibility," she said and blinked as a raindrop splattered on the tip of her nose.

Rogan rubbed it away with his own nose, then looked past her. "The rain is slowing and the clouds scattering."

Emma turned in his arms, resting back against him. The rain was clearing off. The warriors would soon show themselves, leaving their private moment left to memories. She wanted to make a ton of memories with Rogan so that she could cherish each and every one of them through the many years to come.

The warriors were soon gathered and mounted and ready to continue their journey. Emma knew there would be no more stops made. They would ride into the night until they finally arrived home, and that was what they did. They rode nonstop, until they arrived home completely exhausted.

Though it was late, the village stirred upon their arrival. Liam met them at the keep's steps, looking as if he just woke.

Rogan gave no greeting, he asked, "My father?"

"Feverish," Liam answered gravely.

"Take me to him," Emma said and hurried into

the keep.

They quietly entered a sparse bedchamber that appeared more fitting for a monk than the laird of a large clan. Bertha sat beside the bed, her hands knitted in worry, though she stood quickly when seeing they had entered.

"Thank the good Lord you are home," Bertha said, laying eyes on Rogan. "He keeps asking for you."

Rogan approached the bed just as his father's eyes fluttered open.

"Is he here yet, Bertha?" Angus asked with difficulty.

Rogan was at his side instantly, taking hold of his hand. "I am here, Da."

"Good. Good, for I fear I will be joining your mother soon."

As father and son shared a private moment, Emma waved Bertha aside and walked to the hearth with her to speak in hushed tones.

"What happened?" Emma asked.

She shrugged. "I am not sure. He turned feverish one day and it has grown worse."

"Had he complained about anything before the fever struck?"

Bertha shook her head. "Nothing. He was his usual self, eating, drinking, and feeling sorry for himself."

"And you noticed nothing—nothing at all—different about him?"

Bertha shook her head, and then suddenly stopped. "Now that you ask, I thought he was walking oddly one day, though I dismissed it, thinking it nothing more than his drinking."

"How oddly?"

"Like he was tilting or favoring one leg over the other."

"Thank you, Bertha," Emma said and approached the bed.

"Can you help him?" Rogan asked anxiously.

"I need to see his legs," Emma said.

"You will not be looking at my legs, lassie," his father argued.

Emma paid him no mind. She grabbed the blanket before anyone could stop her and threw it off him. The others gasped at the sight of his one swollen and discolored leg. She shook her head and turned to Rogan. "Turn him on his side, so I can see the back of his leg."

"You will not—"

Rogan paid him no mind and did as his wife said and turned his father on his side. He gasped again when he saw the back of his father's leg.

"I took a fall. It is nothing," his father insisted.

Emma bent over to examine it more closely. It held no stench, a good sign. But it would not be long before it did, if she did not cleanse it and attempt to draw out what poison had already settled in. Something caught her eye before she turned away and she leaned closer. She shook her head.

"What is wrong?" Rogan asked.

"He took a splinter of wood when he fell and it rots his leg. I must get it out for the leg to heal."

"You will not be touching my leg, lassie," his father commanded.

Emma ignored her father-in-law and looked to Bertha. "Get plenty of ale and hot water."

"Are you listening to me, lass?" Angus yelled.

"No," Emma shouted as loudly as he had.

"I am the laird of this clan and—"

"Then behave like one and do not be such a coward," she said.

"You dare call me a coward?" Angus said, spitting out his words in frustration.

"Prove to me you are not," she challenged.

Rogan thought to interfere, concerned for his father, then he realized that his wife knew well what she was doing and he stepped aside and let her have her way.

"Get out," Angus yelled.

"You waste your breath, old man, you will not win this," Emma said.

"Old man? Not win this?" Angus turned red with fury.

Before he could say another word, Emma leaned down in his face. "Your fury would be better spent on fighting to live. Do you not want to see grandchildren born? Spend time with a granddaughter perhaps that looks like your Anna and bears her name? And what of your son? He does not wish to lose you. Stop being selfish and fight to live."

Angus glared at her, and then his eyes softened. "You are as bold as my Anna was."

"Then be as courageous as she believed you to be."

"Tell me what I must do," Angus said capitulating.

"Be strong, for it will be painful."

"Nothing is as painful as losing my Anna."

~~~

Rogan woke alone in bed and let a string of oaths fly. Once dressed, he headed to his father's bedchamber. He should have known his wife would not leave his ailing father's side, even though she had insisted that she would come wake him when it was his turn to sit watch over Angus. She had also chased Bertha off to rest, though she had wanted to take the first watch. Emma would not hear of it, insisting it was necessary that she stay and make certain all went well.

He entered his father's bedchambers to find his wife slumped in a chair asleep beside the bed. His father slept soundly and although he was pale, he looked at peace. No pain knitted his brow as it did last night.

Bertha bustled in shortly after him and stood beside him at the end of the bed.

"He looks better," she whispered, "though your wife could do with some rest, since she has been here far longer than needed."

"You will sit with my father?" Rogan asked, though he knew she would.

"I will and I will also see that our two healers alternate time with me so that it is not necessary for Emma or you to sit watch."

"Excellent," Rogan said, knowing his wife would protest and knowing he would not give her a
~~~

choice.

"You best get her to bed and leave her there alone," Bertha said with a poke of her elbow to his side. She went right on talking, not giving him a chance to reprimand her. "I see the love and passion in her eyes every time she looks at you. And being a man, especially one who loves his wife as much as she loves him, you are not going to deny her and she needs rest. She worked hard to save your foolish father's life. So put her to bed and leave her be for her own well-being."

"Her love for me is that obvious?" he asked when he should have admonished her.

Bertha grinned. "You both wear your love for each other openly. A fool could even see it. Now go put her to bed, not take her to bed."

Rogan shook his head. He did not need Bertha telling him what to do. He had had every intention of doing exactly that, though he would have preferred to take his wife to bed.

He walked over to Emma and gently lifted her in his arms.

Her eyes flickered open and she smiled. "Right where I want to be, in my husband's arms."

"I am putting you to bed."

"That is even better," she said and snuggled her face against his chest.

It would be a struggle to leave her alone in bed when he wanted so badly to make love to her and she obviously wanted the same. So, he was relieved when he found Liam waiting outside his bedchamber door.

"We need to talk," Liam said. "Is Emma all

right?"

"Nothing sleep will not cure," Rogan said. "Let me settle her first."

"I will wait in the Great Hall."

"No," Rogan said abruptly. "Wait here and make certain the door stays open."

Liam grinned.

"Not one word," Rogan warned and Liam laughed.

Rogan placed his wife gently on the bed, removed her boots, and pulled the blanket over her. He did not trust himself to remove any of her garments.

"Rogan," she whispered in a husky voice that tempted and invited.

"Later, my love," he said, giving her cheek a tender kiss. "You rest. I have matters I must see to." She went to protest and he pressed a finger to her lips. "Rest."

He quickly left the room, shutting the door behind him, and listened to Liam laugh the whole way down the hall.

Chapter Twenty-seven

The Great Hall was empty except for a few servants. Rogan and Liam sat at one of the trestle tables closest to the hearth. Servants were quick to place platters of food and pitchers of drink in front of them, and then disappear.

"It took a skillful hand and a knowledgeable mind to do what your wife did last night."

"I know. I was in awe watching her."

"The way she handled your father was remarkable. You have an exceptional wife," Liam said and raised his tankard.

"That I do," Rogan agreed and raised his tankard as well. "Now, what did you want to tell me?"

Liam lowered his voice, though no servant stood close enough to hear them. "I have found signs that the ghost warriors watch us and that unsettles me."

Rogan nodded. "If you found signs, then it is obvious the ghost warriors want us to know they watch us. You found these signs while I was gone?"

"I did, and I cannot help but wonder what they want from us."

Rogan shared how the ghost warriors had made themselves known to him and Emma while at Emma's home.

"They warn you to stay away and yet Heather

asks for help. What will you do?" Liam asked.

"There is little recourse left to me that does not have tremendous consequences to it. The Dark Dragon's warriors are superior in every way and their number huge. We could lose hundreds of men to him and still not conquer him, and then what? We become more vulnerable, an easy prey for a mighty warrior clan. And if the King should side with the Dark Dragon, then I bring the King's ire down upon my clan."

"You are caught in a trap."

"The question is, though, who planned and set the trap?" Rogan said.

"It would seem the Dark Dragon."

"At first glance, it would seem that way, but what if that is what the person wants everyone to believe?"

"But who has cause to bring this about?" Liam asked.

"I think that is what I need to learn before I do anything else."

Rogan and Liam continued talking and eating until both men took their leave. Rogan did not trust himself to remain in the keep, away from his wife, so he went off to occupy himself elsewhere.

It was not until several hours later that he returned, hoping his wife had a good rest, for he was eager to join her in bed. He opened the door to his bedchamber quietly in case she still slept.

A growl rose deep from his chest when he saw the bed empty. He headed for his father's room with all intentions of throwing her over his shoulder and carting her back to their bedchamber where he planned to keep her for the next couple of hours.

Then the thought struck that his father had worsened and Bertha had summoned her. He hurried his steps and entered the room only to have Bertha raise a finger to her lips for him to be quiet, and then she shooed him out of the room, though followed.

"He rests comfortably, the fever lingering, though thankfully not spiking. Emma insists he is to rest and not be disturbed."

"When was Emma here?" Rogan asked.

"Hours ago. I told her that she should listen to her own advice."

"I will see that she does," he said and turned and stormed off.

He expected to find her without a problem, a foolish thought on his part. After searching for some time, he came to the disturbing conclusion that she had gone into the woods on her own and had possibly gotten lost. He had quickly summoned Liam and a few warriors to begin searching the woods when he saw her stumble out of the storehouse, brushing dirt off her garments.

"Do not dare grin at me," Rogan warned Liam, who laughed as he walked away. Rogan made his way over to her and was about to release his anger, when she smiled.

"I have missed you," she said, throwing her arms around him and hugging him tight.

She vanquished his anger with loving words and a hug, and his arms circled her, squeezing her tight.

"Hmmm," she sighed. "It feels so wonderful to

be in your arms."

How did he chastise her when she greeted him so favorably? Still though, she needed to know that she could not simply go off and disappear. "I feared something dreadful had happened to you."

"How could that be? Surely, I am safe in your village," she said, informing him of what he should already know.

"Of course you are safe here, but I thought perhaps you had gone off to explore the woods."

"I would never venture that far when your father might require my attention," she said. "I will save that pleasure for another time—"

"You will not go alone," Rogan ordered.

"Do you forget I have tracking skills? I have ventured into unknown woods before and not gotten lost," she said and smiled again, "though I intend to have Liam show me the area before I go foraging in the woods alone."

"Whether you can track or not, you will never venture into the woods alone," Rogan ordered empathically. His hand went up when she looked to protest. "Do not defy me on this, Emma. You will do as I say."

Emma stepped away from him annoyed, her smile fading. She was not accustomed to her freedom being curtailed. She was more accustomed to doing as she pleased.

He did not like that she walked away from him and paced, or that her brow knitted in frustration. "I do not do this to rob you of the freedom you have enjoyed. I do it for my own sanity, so please take pity on your poor husband, for I do not know what I would do without you."

Her smile returned, and she sighed and hurried to throw her arms around his neck once again. "You say the loveliest things to me."

"Then you will do as I say?" he asked, pressing his lips to her brow.

"I will not lie to you, so I cannot promise I will do as you ask, though I will try," she said. "Old habits die hard and sometimes I simply take off for the woods without thinking, especially when I find I am in need of solace."

"You have me for that now," he said and reaffirmed it with a kiss that left no doubt.

"And how long did you intend to take before you introduced your wife to me?" a sharp female voice reprimanded.

Rogan shook his head, smiled, and released his wife as he turned and spread his arms out to the woman, "Ina."

Emma was startled by the red-haired, shapely beauty. That they were friends were obvious by the way she had spoken to him. When she saw Liam approach with a smile, she knew the woman must be his wife.

"Emma," Rogan said, "I want you to meet Ina, Liam's wife and a woman who is like a pesky, little sister to me."

Ina swatted his arm as she stepped out of his embrace. "It is your own fault that I am a pest. You both were forever trying to be rid of me when we were young."

Liam slipped his arm around his wife and

smiled. "But you made that impossible and in the process taught me much about tracking."

Ina swatted him as well. "We three were meant to be family, Rogan my brother and you my husband, and I was not about to have it any other way." She stepped away from her husband and reached out and hugged Emma. "Now I have a sister, something I have always longed for."

Emma returned the hug, having missed the sisterly hugs she had so often shared with her own sisters.

Ina took hold of Emma's hand. "When you have time come and visit with me. There is much I can tell you about your husband."

"Ina," Rogan warned teasingly.

"I would like that," Emma said.

Ina nodded. "Aye, and it is pleased I am that you are here, for the villagers boast of what a fine healer we now have. You have attended many births?"

Emma heard the anxiousness in her voice and wondered over it. "Aye, many. Are you with child?"

Ina's smile vanished. "We have yet to be blessed."

Emma heard the sorrow in Ina's voice and saw the concern on Liam's face for his wife. She understood now. Ina was unable to get with child.

"We should talk," Emma said, hoping that perhaps she could help Ina in some way.

Ina grew anxious. "I would like that."

"My lady, my lady," someone shouted, and they

all turned to see a servant from the keep rushing toward them. "It is the laird. He needs you."

Emma hoisted her skirt and took off in a run. Rogan was quick to follow.

It did not surprise Emma to find that Angus's fever had spiked. She had been expecting it. It was whether she could get him through it that worried her the most. She was quick to examine the wound again and was pleased to see that the swelling had gone done and though the redness remained, it had not grown worse.

"I am dying," Angus moaned. "I am dying."

"Now is the time to fight... not surrender," Emma encouraged and did all she could so his words would not ring true.

Rogan thought he would have to carry her from the room hours later when his father's fever lessened and he fell into a fitful sleep.

"You need nourishment," Rogan insisted his hand firm around her arm so that she could not slip away from him as he escorted her out of the room.

"He may need me."

"You will be summoned if he does, but right now you are going to the Great Hall with me and we are going to eat," Rogan said in a tone that left no room for her to argue, not that she did not try.

"But I am not—"

Her stomach gurgled so loudly that it had both their eyes opening wide.

"I guess I am hungry," she said with a laugh.

They sat in the Great Hall enjoying a meal and talking. He debated sharing Liam's news that there were signs of ghost warriors nearby. He feared she might attempt to find them and try to talk with them. They had, however, been honest with each other thus far and he wanted to keep it that way.

"It would seem they are keeping watch on us," Emma said after he had related the news to her.

"Another reason you are not to go off alone," he said adamantly.

"This is so perplexing," she said with a sigh.

"No, it is simple. You keep me aware of where you go, and no disappearing into woods, until we can make sense of this."

"That is not what I was referring to," she said with a wave of her hand. "None of this makes any sense."

"On that we agree," he said. "And you agree not to cause me worry?"

She kissed his cheek. "I will do my best."

He slipped his arm around her and leaned down to whisper in her ear, "Perhaps I should keep you busy in our bedchamber."

Emma slipped her hand beneath the table and beneath his plaid in answer.

Rogan sucked in a breath as her hand began to toy with him. "Be careful, my love, or you will find yourself upstairs in our bedchamber for the remainder of the day."

"Is that a promise because it certainly fails as a threat," she murmured and gave him a hard squeeze.

He grinned. "You are going to pay for this."

"Again," she grinned, "a promise, for once again it fails as a threat. And whether it is either, I suggest you make good on it posthaste, since I am so very wet and ready for you." She felt him swell in her hand. "Hmmm, and you are so ready for me."

He nuzzled her neck. "That is it. Now you are my prisoner."

She giggled softly. "Will you tie me up?"

"Do not tempt me," he groaned at the image her words provoked.

He grabbed her hand and moved it off him. "Our bedchamber now," he ordered.

Before they made another move, one of Rogan's warriors hurried into the Great Hall and approached him with haste.

"A problem with two warriors, my lord," the man said anxiously.

Rogan knew he would not be summoned if the problem between the two men had not gotten out of hand. He turned to Emma. "You will remain right here until I get back."

She pressed her cheek to his. "I will be waiting for you naked in bed."

"Emma, so help me—"

"Do not make threats or promises you will not keep, for you will sorely disappoint me."

"Never would I disappoint you," he whispered and kissed her gently.

She sighed, her elbows on the table and her chin resting in her hands as she watched him walk away. She could not be more pleased that she had wed such a loving and wonderful man. She was truly blessed.

She finished the cider in her tankard before she headed for their bedchamber, only to be stopped by a servant. It seemed the cook wished to speak with her if it was a convenient time.

Surely, Rogan would be several minutes at least. So, there were a few moments to spare. She followed the servant to the kitchen and one look told her that much work needed to be done here.

The cook, a stalwart, solidly built woman asked if Emma would inspect her kitchen and pass on any advice necessary. That was all Emma needed. She set the whole staff to cleaning the kitchen. While they did, she went to inspect the kitchen garden.

It was a poor excuse for one. She bent down and scooped up a handful of soil. She squished it between her fingers, weighed it in her hand, and then let it fall between her fingers. It felt tired. The monk had taught her how to judge the soil for planting. It was one of the reasons Macinnes crops did so well. Now she would see that the MacClennan crops did the same.

Some parts of the soil required rest while the whole patch required feeding. She would have the patch cleared and made larger, then see to nourishing it. In a couple of weeks it would be ready to receive seeds and produce hardy plants.

She turned to return to the kitchen and was startled by a man draped in a worn, tattered cloak that smelled so bad she took a step back.

"Sorry, my lady, I mean no offense, but I must speak with you."

Emma stepped closer, the voice having a familiar cadence to it.

"Please, so no one suspects anything, bring me food and drink. I will wait by the large oak tree," he said with a bob of his head, then slowly plodded over to the tree, a few feet from the kitchen garden.

Emma quickly gathered a loaf of bread, cheese, and a pitcher of ale and joined the stranger, under the tree.

"Thank you, my lady," he said and raised his head for their eyes to meet as he accepted the items she handed him.

Her breath caught and for a moment words were lost to her. It was Bruce, one of Patience's most trusted warriors.

Chapter Twenty-eight

"Is my sister well and why do you disguise yourself?" Emma asked and stopped before she flooded him with more questions.

"Let me explain, and then if you have questions I will answer them as best as possible," Bruce explained calmly.

"First, I want to know about my sisters," Emma said adamantly.

"Patience is fine and you are not to worry about her, but we have yet to find Heather, though we know for certain the Dark Dragon has taken her. Patience now searches for his lair."

"Surely, she does not mean to try to rescue Heather," Emma asked worried that she would do something foolish in an attempt to bring Heather home. Not that she could blame her, for she would storm the Dragon's lair herself if it meant freeing her sister.

"Patience understands full well that it would take several armies of warriors to try to win against the Dark Dragon and that would mean too much loss of life, thus leaving many clans vulnerable. But she believes two or three people could possibly succeed."

Emma's stomach clenched at the thought that

she could possibly lose two sisters to the Dark Dragon if Patience should attempt such a feat. She wished she could warn her against taking such a chance, but her advice would be wasted, for Patience would not listen. And she could not blame her. Heather had to be rescued.

"You must take a message to my sister," Emma said and told Bruce of the incident with the ghost warriors and Heather's ring, though there was no reason to explain the significance of the ring to him. She also told him that the ghost warriors continue to watch them. Her eyes turned wide. "That is why you have disguised yourself, so they do not know that you have come to speak with me."

Bruce nodded. "They are everywhere. Patience feels it is because they know that she and you will stop at nothing to see your sister returned home, and they intend to be prepared for what comes. She wants you to return home and wait to hear from her. And you are to tell Rogan MacClennan that he is to do nothing as well. She wants no one getting in the way of her plans."

"I cannot return home, for I am already home," she said and explained that she and Rogan were wed.

"Patience will want to know if you are pleased with this arrangement."

"Aye, I am," she said without hesitation. "Tell her I am very pleased. Also tell her that our father does well, thanks to Maura looking after him. And, please, tell her I miss her greatly and to bring herself and all with her home safe."

"Patience would not have it any other way. I

should go. It does not look right for you to speak at any great length with a beggar."

"Let me get you some food to take with you," she said, standing.

"I will take what is left. You must go and know that your sister misses you greatly as well."

Emma choked back the tears as she hurried away. In a way, she was relieved to have heard from Patience and know she was well and continued the search for Heather. In another way, she wished she was with her or at least able to somehow help more. She did not like feeling so helpless.

She ached for the cottage in the woods where she had sought solace, but that was no more. She had no place to slip away to seek comfort from her troubled thoughts.

Rogan.

He was her solace now, and she hurried off to find him.

~~~

Rogan stood a step inside his bedchamber shocked to find it empty. Before he lost his temper completely, he decided to see if his father had needed her. When he did not find her there, he grew annoyed. She had been so eager for them to make love. What could have been more important than making love with her husband?

His temper was mounting with each step he took when suddenly he stopped. He had spoken to her about this and she had promised to try. If he knew
~~~

anything about his wife, it was that she spoke the truth to him. Anger would do him no good. She needed time to adapt to her new life, time to accept that she had a husband who loved her and that she was no longer alone.

He headed for the stairwell, wondering if someone had required her help. He would see if anyone in the Great Hall knew of her whereabouts. With quick steps, he hurried down the stairs only to find his wife, her skirt hoisted to hasten her steps, hurrying up them.

When he saw her eyes flooded with tears that had yet to fall, he reached out and yanked her into a tight embrace. As soon as he did, she buried her face in his shirt and began to sob.

He had her up in his arms and into their bedchamber in minutes. He sat on the edge of the bed and held her as she wept.

When her tears were finally spent, she raised her head. "You truly are my solace now."

"Always," he whispered, pleased that she had taken his words to heart and had come to him for comfort, though wondered what had upset her so. He did not ask her. He waited, knowing she would tell him.

And she did, the words spilling from her lips almost as fast as her tears had fallen.

"I am relieved to know that Patience is well and still pursuing Heather," Rogan said after she detailed her talk with Bruce. "I am also glad to know that Patience is wise to the ways of the ghost warriors, though I am sorry that you and your sisters remain separated. With Patience attempting to locate the Dark Dragon's lair and your father sending the missive to the king, I am confident that all will be resolved soon and Heather brought home." He gave her a loving and reassuring squeeze.

"It will take longer than I had hoped, and what does Heather suffer while she waits for us to rescue her?"

"Heather sent you that ring to let you know she needed help. The message also told you that she knew you would come for her. She will do what is necessary to survive until you find her. Heather will not give up. Patience is not giving up and neither are we. My men are prepared to leave as soon as word reaches us. And your father assured me before we left that Macinnes warriors stand ready as well. It may not go as quickly as you would like it to, but there is no doubt that Heather will be coming home."

"I have found a better place of solace than I once had," she said and kissed him gently.

They were words he was truly pleased to hear and he returned her kiss, though it was far from the passionate ones they usually shared. And while he would not mind making love, he knew it was not what she needed right now.

"I need to talk with Liam about this and about our preparations. Why don't you go visit Ina while I do?" he said.

She rested her cheek against his and whispered, "Thank you."

He turned his head so that his lips brushed

across hers. "What for?"

"For being you." She kissed him again.

He eased her off his lap before she felt the effects of her innocent kisses. The woman could arouse him much too easily. "I will walk with you to Ina and Liam's cottage and retrieve you when I am done."

Emma laughed softly. "Is that your way of telling me to stay put?"

"It is my way of trying," he said and took her hand after he stood, "though shackling you to me might be a better idea."

"There you go tempting me," Emma said teasingly, and found her own words igniting a spark of passion in her.

"Fair play, since you tempt me with one look or one word." He found himself walking much too slowly to the door, but then his wife did not seem in a hurry.

"You are hard for me?" she asked innocently enough, though she felt anything but innocent.

Rogan stopped and turned to her. "And if I am?"

Her hand moved to see for herself, but he grabbed it, stopping her. "Do not... unless you are prepared to deal with the consequences."

Emma closed her eyes, thoughts and concern for her sisters replaced by a need for her husband. No matter how she tried to chase that need away, she could not. It consumed her like a burning fever, licking at every inch of her flesh. She wanted his hands on her, his lips on her, and, good Lord, she wanted him buried deep inside her. She wanted to explode in climax again and again.

She took a few steps away from him.

"Emma?"

She did not look at him. She kept her gaze fixed on the burning hearth. "How? How can I want you so badly after only hearing news from my sister? It is not right."

Rogan approached her, though he did not reach out and touch her. "You cannot suffer for them, Emma. You do them more justice by loving and living life. It assures you and others that they cannot take that from you, that you will not crumble or surrender. That you will stay strong and fight, as your sisters do."

Emma hurried to his side, but before she could reach out and grab him, he scooped her up and rushed her to the bed. In minutes, he had both their clothes off.

"Quick," she whispered, "I cannot bear to wait."

Rogan felt the same, feeling as if he would climax before he even entered her. He did not have to spread her legs. She threw them apart wide, welcoming him. He could not stop from reaching out and running his fingers through the mass of dark curls between her legs and teasing her soft nub with quick strokes.

"Do not, please, I beg you. I am ready to come."

He leaned down, spread her soft curls and delivered wicked licks that had her erupting in a breath-catching climax. He slipped into her quickly and easily, she was so wet, and then drove into her hard and fast, making certain to not only prolong her climax, but to make her come again. And this time he came along with her.

They lay side by side, hands joined, breathing labored, and all thought of leaving their bedchamber gone. Emma was soon snuggled in his arms and they talked and laughed and touched. And before they knew it, they were making love again. Only this time it was the slow and easy kind, the kind that explored and allowed them to learn something more about the other.

What Rogan loved about Emma was that she was not shy about asking if she was unsure or thought something improper. She was quickly learning that nothing was improper when it came to them making love. And she was also quick in trying the things she had asked about and finding to her pleasure, and definitely to his, how much she enjoyed them.

It was not until hours later, both of them completely spent, that Emma said, "I think the visit to Ina must wait until tomorrow."

Rogan laughed. "The discussion with Liam as well. The rest of the day is ours."

"You mean night. We have been here for hours."

"And still I have not gotten enough of you," he teased, nuzzling her neck.

Her stomach protested loudly, reminding them how long it had been since they had last eaten.

"I will summon a servant to bring us food," he said and got out of bed and slipped into a robe.

"Perhaps I should see how your father does," she suggested, moving to the edge of the bed.

Rogan held his hand up, stopping her. "If you

leave here, it may be hours before I find you. And I am greedy, I want you to myself. I will have a servant inquire as to how he is doing."

Emma dropped back on the pillows.

"You are exactly where I want you," Rogan said and licked his lips. "I will be having another taste of you before the night ends."

"Only if I get to taste you as well."

"The servant may have to wait," Rogan said, walking back to her.

A knock at the door stopped him and he walked over and opened it to find Bertha. As soon as he saw her face, he called out to his wife, "My father needs you."

The fever had worsened and though the wound looked to be fine, Emma could not help but worry that she had gotten to the leg too late. She reminded herself that fevers always seemed to spike at night until the worst of it had passed. She hoped this was the worst of it and the fever would finally leave him. If it lingered much longer, his chances of surviving were not good, and everyone knew it.

She doubled the ingredients of the brew she was giving him. She had tried it before with some success and also some failure, but there was little else she could do, so it was worth the try.

Surprisingly, and to everyone's relief the fever dropped and Angus returned to sleeping soundly.

Rogan and Emma returned to their bedchamber and servants brought food for them. The day quickly caught up with them as did the worry over her sisters and Rogan's father. And when they took to their bed this time, they snuggled together and fell asleep.

~~~

Emma woke before Rogan and contemplated remaining in bed until he stirred, but she got restless after a few moments. There was much to be done in and around the keep, and she so wanted to start exploring the surrounding woods before spring was in full bloom. So after what seemed like hours, though probably was nothing more than mere minutes, Emma quietly slipped out of bed, so as not to disturb Rogan, dressed, and left the room, plaiting her hair as she went.

The keep was just stirring to life and she made her way outside to the kitchen. She was determined that a more favorable morning meal was prepared for her husband and those warriors who frequented the Great Hall for their meals.

She showed the cook how to make the oatmeal porridge tastier. She also taught the cook how to prepare a more flavored fish with potatoes, well-seasoned with wild onions and the few tasty herbs she could find.

While the servants saw to the preparation of the dishes she had demonstrated, she and the cook looked over the larder. Emma was not surprised to find it poorly stocked. She decided there and then that a hunt was necessary to fatten the larder. In the meantime, she set what birds were fresh enough to cooking on spits, after soaking them in ale and herbs to the surprise of the cook.
~~~

Then she set a crew to expanding the kitchen garden. She left them all busy with their chores, wanting to explore at least the outskirts of the woods and see what it had to offer.

She was waylaid by Ina before she reached the edge of the woods.

"Have you time to talk?" Ina asked anxiously.

"Aye," Emma agreed, sensing the woman was eager to speak with her.

"What a lovely cottage," Emma remarked as she entered the sizeable home. It had two good sized rooms, a fireplace in each. It was cared for with love and kept remarkably clean with fresh rushes on the dirt floor. But it was the beautifully hand-crafted, though empty cradle near the hearth that drew her attention, and she did not waste time in asking, "You have had difficulty getting with child?"

Ina sunk down on a chair by the table, tears in her eyes. "We have tried so hard that it has become a chore. I fear I am one of those women that," —she paused, fearing to say it— "that is barren." Ina stood quickly. "Forgive me for not offering you something. Have you eaten?"

Emma shook her head. "No, but—"

"I will fix you something," Ina insisted before Emma could object.

They were soon feasting on a fine fare, the cake like bread being exceptionally tasty.

"This is very good," Emma said. "Much better than anything the cook at the keep has prepared."

"Something I have perfected over time," Ina

said. “I so want to give Liam children. He wants a whole gaggle of them, though of late he tells me differently. But I know it is to soothe my worries of not giving him a child.”

“Did your mum have only you?” Emma asked.

Ina shook her head. ”I have three brothers who serve Lord Rogan well.” Ina sighed. “I would be ever so grateful if you could help me. I feel such a failure as a wife that I cannot bear my husband a son or daughter.”

“What goes into this bread?” Emma asked, trying to decipher the taste.

Ina did not wish to talk about her bread, but she could not refuse the lady of the keep. She detailed the ingredients, though Emma stopped her at one point.

“Wild carrot? You put wild carrot in this? And you eat this frequently?”

“Aye, every day.”

Emma took what was left of the bread and threw it into the fire, the flames greedily eating it up.

Ina gasped and looked devastated. “Have I done something wrong, my lady?”

“Emma, call me Emma, please,” she said, “and no you have done nothing wrong. But I can assure you that that if you stop putting wild carrot in your food, then you will finally get with child. Wild carrot is known for keeping a woman from getting with child or disposing of a child when only carrying it for a few weeks.”

Ina’s eyes turned wide. “Truly, you think this is why I have not gotten with child?”

“I cannot be completely certain, though I do

believe it is likely."

Ina smiled. "I cannot believe it could be that simple, but I will do as you say."

"Then I have no doubt you will be welcoming a child in the winter."

"I pray you are right," Ina said with tears filling her eyes. "And I am glad you are here, for I would want you with me when I birth my babe and I will be with you when you birth yours."

Emma's cheeks flamed.

"Are you already with child?" Ina asked eagerly. "Rogan would make a wonderful father."

"That he would, but not yet. We have only wed," Emma reminded her.

"Many a lassie finds herself with child right after being wed," Ina said with a laugh.

Emma was well aware of that and it made her realize that she could very well be with child by now. The thought thrilled her, though it also upset her. If she was with child, it could prevent her from rescuing her sister and that would not do. She had to be available to Patience if she should need her. The thought weighed heavily on her, but there was nothing she could do about it. She could not start taking the wild carrot now for fear of aborting a babe she could already be carrying. And she certainly was not going to stop making love with her husband.

"If you have a son and he is anything like his father," Ina said with a chuckle, "you will have your hands full."

"Tell me about Rogan when he was a young

lad," Emma encouraged, and Ina soon had Emma laughing with tales of Rogan's childish antics.

By the time Emma left Ina, she was hoping she would have a son as adventurous as his da and mum.

"Do I have to tie you to my bed, wife, so that you wake by my side?"

Emma turned with a grin to face her husband and crossed her wrists, holding them out to him. "We could practice if you like."

Rogan grabbed her around the waist. "Do not tempt me." He went to kiss her and the horn sounded, alerting the village of approaching riders.

Rogan swore and barked orders for her to return to the keep before he turned and hurried off.

Emma waited only a moment, and then followed him.

Chapter Twenty-nine

Emma held back until she saw that it was MacClennan warriors, worn, injured, and returning home. She ran to help, realizing they had to be the warriors that had still been unaccounted for and she hoped they brought news concerning Heather.

She flew past her husband and went straight for the warrior who appeared the worst of the lot.

Rogan shook his head and wondered why he even bothered to give her any orders. He would send her back to the keep, but his men needed her and they greeted her eagerly, knowing full well she would tend their wounds.

A few women hurried forward, tears in their eyes as they ran to hug their husbands.

Rogan slowed as he approached, giving his wife time to look over his men and to determine the extent of the various injures and for the wives to greet their husbands. Then he stepped forward, and the men squared their shoulders and gave him their full attention.

"You are all to go to the Great Hall where my wife, that raised brows and turned eyes wide since these men had not been aware of the marriage, will tend you and you can get some nourishment." Rogan knew it went without saying that he expected to talk with them.

Liam and several other warriors help the injured and Ina was waiting at the keep with several other women ready to help. Food and drink were brought out and the warriors ate while waiting their turn for Emma to tend them.

Rogan joined a couple of unwed warriors who looked to be enjoying the food.

"Congratulations, my lord, on your marriage," the one said and the other nodded in agreement, his mouth too full to speak.

"Thank you," Rogan said, refilling their tankards with ale.

"What happened to the cook?" the other warrior asked before shoveling another spoonful of porridge into his mouth.

"My wife made some changes to the kitchen," Rogan said, aware of what the warrior meant. The food was much tastier than usual. Having enjoyed the morning meal immensely, he had taken the time to go to the kitchen and inquire. The room was so clean that he had to look twice at it to make certain he was in the right place. The smells were delicious and the servants even seemed happier. The cook had praised Emma's changes and told him she looked forward to learning more from the new lady of the keep.

"God bless her," the two warriors said in unison.

Rogan could not help but grin. "I could not agree more." His smile faded. "Now tell me what happened."

The one warrior downed some ale, wiped his arm across his mouth, then explained, "We were herded together, our weapons and horses taken from us, and we were forced to walk deeper into the forest. We were left there, we thought, alone. After seeing to our injures as best we could, we tried to make our way back, but we found out fast enough that we were not alone. We were captives."

The other warrior continued explaining. "Lem is right about that. As soon as any one of us stepped past an invisible boundary, the ghost warriors would show themselves, reminding us that they were there and we were not free."

"How did you manage to escape?" Rogan asked, hoping his men had found a weakness in the ghost warriors.

"We didn't escape," Lem said and nodded to the warrior beside him. "Connor woke one morning to find our weapons and our horses right there waiting for us. He woke us and we got out of there as fast as we could, and we never saw another ghost warrior again."

"We were herded away so fast that we had no chance to see what had happened to you and my lady," Connor said. "We searched the area on our way home and found a few signs that gave us hope you survived. Never in all our fighting days have we ever come up against men like the ghost warriors. They seem invincible."

"No one is invincible, but I will admit that the ghost warriors are the most highly skilled warriors I have ever battled," Rogan said, knowing future skirmishes with them could prove deadly.

Emma approached the table and the two

warriors scurried to stand. "Sit," she ordered firmly and the two obeyed. "You both look well, though worn out. Have you any injures?"

"Bumps and bruises is all, my lady, and this delicious fare has helped ease any pain," Lem said, smiling and Connor agreed with a nod and a grin.

Emma leaned in close as if she was about to share a secret with the two. "Wait until you taste the seasoned birds that are roasting and the wild onion mash cooking for supper this eve."

"We will be the first ones here, right, Lem?" Connor said with a poke to his friend's rib.

Lem winced.

"You have pain. Let me have a look," Emma said, stepping around the table to where he sat.

"It is nothing, my lady," Lem insisted.

"Let her have a look," Rogan ordered and the warrior obeyed.

At first glance, Emma feared the deep bruise could be a problem, but after asking him some questions and giving the area a closer examination, she smiled, claiming him fit. She suggested that he not swing a sword for several days unless necessary.

With all the warriors having been looked at and most having taken their leave after speaking with Rogan, he escorted his wife to an empty table where they could talk.

"What did they have to say to you?" Emma asked eagerly.

Rogan explained what Lem and Connor had told him. "I will speak to the other men eventually, but the two warriors' accounts are enough to determine why they were held captive and then released."

"Time," Emma said. "The Dark Dragon wanted time for us to return home and receive that false message from Patience and to learn once and for all that he was the one who had captured Heather."

"It would seem that way," Rogan agreed.

"You sound doubtful."

"Not about why my warriors were detained." He rubbed his chin and thought for a moment. "I have wondered if someone helps the Dark Dragon. He seems to have been steps ahead of us at various turns."

"That is impossible," Emma argued. "Who would help him? The Macinnes clan is a loyal lot. Besides, Heather is loved by the clan. They would never want to see her meet such a horrible fate."

"Promise of wealth can be a temptation too hard to refuse."

Emma shook her head slowly. "I cannot, or perhaps I do not want to believe that someone in our clan would do such a thing to Heather, but I would be a fool to deny it a possibility."

"Has any strangers recently stayed with your clan for an extended period of time?" Rogan asked, thinking of another possibility.

"Are you suggesting we have or had a spy in our clan?"

"We cannot rule out anything," Rogan said.

"I would hate to think that someone in the Macinnes clan betrayed Heather."

Rogan reached out and took her hand.

His simple touch made her smile and eased her

worries. "I am glad I have you, husband."

"We have each other." He raised their joined hands and kissed the back of hers. "So tell me, is there a chance that you could have had or perhaps continue to have a spy in your midst?"

Emma thought it over and shook her head. "The only recent stranger was Duncan, the monk, and he died before any talk began about a marriage arrangement."

"Who most recently joined your clan?"

Emma had to think a minute. "Maura, but she has been with us over a year now."

"How did she happen to join your clan?"

"She appeared one day like any stranger does, in need of food and rest. Heather saw to her and once she learned that Maura had no one, she suggested that Maura stay, and so she did. But I cannot believe that Maura is anything more than she claims to be—a widow who lost home and hearth when her husband died."

"She does seem a kind soul," Rogan admitted.

"And she takes good care of my da." Emma shook her had more vigorously. "It cannot be Maura. Perhaps the ghost warriors have been watching the Macinnes clan longer than we have realized."

"I never thought of that, but it is a distinct possibility," Rogan said, though wondered if there was not more too what was going on than they had allowed themselves to realize. The question remained... what could it be?

"I hate that there are more questions than answers," Emma said, letting go of Rogan's hand to fill two tankards with cider.

"But the questions do get answered, though not as quickly as you would like. And need I remind you that Patience prefers us to wait while she locates the biggest piece of this puzzle?"

"The Dragon's lair," Emma whispered, not wanting to say it aloud.

"I know right now time seems an enemy to you, but it could prove to be your best friend. In time we will learn more and be able to formulate a plan that will succeed in rescuing your sister. If we continued to search for her, the ghost warriors will only claim more of our warriors, which I am certain would delight the Dark Dragon, for it would weaken our forces. We will be ready and fit to strike when the time comes."

"You are right," she said on a sigh.

"What was that you said?" Rogan asked with a grin.

Emma laughed. "A slip of the tongue."

Rogan held three fingers up, wiggling them. "Three times now you have told me I am right. So, you admit that you have a wise husband?"

She laughed again. "Yes, dear husband, you are wise."

"Since you admit I am wise, then you should have no problem obeying me."

Emma glared at him, though her smile remained wide as she accused, "You trapped me with your words."

"Wise words," he said his grin growing.

She reached out and took his hand in her two. "I

fear I will never be the obedient wife you want me to be. I tried hard this morning to remain in bed until you woke, but I was eager to explore."

"You could have woken me."

"I thought about it, since I woke with a need for you. But I feared I wore you out yesterday, since your slumber was heavy and your snore light. So, I felt it was best I left you alone."

Rogan took hold of both her hands in his large one. "I do not know how many times I must remind you that you could never wear me out. When you are in need of me, you simply need to tell me, for no doubt I would be feeling the same, my need for you just as great. Also, I would love to wake to your touch in the morning. It would please me and pleasure me beyond belief. And lastly, I do not snore."

"My lord," a servant said softly to announce her approach.

Rogan nodded, keeping hold of his wife's hands.

"Your father wishes to speak with you," the servant finished.

Emma yanked her hands away from Rogan and popped up off the bench. "Is something wrong? Is he not feeling well?"

"No, my lady, the laird is doing fine. He simply wishes to speak with his son."

"I will be right there," Rogan said relieved that his da felt well enough to talk with him.

The servant bobbed her head and hurried off.

"I have things to see to," Emma said, walking around the table.

Rogan swung his feet out from under the table and over the bench and hooked his wife around the waist as she went past him and tugged her down on his lap.

"Your father—"

"Will wait a moment, while I tell my wife how much I love her."

Emma wrapped her arms around his neck and kissed him, not softly, though not ravenously, since it would be difficult to let him go if she did. Rogan added to that difficulty by nibbling at her neck after the kiss was done. Between his lips and teeth nipping along her sensitive skin, he had her growing wet in seconds.

Then he did something that had a soft moan slipping from her lips as she rested her brow against his. He moved her so that her backside nested on his thick, hard manhood.

"You are not being fair," she whispered.

"To either one of us," he murmured and nipped at her neck. "After I finish speaking with my father—"

"Find me." She grabbed his face in her hands and brushed her lips across his. "I will be wet and willing."

"Our bedchamber," he commanded.

She pushed her way out of his embrace, since he was not willing to let her go. "No, I fear if I wait there for you I will—" Her cheeks burnt red.

He stood, his arm going around her waist once again. "You will what?"

"I dare not say it. It was wicked of me to even

think it."

"Are you so impatient or are you in such need that you think of pleasing yourself?"

She gasped softly, but then he knew her too well for his response to have startled her. Still, embarrassment stained her cheeks red. "That is improper."

"Only if I am not there to watch," he whispered.

Her cheeks continued to flame, but her curious nature had her saying, "If it pleases you, it most certainly will please me."

Rogan smiled and kissed her quick. "I do love you, wife."

She stepped away from him. "Then go and speak with your father, and then come find me so that I can show you how very much I love you." She hastily left the Great Hall and Rogan left with equal haste to speak with his father.

Chapter Thirty

Rogan entered his father's bedchamber, pleased to see him sitting up and looking so alert. He had thought to rush this talk with his da, but seeing him looking better than he had in some time and not being into his cups made him change his mind.

"You are looking well, Da," Rogan said, approaching the bed.

"Like his old self," Bertha said with a smile and continued on before Angus could say a word. "I will be leaving you two to talk." She wagged her finger at Angus. "And don't you be getting out of that bed." She turned her wagging finger on Rogan. "And don't you let him be talking you into helping him out of bed." She emphasized her point with one sharp wag of her finger and marched out of the room.

Both men looked at each other as Rogan took a seat in the chair by the bed. "I do not know about you, Da, but I would not cross Bertha and I would not dare cross my wife." He smiled and it spread slowly into a huge grin.

"Sometimes it is good to let women think they have some control," Angus said with a nod and a grin of his own.

"I think you mean that women let *us* think we

have some control when we have none."

Angus laughed. "Aye, it was like that with your mum, though she always insisted she was an obedient wife. I still do not know how she got her way all the time."

"Love," Rogan said. "She loved you and you loved her."

"You are right. It does make all the difference, and I am sorry that you got stuck in a loveless marriage. I wanted more for you."

"Fate saw that I got what you wanted for me. I love Emma and she loves me. I could not have asked for a more loving, generous, and stubborn woman."

A tear came to Angus's eye. "She reminds me of your mum, and she is prettier than I first thought."

"She is beautiful, Da, and I am lucky to have her as my wife."

"I am happy for you, my son, and knowing you have a loving and supportive wife, gives me all the more reason to make you Laird of the MacClennan Clan." Angus raised his hand to stop any protests from Rogan. "It is time. You are young, strong, and more than capable of leading the clan. Besides, you have been leading this clan since soon after your mother died. You had no choice with me failing to attend to my duties. You have the right to carry the title of Laird of the MacClennan Clan."

"If you are certain, Da, I will accept the title with honor." Rogan had expected this, though now that the time had come it seemed surreal. That his father thought enough of him to declare him laird of the clan while he, himself, still lived was a great honor. However, he could not help but wonder if his father would once again suffer a great loss as he had when Rogan's mother had died. He prayed and hoped that this loss would not affect his father as badly as losing his wife had.

Angus sighed. "I am certain and relieved to officially hand the title and all that goes with it over to you. We can have a celebration once I am well and can stand firm on my two feet. For now, tell me of any news I have missed."

~~~

Emma talked with the men working on the kitchen garden, explaining exactly how she wanted the patch extended and designating where paths were to be situated between the rows of plants. When she finished, she went to the planting fields to examine the soil and see what the farmers planned for spring planting. She noted changes that would need to be made and as with the kitchen garden the planting fields also needed to be extended and more of a variety of plants added.

She put off examining the animals and pens where they were kept for another day. It was not where she wanted Rogan to find her when he came looking for her. It would not be a place conducive for making love, and she so wanted to make love with her husband. He had left her with a lovely throb in her loins and she could not wait to have it satisfied.
~~~

Sometimes she wondered if it was proper for her to enjoy making love with her husband so much. She had heard more women speak of it as a duty or a chore one suffered through rather than enjoyed. It was no duty to her and far from a chore, though she thought much too often on it.

She shook her head as she walked through the village. She had to stop thinking of all the delicious things her husband did to her and the thoroughly delicious things she was learning to do to him. She had matters that needed her attention and her body crying out for her husband to mount and ride her hard fast should not be foremost on her mind.

Her cheeks flamed. Good Lord, what was the matter with her? She was not at all a proper wife, demanding that her husband pleasure her. But Rogan seemed to find nothing wrong with it and even encouraged her, so why should she feel improper about wanting her husband?

She had a lot to learn about being a wife and she smiled at the prospect. After all, she did love to learn.

She slowed her pace, her eyes catching sight of many things that needed repairing and refreshing now that spring had set in. Several roofs needed thatching, pens needed repairing, tools needed tending, and garments needed mending. She realized then that the village and its people had declined along with its laird. But that would be no more. Angus MacClennan had requested her help and he was about to get much more help than he expected.

Her eyes caught sight of an abandoned cottage.

It looked so forlorn sitting off by itself, as if purposely separated from the others. A bench, broken and rotted sat under a large oak, the branches looming over the cottage like a protective shield. Remnants of a garden were overgrown with weeds and brush. For some reason, her heart went out to the neglected little cottage.

"It belonged to Lady Anna, Rogan's mother," Ina said, coming to stand beside Emma.

"Why did she have a cottage?"

"She wanted a place where only women could come and bring their troubles, a place where they would feel free to speak with her and not worry of repercussions. Lady Anna would listen and if she could help in any way, she would find a way to do so without betraying their trust. Her husband, at first, thought it foolish, but he loved his wife and allowed her to use the cottage as she wished. I do not think he knows how much that cottage helped, not just the women, but his warriors. The women miss it and Lady Anna very much."

"Then perhaps we should give it life again," Emma said with a smile and headed for it, Ina following.

As soon as other women saw Emma and Ina cleaning Lady Anna's cottage, they joined in to help. Word spread and before they knew it, women were weeding the garden and others cleaning around the tree, carting off the broken bench. Another woman had her husband up on the roof repairing the thatching. Chatter and laughter filled the air as the women worked together, pleased that once again Lady Anna's cottage would be open to them and even more pleased that the new lady of the cottage was a fine healer.

Bertha entered the cottage and grinned from ear to ear while tears stung her eyes. "Lady Anna would be proud and pleased to see her cottage cared for once again." She nodded to the narrow bed in the corner. "Women who needed a night or two away from their husbands spent it there." She wiped at her wet eyes. "I will fetch fresh linens for it and a nice soft blanket."

Ina turned to Emma when the woman left. "You have brought not only life back to this place, but hope as well." She placed her hand to her stomach.

"Do not be disappointed if you bleed this month. It may take a month or two for the wild carrot to leave your body."

Ina smiled. "Thank you for letting me know that or I would have wound up crying my eyes out."

"I think soon it will be tears of joy you cry."

"It is so very good you are here. You have brought much happiness with you."

Emma's smile faded and she turned her head away.

"I have a foolish tongue. I am sorry," Ina said apologetically. "Here I talk of happiness when your sisters are still missing. Please forgive my selfishness."

Emma turned around, shaking her head. "You are not selfish, and I am glad you are here to help me as I am appreciative of all the women who help." She reached her hand out to Ina and the woman took it. "I do not feel alone with you here and my sisters would be so pleased to know that."

The two women continued working and that was how Rogan found his wife, busy cleaning his mother's cottage and it gave his heart a jolt. His mum had loved the time she spent there. She would return to the keep feeling renewed as she would say, though there had been times a woman's problem would weigh heavily on her. Never, though, had she ever betrayed any of the women's confidences.

Emma turned when a large shadow blocked the light coming through the open door. She smiled as soon as she saw it was her husband. Then she recalled what she had told him. *Find me. I will be wet and willing.* Her smile faded, for how did she desert these women who so generously and eagerly had come to help her? And how did she deny her husband, especially when it was the last thing she wanted to do.

Rogan saw the dilemma on her face and walked over to her. "What can I do to help, wife?"

Emma threw her arms around him and hugged him tight. "I will make this up to you," she whispered.

"All night," he whispered back.

"And morning too," she murmured before stepping away from him.

He grinned, so very pleased to know she would be in his arms in the morning.

A few hours later Rogan and Emma stood in front of the cottage along with Liam and Ina and several women. All of them were smiling. The small cottage had been brought back to life. A lovely twig wreath decked with spring flowers hung on the repaired door and a new bonnet of thatching graced her roof. The garden was cleared of weeds, revealing a patch of blooming pink rock daisies. A fresh wood pile was stocked on the side of the cottage and two benches now welcomed women to sit and enjoy the shade of the towering oak.

Emma loved it and her beaming smile showed how pleased she was.

Rogan kissed her cheek. "Thank you. Mum would be grateful." He raised his voice for all to hear. "What say we all celebrate our hard work? A feast for all in the Great Hall."

A cheer went up and word spread and soon the Great Hall was filled with talk and laughter and joy that had been absent too long. Flute music filled the air and Ina was soon encouraged to sing.

Emma was startled by her beautiful voice and sitting there listening to her and seeing all the happy faces made her realize that this was her clan now... her family. Joy, along with sadness, filled her heart. She loved her life with her father and sisters and her clan, and she would sorely miss it. But she felt an excitement and hope for a good future here, starting a new life with her husband. Guilt washed over her for feeling so happy.

As soon as Rogan's arm slipped around her, she leaned closer to him, seeking the solace she knew he would offer.

"What troubles you?" he whispered.

"I am happy," she admitted, guilt still weighing heavily on her.

"You have a right to be."

"My sisters—"

"Will one day find happiness and you will rejoice for them as they would for you now. Happiness comes in its own time, Emma. Your sisters will find it when it is their time. This is your time. Do not let senseless guilt rob you of it. From what you tell me of your sisters, they would be disappointed in you if you did."

Emma smiled. "You are ri—"

Rogan grinned. "What was that you were about to say, wife?"

Emma shook her head, though kept smiling. "You are right, husband."

Rogan turned to Liam to his left. "Did you hear that, Liam? My wife says I am right."

Liam raised his tankard. "Enjoy the one time."

"It is the fourth time she has told me I am right," Rogan beamed.

"Then you are truly a lucky man," Liam said and Ina who had finished singing and returned to her husband's side playfully punched him in the arm.

Rogan turned to his wife. "I am a very lucky man."

Emma kept her voice low. "You will be even luckier when we retire for the evening."

Rogan gave an exaggerated yawn. "I am tired. It is time to retire."

"Another drink first," Liam said, raising his tankard and getting a warning look from Rogan.

Emma laughed and filled Rogan's tankard. "A few more minutes with our clan, and then the evening will be ours."

Talk continued and soon tales were being told about the mighty MacClennan clan and Rogan was forced to remain and listen to his warriors boast about their feats. He soon joined in and had the hall laughing out loud with funny mistakes made by various warriors. The evening went on until finally the hour grew late, and Rogan announced he was retiring. It was another hour before Emma and he could take their leave, warriors and wives rushing to thank him and Emma.

Emma remained seated while Rogan stepped around the dais to speak with one of his warriors. Liam and Ina had taken their leave and Emma smiled, knowing Ina was doing all she could to make certain she would soon carry a babe.

"My lady," a soft voice said.

Emma turned to see a petite, slim woman with pure white hair that hung in a braid over her shoulder to rest on her right breast, standing to the side of the dais. A few wrinkles framed her lovely blue eyes, though barely any marred her soft smile. She recognized her as one of the women who helped at the cottage today.

"I am Murdina and I wanted to tell you how grateful I am that Lady Anna's cottage is now available to us once again. Lady Anna was a great help to me when I lost my Harold. I would be pleased and feel it a privilege to help you whenever needed."

"That is very generous of you, Murdina. I truly appreciate it. How long has it been since your Harold has passed?"

"Four years now and I still miss him greatly. He was a good man and a wonderful husband."

"There is much work yet to do at the cottage. I would be only too glad for your help."

"Thank you, my lady," Murdina said with a bob of her head.

"I will see you tomorrow, Murdina," Emma said and the woman bowed her head before walking away.

Emma eased herself out of the chair, her body letting her know that she had done more than her fair share of work today. She saw that Rogan had finished speaking to the warrior and was pleased. She was eager for them to retire to their bedchamber and make love.

"You are tired," Rogan said as he curled his arm around his wife's waist and eased her to rest against him.

"Not too tired to make love," she whispered, though a sudden yawn spoke differently.

Rogan took the stairs slowly, though he would have preferred to run up them, his desire for his wife burning his loins. He was concerned that she was too fatigued to make love, though she would never admit it.

His suspicions were confirmed when he watched how slowly she disrobed as soon as they entered their bedchamber. It was obvious her limbs were sore from all she had done today, and he hurried to her side to help her undress.

She rested her brow to his chest after her garments lay discarded to the floor, and realizing he still wore his shirt, her hands tugged at it, trying to get it off him.

He brushed her hands away and scooped her up in his arms and carried her over to the bed. He laid her down gently and pulled the soft wool blanket over her.

"I will undress and join you," he said and gave her a quick kiss.

She grabbed his hand before he could step away. "Hurry," she urged a yawn following.

Rogan could have shed his clothes in an instant and joined with her fast. But he could not bring himself to do it with her so exhausted and half asleep.

He nodded and walked over to the fireplace, knowing if he took his time returning to her, she would no doubt fall asleep. He took a few moments to add more logs to the fire, and then he took even longer to shed his clothes. By the time he returned to bed, his wife was fast asleep.

With a sigh of resignation, he climbed in beside her and eased her against him to cuddle his body around hers, and though he thought sleep would elude him, it claimed him in mere minutes.

Chapter Thirty-one

Emma snuggled deeper into the delicious warmth. It felt so good that she wanted to linger in it forever. And the woodsy scent tickled her nostrils and had her thinking of her morning walk in the woods.

Her eyes sprang open and she looked up to see that her husband was sound asleep. She glanced over at the hearth and saw that the fire had died to embers. They had slept the night away, never having made love.

Anger stirred in her for a moment, though she brushed it away before it could take root. She knew her husband well, and she realized he had sacrificed his own need so that she could get the rest she had needed. It was a loving gesture for sure and she smiled, for he certainly deserved a reward for his thoughtfulness. And she had promised him she would be in bed when he woke.

She ran her hand softly across his chest, marveling at how firm and muscular it felt, yet it pillowed her head so gently. She circled his nipples with the palm of her hand, and the exquisite sensation sent tingles shooting through every inch of her. This was going to be more delightful than she had thought.

Eager to learn and experience more, she moved her hand down along his midriff, feeling the tight cords there, and again she lingered enjoying the feel of him. Her hand drifted lower. She spread her fingers as she went and watched as they disappeared into the thatch of dark hair where his manhood nested and started growing hard before her eyes.

She could not help but reach out and tease him with gentle strokes. He grew harder and she grew more curious and eager to further explore. She scooted down along the bed, pushing the blanket off them as she went and settled herself between his legs. After stroking, exploring, and familiarizing herself with all of him, she set her mouth upon him and enjoyed.

Rogan groaned, not wanting to wake from his wicked dream. Damn, if it was not the best dream ever. Never had a woman tasted him with such eagerness and skill. And damn if it did not feel real.

His eyes sprung open. "Emma!"

Her response was a sensual groan and he grew harder. He fought back the climax that was edging ever closer, enjoying this moment far too much to see it end. Besides, he wanted to be inside her when he came, and he wanted to make her come along with him.

"I love the taste of you," she said on a wispy breath when her mouth left him for a moment.

He took advantage of it and reached down to grab her, yank her up, over, and under him, to her utter surprise. She grabbed onto his arms when he drove into her like a sword finding its sheath and settling in, though this sword did not remain still.

Emma held on, meeting his every thrust with her own, the urgency of their joining, growing ever more powerful.

"I am going come," Emma moaned.

"Not yet," he ordered.

"I cannot stop it," she groaned.

He dropped his head down between his taut arms that kept him hovered only inches above her chest. He brought his lips to rest a mere breath away from hers. "Now," he ordered and claimed her lips in a possessive kiss, his tongue thrusting into her mouth.

Emma exploded, her climax consuming every inch of her and sending ripple after ripple of divine pleasure racing through her.

Rogan pulled his mouth off hers, tossing his head back and releasing a loud groan as he climaxed with such intense fury that he thought the pleasure would rip him in two. When he finally gave one last thrust, he felt his wife move beneath him and knew she was on the verge of coming once gain. And he made certain that she did.

When they were both finally spent, Rogan rolled onto his back, though reached out and took hold of her hand.

They both lay silent for several minutes, waiting for their breathing to calm.

Rogan was the first to speak, turning on his side to face his wife. "Good God, wife, you almost killed me, though I would die a very happy man."

Emma chuckled.

Rogan rested his brow to hers. "Truly, wife, you

pleased me beyond belief, and I will return the favor one morning."

Emma shivered at the thought. "Morning, noon, or night, you always please me beyond belief."

"God, but I love you," he said and kissed her softly.

"And I you," she said, snuggling against him.

"It is good to have you here in bed when I wake," Rogan said, "but I do not expect you to do so every day."

Emma turned startled eyes on him.

"I know how much you love your mornings alone and I do not wish to rob you of them. I would, however, ask that you spare me a few and invite me for a morning walk or two every now and then."

"I would truly like that. There is much I can teach you about the woods," she said excited to share her knowledge with her husband.

"I look forward to it," Rogan said and meant it.

~~~

Emma continued to make changes to almost everything over the next few days, though no one complained. After a harsh winter, the beautiful spring weather had everyone eager to be outdoors and busy. Many in the clan followed Emma's lead and began making their own repairs to their cottages and most of the women were busy extending their garden and inquiring about what Emma had planted in her garden.

Murdina had proved more than helpful and Emma had been thrilled to discover that she was
~~~

extremely knowledgeable when it came to plants. Emma gladly shared the planting and caring of her garden with Murdina. Ina brought breads and honey cakes to the cottage for anyone who stopped by. Another woman brought a basket of freshly cut heather, others brought wildflowers. The women were generously showing their support for the cottage and each other.

"It will be a lovely garden," Murdina said after Emma finished seeding a patch.

"What goes on here!"

Emma and Murdina turned to see Angus MacClennan standing a few feet away from them.

Emma ignored his question and asked, "Where is the walking stick I gave you to use?"

"I do not need it," he barked. "Now answer me. What goes on here? Who gave you permission to use this cottage?"

Emma dusted the dirt from her hands and walked over to Angus. "The cottage did. It sat here neglected and forlorn, so I gave it life again."

"It was not your decision to make," Angus shouted. "It belonged to my Anna and—"

Murdina stepped forward. "And Lady Anna would be pleased to see that the new Lady MacClennan was using it as she once did."

Angus looked ready to argue, but Murdina continued before he could.

"Though you will never forget the one you loved with all your heart, there comes a time you must let go. I know how hard that seems, but my Harold told me before he died that he would not rest if I did not continue to live as I should. I imagine Lady Anna said something similar to you."

Emma eased away from the pair. Murdina was telling Angus what he needed to hear and being she truly understood how he felt... he might listen to her.

Angus remained silent for a moment and Murdina took another step closer to him.

"My Anna did tell me I was not to mourn her for long, but..." He turned his head away.

"Why not come and see what we have done to Lady Anna's garden. She would be so happy and proud to see how beautiful it will be once again."

Angus coughed away the tears that threatened. "Aye, I would like to see what you are doing."

He followed Murdina who explained with a smile what plants and flowers would flourish in the spacious garden. The two were soon talking. Angus was even smiling and when he stumbled, his leg having yet to fully heal, Murdina caught him and slipped her slim shoulder beneath his arm to help him to the nearby bench.

Angus protested. "You are too petite to take my weight."

"Nonsense, my lord," Murdina said and shouldered his weight with ease as she helped him to the bench. "I may not have much size to me, but strength I have an abundance of."

Angus smiled and patted the spot beside him. "Sit and talk with me and call me Angus."

Emma saw her husband approaching and ran off, wrapping her arm around his and turning him around to walk back the way he came.

"I was going to speak with my father," Rogan said.

"He is busy talking with Murdina," Emma said with a smile.

"But I wanted to tell him," —Rogan stopped abruptly and turned wide eyes on his wife— "I saw him sitting on the bench with her."

"He invited her to sit with him and to call him Angus."

Rogan grinned. "Finally, he shows interest in a woman. He is not dead after all."

"And is a woman dead if she shows no interest in a man?"

"She might as well be."

Emma took a step away from him. "Then I guess I was dead all those years I found no interest in men."

He grabbed her around the waist and yanked her to him, ignoring her hands that slapped at his arms. "You were waiting for an exceptional man... me."

"You did not wait," she accused, though with a smile.

"I had to make sure I found the right woman."

"Then how do I know I found the right man when he is the only man I have ever known intimately?" she asked.

He leaned down and stole a quick kiss. "Because he proves it to you every day in everything he does for you and every time he makes love to you." He lowered his voice. "His love knows no bounds for you. He cannot spend enough time with you or make love enough to you. You consume his every thought, word, and deed. And there would be no life without you."

Each word melted her heart and sparked her passion. She did not think she could love him anymore than she already did, but somehow he continued to prove her wrong with his words, his deeds, and his love.

She wiggled out of his embrace and took hold of his hand. "I need to show you something."

Rogan glared at her. He pours his love out to her and her response is to show him something?

"It is important," she insisted and tugged at his hand for him to follow.

He shook his head and went along with her. He shook his head harder when she hurried him into the stable, though he was pleased to find that it had a fresh scent to it when normally it stunk.

Rogan followed her to the back of the stable and when she turned into the last empty stall, he wondered what was so important that she wanted him to see. He was shocked when she hopped up on a crate and flung herself into his arms, wrapping her legs around his waist. He grabbed her tight as he stumbled slightly from the brunt of her body slamming against his, and then settled her firmly against him.

"Now to show you how much I love you," she said with a smile.

Sometime later, they lay panting and sweating in the fresh hay on the ground.

"You are sure to kill me, wife," Rogan said with a chuckle.

She balanced herself on her elbow and rested

her head in her hand after she turned on her side to face him. “But at least I will know you died happy.”

“Extremely happy,” he confirmed with a growing grin.

“But first you will give me many children,” she instructed sternly, though smiled.

He laughed. “With as much as we make love, we are bound to have a large brood.”

“It is your fault I want you so much,” she said with a serious tone, though her smile grew, telling a different story.

His arm came around her waist quickly and with an effortless tug and lift she was stretched out over him. “Now tell me why it is my fault, wife.”

She rested her elbows on his hard chest and her face in her hands. “You awakened my body and once I got a taste... I craved more.”

“Have no fear, wife, I will be sure to satisfy all your cravings.”

“Though it may kill you?” She giggled.

“It is better to die a happy man than a miserable one,” he assured her.

“I will keep you very happy, husband.”

“You already have,” Rogan said and kissed her softly.

Chapter Thirty-two

Emma made her way quietly out of the keep. It was the first morning in days that she left her husband to wake alone. The urge to explore the woods on this beautiful morning was too strong to ignore. This place would not entirely be her home until she made her personal acquaintance with the woods.

She was not surprised to see Murdina walking toward the cottage. She had found the woman was an early riser like herself. And over the last few days, she had found that Angus would join Murdina shortly after she began tending the garden and they would spend several hours talking.

Her thought had her asking Murdina, "Will Angus join you today?"

Murdina's cheeks blushed pink, and she smiled. "I would not mind if he did."

"You have given him reason to start living again," Emma said happy for the pair.

"And he has given me reason to smile more often," Murdina admitted, her smile growing. "You are here early this morning. Is there something or someone who needs tending?"

"No, I hoped to take a walk in the quiet and peacefulness of the woods as I did daily at my home."

"And Lord Rogan permits you to go alone?" Murdina asked.

"I fear I have not yet grown accustomed to asking permission."

"Do you think it wise not to at least let your husband know where you go? After all, you are not familiar with these woods yet."

"My sister Patience taught me how to track, so I rarely get lost," Emma said, hoping to alleviate the woman's obvious worry. "And you know where I will be."

"Aye, and glad I am that I do," Murdina said like a concerned mother.

"I will see you in an hour or so," Emma said. "I do not intend to go far this morning."

"Good," Murdina said with a nod and a sigh of relief.

Emma left the woman to open the cottage door, a signal that it was available to anyone who needed it. She made her way into the woods behind the cottage and through a thick wooden door in the stone wall surrounding the village. She took only a few steps in before she was surrounded by lush growth, and she stopped to breathe in the earthy scent.

There was something about the woods on a spring day. It was like watching it wake after a long winter's nap. She closed her eyes and listened to the birds tweeting and the rustle of the new leaves on the trees. Her heart soared, for she felt she was finally home.

She opened her eyes eager to explore and

dropped down like a dead weight when she heard footfalls not far off. Patience had taught her to never wait to see who approached, for by then it might be too late to escape harm.

Emma maneuvered herself behind lush foliage and waited and listened. The footfalls were light, almost faint, but she heard them. She was sure of it. Her hand flew to her mouth when a ghost warrior appeared a few feet away. She kept still, not making a sound, though she feared he would hear her heartbeat, it pounded so hard in her chest. She watched as he walked with guarded steps and cautious eyes.

Seeing him was proof the MacClennan clan continued to be watched.

A thought hit her then. If they were being watched, why could she not do the same to them? Perhaps she would be able to learn something about them or was she being foolish?

She had no time to debate the matter. The ghost warrior would be out of view soon and her chance gone. Foolish or not, she followed.

Emma kept as light on her feet as possible and kept to the bushes, trees, rocks, whatever she could find to duck behind so that he would not see her. When he went over a small rise, she held back and crept slowly toward it, not sure what would be on the other side. It was nothing more than a glen and the warrior was heading up the other rise. She waited and approached with the same caution. She did not know how long she followed him, though she had cautiously marked the trail as she went, so she would be able to find her way back.

It was when she approached another rise and peeked over it that she almost let out a gasp. There in a campsite sat her sister Heather surrounded by several ghost warriors.

~~~

Rogan turned as he woke to wrap his arm around his wife, but met empty space. He could not say he was not disappointed to open his eyes and find her gone. It had been nice the last few days to have her there beside him, on top of him, or under him after waking. He smiled at the memories. He could not be angry with her. He had been expecting this. He had seen the way she had glanced with longing at the woods. It had only been a matter of time before she answered the need.

That did not mean he would not worry about her until she returned. She was a good tracker, so he was not concerned she would get lost. But the woods could harbor danger and the one thing that did concern him was that the ghost warriors were out there watching them.

He doubted she would venture too far, but a few feet into the woods could prove dangerous enough. He hurriedly got dressed and went to the Great Hall. Liam was at a table, and he hurried over to him.

"Have you seen my wife?" he asked anxiously.

Liam saw the worry on his friend's face and quickly answered. "I saw her talking with Murdina by the cottage just after daybreak."

Rogan felt his apprehension fade, and he joined
~~~

Liam at the table. "Why are you not eating with Ina this morn?"

"An early morning romp has left her exhausted and she sleeps," Liam said with a grin.

"An early morning romp wakes my wife and off she goes full of strength to start the day."

"So you are the one left exhausted," Liam teased.

"And famished," Rogan said, reaching for a hunk of bread and a bowl of porridge.

~~~

Emma stared in disbelief. Heather sat only a few feet away from her, yet it might as well have been miles. At least, she appeared to look well, none the worse for wear. No bruises marred her lovely face and her long blond hair fell neatly in waves as it always did. She wore different clothes than Emma remembered, but otherwise she looked as she always did... beautiful. And Emma was overwhelmed with relief.

The problem was... how did she rescue her?

There was no way that she would simply walk away and abandon her sister. If she took a chance and hurried back to the keep to get help, Heather could be gone by the time she returned. And the search for her would begin again.

No, she would not take the chance. Her sister was here in front of her, and there was no way she would desert her. She had to think this through, and it suddenly dawned on her. She had not followed the ghost warrior here—he had led her here.
~~~

Whatever was the matter with her to think that she could follow a ghost warrior without being detected? It had been a trap. They wanted her to follow, but the question was why?

Emma was about to find out. She tucked the loose strands of hair that had fallen free from her braid, brushed leaves and twigs from her clothes and with her head held high, she stood and marched into the camp.

~~~

A couple of hours later Rogan walked with Liam to the cottage. Liam was certain his wife had woken by now and he would find her there. Rogan was eager to see Emma and find out if she enjoyed her walk in the woods and perhaps entice her to take a walk with him.

Ina and Murdina hurried over to Rogan as he approached, and his heart slammed in his chest. Something was wrong. He could feel it.

"She has not returned," Murdina said. "I was telling Ina that Emma left for a walk in the woods and she has yet to return. She told me that she was not going to go far and would be but an hour."

"When did she leave?" Rogan asked, fearing he already knew.

"Just after sunrise," Murdina said. "I should have realized sooner that she had not returned, but your father was here and we talked and he left a short time ago and that was when I realized she had not returned. I was just coming to find you."
~~~

"Gather the men," Rogan ordered Liam. With rushed strides, he returned to the keep. He cursed himself ten times over. While he had sat joking and laughing with Liam, Emma had been in danger. Never. Never again would he allow her to go into the woods alone.

He rolled up the sleeves to his shirt as he made his way to his bedchamber. Once there he slipped on his chest straps, crisscrossing them over his chest and back and sheathed his sword in the back sheath. A dirk went in the sheath at his waist and he tugged on his leather arm guards tying them at his wrists.

He walked out of the room prepared to get his wife back no matter the cost, and God help anyone who stood in his way.

~~~

"Emma!" Heather shouted, scrambling to her feet and ran to her sister.

They threw their arms around each other and hugged tight. Emma noticed that the ghost warriors did not stop Heather from going to her, nor had they come after her when she entered the camp. Her instincts had been right. They had led her here.

Heather stepped away from Emma, though kept firm hold of her arms. "You got my message. You came for me."

"I have," Emma said happy to be holding her sister tight.

"But now you are trapped. They will not let either of us go," Heather said sadly.

"At least, we will be together," Emma said,
~~~

though her heart filled with sadness at the thought that she would be separated from her husband. Still, though, she could not leave her sister alone with that monster.

"Are you alone? Is there no one protecting you? And how far are we from home." She shook her head annoyed. "I get no answers, though I have asked many questions."

"To start with, Patience still searches for you and Da has improved some. Maura watches over him. We are on MacClennan land and—" Emma stopped. How did she tell her sister that she was wed to the man Heather had been promised to?

"What is it, Emma? What is wrong?" Heather asked anxiously.

Emma blurted it out quickly. "I am wed to Rogan MacClennan."

Heather shook her head. "Nothing makes sense anymore. Come by the fire and tell me how your marriage came about and if you are happy."

"You are not angry?" Emma asked. "You had been promised to him."

"I will be angry if you tell me this was forced upon you and you do not wish to be wed to Rogan MacClennan."

"Though it was forced, I love him with all my heart," Emma said.

Heather walked Emma to the campfire and they sat side by side with their arms around one another, without one ghost warrior approaching them. And Emma began explaining why Rogan was now her husband.

~~~

"She leaves a clear trail," Liam said, "but then so does the ghost warrior."

Rogan sat impatiently on his stallion. He wanted to rush ahead and find his wife, but it would be an unwise move and one that could prove harmful to Emma. This news now filled him with foreboding.

"Are you telling me that this was a trap?" Rogan asked. "That the ghost warrior wanted Emma to follow him?"

"It appears that way."

"Then that would mean they lead us to her as well," Rogan said.

"And into another trap."

"That we have no choice but to follow." Rogan shook his head. "Why? Why lay in wait for Emma and leave a clear path for us to track her? Unless someone wishes to meet with me on his own terms."

"You think the Dark Dragon is near?" Liam asked anxiously and cast a quick glance around them.

"I do not know, but we will find out soon enough."

~~~

"I am happy for you, Emma," Heather said after her sister finished telling her bout the marriage and gave her hand a squeeze. "It gives me hope, for surely your husband will come and rescue us."

Emma had expected Rogan by now. There did

not seem to be many ghost warriors lingering about, though there could be more hiding away, and waiting. She hoped not, for there was a chance of a rescue. There was a chance to bring Heather home.

There was one thing Emma had to know. "The Dark Dragon has not hurt you, has he?"

Heather paled. "The Dark Dragon?"

Surely, her sister knew who had captured her. "These are his warriors."

"But they wear no white faces."

"The one I followed did," Emma said, looking around to find him and seeing not one warrior with a face painted white.

"I thought a band of mercenaries abducted me and were demanding money from Da. They wanted something to send to Da to prove they had me. I was so frightened of what they might do to me, I chose to send the ring so you were aware of how dire my circumstances, instead of Mum's pin." Heather shook her head. "Surely, you are wrong about the Dark Dragon."

Emma watched as fear turned Heather's face deathly pale and she hurried to offer encouragement, keeping her voice low. "Rogan will be here soon and we will both be safe. You will come home with me. Rogan will protect you."

"Tell me, Emma, tell me how you know that it is the Dark Dragon who is responsible for my abduction," Heather urged.

Thunder cracked and lightening sparked, causing the two women to jump.

Emma looked up, shocked to see the dark storm

clouds overhead. It had been a beautiful day when she had started out this morning. When had the sun disappeared, and the clouds turned so ominous?

The Dark Dragon brings them. The thought shivered her down to her bones.

It was with heavy sorrow that she detailed to her sister all that had happened since her capture.

~~~

The horses had turned skittish and the men leery the further they traveled into the woods. Their eyes were constantly going to the trees and bushes, expecting ghost warriors to surprise them at any minute.

Rogan could not help but feel the same. After all, this was a trap and he was waiting for it to be sprung.

Tales of the Dark Dragon's exploits only served to make it worse. From stories being told, it would seem that the Dark Dragon was spawned from evil and that even the devil feared him. It was nonsense of course. Riding through the dense forest that grew ever more ominous and the darkening sky blotting out light and the mist swirling along the ground like a slithering snake, made one think that the Dark Dragon had called on his evil minions for help.

Evil or devil, Rogan would fight both and go to hell if necessary to rescue his wife.

~~~

Emma kept her arm around her sister, fearing that any moment she would faint, she turned so pale.

"It cannot be. It just cannot be," Heather kept saying. "Why? Why would he want me?"

They both shivered at the possibilities.

"Do you have the ring I sent you?" Heather asked.

Emma nodded.

"Give it to me," she said. "I feel so vulnerable when I am not wearing it, and right now I could use some strength."

Emma slipped it out of her pouch and Heather slipped it around her neck, giving it a squeeze before tucking it beneath her blouse.

There was sudden movement in the camp. More warriors poured out of the woods and every one of their faces was painted white.

"Oh God, Emma, he is come for me," Heather said, grabbing onto her sister as they stumbled to their feet.

Emma wished they could run, at least have a chance of escape, but ghost warriors surrounded them. There was no place for them to go.

One large warrior stepped forward and beckoned with his outstretched hand. "Come, we leave now."

Both women stepped forward, clinging tightly to each other.

"No," the warrior commanded. "Only you." He pointed to Heather.

They clung even tighter to each other.

“I go where my sister goes,” Emma said her tone threatening an or else, though she knew not what the or else would be.

The warrior shook his head. “Only Heather.”

“No,” Emma shouted at him, frantic to keep her sister safe, but not sure how she could. She feared Heather being taken from her again, never able to find her.

The warrior stepped forward.

“Touch her and you die,” Rogan roared.

Chapter Thirty-three

Emma watched as her husband fought to control his stallion, the animal pawing the ground and appearing as angry as Rogan and just as intimidating. She had to smile. Never had he looked more the mighty Highland warrior astride his steed, ready and fearless of the battle ahead.

He guided his horse down the rise, his men following behind him.

The ghost warriors remained as they were, not moving an inch. It was as if they had frozen in place. They made no move even as Rogan drew closer. They kept a tight knit circle around Emma and Heather, and Emma feared her husband would have to battle his way through them.

Rogan kept his eye on the large warrior, standing a few feet away from his wife. He still was not close enough to stop him from reaching out and grabbing Emma. He had been shocked to see Heather next to Emma, though pleased. He hoped to rescue them both, though wondered if it would be possible. After all, this was a trap, but for who or why still went unanswered.

They were only a few feet away when it happened. The big warrior rushed at Emma and Heather, and the other warriors rushed to close the circle. Then in mere seconds, almost in the blink of an eye, the ghost warriors vanished into the woods as if they had never been there at all. And they left only Emma behind.

It took Emma a moment to realize what had happened and when she did, she let out such a furious scream that the horses startled and the MacClennan warriors cringed.

Rogan rode straight for her, dismounting before his horse came to a complete stop and tried to pull her into his arms.

Emma refused to be comforted. She pushed her husband away and screamed, "Heather, I will come for you. Patience and I will come for you. I promise." Her scream grew to a fury. "And you, Dark Dragon, hurt my sister and I will see you dead. Do you hear me, I will see you dead! On that you have my word!"

A mist began to creep down the hill, claiming everything in its path. The horses grew skittish as it settled around their feet, as if they feared it touching them. The warriors drew their legs up fearing the same.

Thunder suddenly rumbled over the land like an angry beast and the dark gray sky seemed to grow darker. The thunder grew louder, cracking and rolling in thunderous roars.

One of the warriors cried out, "A beast approaches."

Rogan turned a furious warning glare on him and the warrior froze, frightened more of Rogan than the beast. He then turned back to his wife. "They are on foot. We ride after them."

She nodded, grateful he was a fearless warrior.

Before either of them moved, one of the warriors cried out, “The Dragon.”

Everyone turned to look. There on the rise, the mist licking at his feet stood a figure shrouded in black, the wind blowing at his cloak, making it appear as if he had wings.

Emma stared. The figure in her dream had come alive and was standing before her very eyes.

A ghost warrior suddenly appeared a few feet away from them.

“You will hear from your sister again, but if you dare follow, then you will never hear from or see your sister again.” He disappeared as fast as he had appeared.

Emma turned to her husband and collapsed in his arms in tears.

~~~

The wind and rain blew fiercely and Rogan was glad they were tucked safely away in the castle. He had had food brought to their room so they could sup in private, Emma having suffered bouts of tears since arriving home hours ago.

“He is a monster, letting me see my sister and then taking her from me,” Emma said.

“It was his plan and one that worked well,” he said, handing her a goblet of wine. “He let you see that she was unharmed, though warned that harm would come to her if you tried to follow and showing himself as he did was meant to instill fear
~~~

so we would keep our distance. It worked, for stories now spread about the incident and many in the clan want no trouble from the vengeful Dark Dragon."

"The look on my sister's face when I told her it was the Dark Dragon who abducted her haunts me. She had not known. He had never made himself known to her. I can only imagine her fear now." Tears rolled down her cheeks.

Rogan hunched down in front of his wife, snug in a chair by the hearth. "If he intended to harm her, he would have done so by now. She appeared well cared for and the ghost warrior did say that you would hear from her again. So evidently, the Dark Dragon intends to allow her to communicate with you."

"But it is what he wants from her that worries me," Emma insisted.

"We still have to hear from the King," Rogan reminded. "He may be able to intervene and bring an end to this."

Emma shivered. "Seeing him on that rise as he had appeared in my dream, makes me doubt that anyone would be willing to go up against him."

"I would," Rogan said without hesitation.

She rested her hand against his warm cheek. "I do not want to exchange your life for my sister's."

"You have little faith in me, wife," he said, taking her hand and placing a gentle kiss on her palm.

"I have all the faith in the world in you, husband, but faith will not help you when you face an army of the Dark Dragon's warriors. I thought I was prepared and hoped that perhaps Heather and I could fight them off until you reached us. But they moved so fast that I did not even see them move. There were a few steps away from us and in an instant they were on top of us, and in the next instant they were gone. I did not even feel them separate Heather and me. How do you fight warriors you cannot see move?"

Rogan had to admit she was right. He had seen it with his own eyes and not believed it.

"We will find a way," he assured her.

"That we will, for I will not leave Heather in the claws of the Dark Dragon." She yawned, not wanting to sleep, yet yearning for the oblivion it would bring, if only to ease her worries for a few hours.

Rogan did not bother to tell her that she needed sleep. He simply scooped her up out of the chair and carried her to bed. He intended to leave her to sleep, but she reached her hand out to grab his arm when, after tucking her in, he turned to walk away.

She realized as soon as she was in his arms that she much preferred to seek the solace he could offer, rather than the oblivion of sleep. "Make love to me."

Rogan did not think to deny her. He undressed, climbed into bed, and took her in his arms.

Chapter Thirty-four

Emma stared out at the woods. She had been coming here daily since she had last seen Heather about a month ago, hoping that a ghost warrior would once again show himself and lead her to her sister. Though life went on, she could not shed the guilt of failing to rescue Heather.

Rogan had insisted on accompanying her and the times he could not, he sent one of his warriors with her. She had managed to evade the warriors more often than not. Today was one of those days, and she was grateful for it. She desperately needed time alone, if for nothing else than to mourn her two sisters' absence.

She missed them so very much, though she could not say she was not happy in her new life. Her husband was wonderful, and she had made good friends with Ina and Murdina. She smiled. Murdina and Angus were inseparable, and while Angus still enjoyed his ale, it was far less than before. Everyone in the village was wagering when the wedding would be. Ina was certain she was with child, since she was a few days late in bleeding. She insisted she could feel a babe nestled in her and no one could tell her otherwise. Liam was worried she would once again be disappointed. But Emma had learned to trust a woman's instincts, they were rarely wrong.

Emma said nothing of her own suspicions that she was with child. She wanted to be certain so as not to disappoint anyone.

The land was flourishing along with the clan and all was good, but would be far better if her sisters where here to enjoy it with her.

She walked a bit more, taking note of seedlings she intended to replant in the garden as soon as they were strong enough to move. Then she started back to the keep, meeting up with her husband as she stepped from the woods.

"When are you going to take pity on me and learn to obey me?" he said.

She hooked her arm around his. "I do obey you."

He laughed. "When it suits you."

"It suits me now to spend the rest of the day with my husband."

"That is good, since I was going to order you to do just that."

Emma patted his arm. "You see what a remarkable wife I am, obeying orders you have yet to issue."

"I agree you are a remarkable wife," —he lowered his voice— "in so many, many ways."

Emma leaned in close. "Perhaps we should explore those ways, especially since I missed exploring them this morning."

Rogan slipped his arm around her waist. "Let us hurry before someone stops us."

They made it to the steps of the keep when Liam

called out to them.

They turned reluctantly.

"A message from your father," Liam called out to Emma as he ran to them. "Your sister Patience has returned home and she is well."

Emma squealed with delight. "Patience is home and safe." She flung herself at her husband and hugged him tight. "I cannot wait to see her. I will have the servants pack. We will leave immediately."

"On the morrow," Rogan said firmly and was surprised when she did not argue.

"Aye, on the morrow," she said and turned to hurry off.

Rogan grabbed her arm, stopping her. "You will not sneak off without me. We will leave together tomorrow. I will have your word on it."

She kissed his cheek. "You have my word, husband. We will leave together tomorrow."

Rogan watched her hurry up the stairs and into the keep.

"She obeys you well... this time," Liam said, grinning.

"That is what I'm afraid of." Rogan shook his head. "Just when I thought things had settled to a relative calm... they start all over again."

THE END

Look for Patience's story Highlander's Rebellious Love available fall 2014

Titles by Donna Fletcher

Single Titles

San Francisco Surrender
Rebellious Bride
The Buccaneer
Tame My Wild Touch
Playing Cupid
Whispers on the Wind

Series Books

Wyrrd Witch Series

The Wedding Spell
Magical Moments
Magical Memories
Remember the Magic

The Irish Devil
Irish Hope

Isle of Lies
Love Me Forever

Dark Warrior
Legendary Warrior

The Daring Twin
The Bewitching Twin

Taken By Storm
The Highlander's Bride

Sinclare Brothers' Series

Return of the Rogue
Under the Highlander's Spell
The Angel & The Highlander
Highlander's Forbidden Bride

Warrior King Series

Bound To A Warrior
Loved By A Warrior
A Warrior's Promise
Wed To A Highland Warrior

Highlander Trilogy

Highlander Unchained
Forbidden Highlander
Highlander's Captive

Rancheros Trilogy

Untamed Fire
Renegade Love
Third book yet to be titled

Sexual Appetites of Unearthly Creatures Novella Series

Sexual Appetites of Vampires

Macinnes Sisters Trilogy

The Highlander's Stolen Heart
Highlander's Rebellious Love, Fall 2014
Highlander: The Dark Dragon, Winter 2015

About the Author

Donna Fletcher is a *USA Today* bestselling romance author. Her books are sold worldwide. She started her career selling short stories and winning reader contests. She soon expanded her writing to her love of romance novels and sold her first book SAN FRANCISCO SURRENDER the year she became president of New Jersey Romance Writers. Donna is also a past President of Novelists, Inc.

Drop by Donna's website www.donnafletcher.com where you can learn more about her, get a printable Book List, and read her blog.

Made in the USA
Middletown, DE
20 October 2015